YOUR HUSBAND'S FAULT

BOOKS BY KERRY WILKINSON

THRILLER NOVELS

Two Sisters

The Girl Who Came Back

Last Night

The Death and Life of Eleanor Parker

The Wife's Secret

A Face in the Crowd

Close to You

After the Accident

The Child Across the Street

What My Husband Did

The Blame

The Child in the Photo

The Perfect Daughter

The Party at Number 12

The Boyfriend

The Night of the Sleepover

After the Sleepover

The Call

The Missing Body

Home Is Where the Lies Live

My Son's Girlfriend

Romance novels

Ten Birthdays

Truly, Madly, Amy

The Jessica Daniel series

The Killer Inside (also published as *Locked In*)

Vigilante

The Woman in Black

Think of the Children

Playing With Fire

The Missing Dead (also published as *Thicker than Water*)

Behind Closed Doors

Crossing the Line

Scarred for Life

For Richer, For Poorer

Nothing But Trouble

Eye for an Eye

Silent Suspect

The Unlucky Ones

A Cry in the Night

The Andrew Hunter series

Something Wicked

Something Hidden

Something Buried

Whitecliff Bay Series

The One Who Fell

The One Who Was Taken

The Ones Who Are Buried

The Ones Who Are Hidden

Silver Blackthorn

Reckoning

Renegade

Resurgence

Other

Down Among the Dead Men

No Place Like Home

Watched

YOUR HUSBAND'S FAULT

KERRY WILKINSON

bookouture

Published by Bookouture in 2025

An imprint of Storyfire Ltd.
Carmelite House
50 Victoria Embankment
London EC4Y 0DZ

www.bookouture.com

The authorised representative in the EEA is Hachette Ireland
8 Castlecourt Centre
Dublin 15 D15 XTP3
Ireland
(email: info@hbgi.ie)

ISBN: 978-1-83618-722-6
eBook ISBN: 978-1-83618-721-9

ONE

TUESDAY

There is only one thing worse than other people's children – and that's other children's parents.

Sarah slowed her pace and clutched Oliver's hand a little tighter as they rounded the corner, putting the seven-year-old's new school in sight. A gaggle of adults were huddled on the pavement, a separate circle of children nearby. Everyone was waiting for the gates to open and Sarah had a flashback to her own first day at secondary school, decades before. She'd been walking side by side with her friend up the hill – nervous then, too. Wondering whether they'd make friends and fit in, fearing she'd catch the eye of some bully.

And now...

It wasn't that different.

The other women stood tightly, chatting amiably, as if they'd known one another for years – which they probably had. There was one man, taller than the others, beard that made it look like he enjoyed IPAs, watching, not saying much.

Oliver didn't appear to match his mother's nervousness. He wriggled his hand against her grip and sped up, his red rucksack rhythmically jostling against his new coat and riding up to the nape of his dark blond hair. Within moments, he'd wedged himself in with the group of other children, with none of the apprehension Sarah was feeling. She sometimes saw herself in him, other times – like now – she couldn't believe someone so different had come from her. Barely a second and he was chatting away to another boy of a similar age, as if they were old friends.

'Bye...' she said, although her son wasn't listening.

With Oliver blending seamlessly with the other children, Sarah was left alone nearby. The school gates remained closed, though there were a couple of teachers on the other side, near the main doors, making a slow walk towards the gates.

'Hi,' a woman said.

Sarah turned to see someone hovering a short gap from the main group of parents. She was late-sixties or seventies, smiling and bright, wearing a layer of clothes too many. There was a slight stoop, as if her knees had long since given up.

'I'm Pamela,' she added quickly. 'Did you just move into Puddlebrick Cottage?'

Sarah gawped for a moment. She had grown up in a city, living in various flats, where it was easy to be anonymous. She had moved to this village barely a day before and her husband had warned her it would be different.

'Uh... yeah,' Sarah managed. 'The estate agent said that's what everyone calls it.'

Despite 'Puddlebrick' being nowhere on the actual address, that was apparently the name. Sarah didn't think she liked it.

Pamela seemed aware as she nodded along earnestly. 'I saw the moving van,' she said.

Sarah wasn't sure she wanted to get into the conversation and smiled weakly as she shot a glance towards her son. Oliver was still chatting to his apparent new friend as the teachers reached the gates. One of them undid the latch and creaked open the heavy metal, as children offered varying degrees of 'bye' to their parents. Some gave hugs, others barely a glance backwards. Sarah looked for Oliver, who had slipped around his friend. He waved, ignoring her mimed requests for a hug, as he disappeared towards his new school. Sarah continued watching, hoping her son might at least look over his shoulder to make sure she was still there.

He didn't, of course. He was busy talking to his new friend. She told herself this was a good thing. New home, new village, new school. He needed friends.

Still, it would've been nice if he'd shown the merest indication he might miss her. She had given birth to him, after all.

'How did you choose the village?'

Sarah turned back to Pamela, who hadn't moved. The other adults had started to drift away, though there was one woman whose young daughter was stuck to her leg, refusing to let go.

'My husband grew up here,' Sarah said, watching as the other mum prised the girl away, telling her that school wouldn't be so bad. The girl was coaxed towards the teacher who had remained at the gates.

'Really?' Pamela replied, sounding interested. 'I've lived here seventy years, just dropped off my great-granddaughter. What's your husband's name? I probably know him.'

Sarah watched the daughter sob her way past the gates, alongside the teacher. Meanwhile, her mum was blowing her own nose. The other mum offered a sad *What can you do?* smile towards Sarah, then turned and started walking away. A moment later and it was only Sarah and Pamela left at the gates.

Pamela had the air of a person who would happily spend fifteen minutes telling a cashier about the catalogue of pills she had to take each day.

'James Parkinson,' Sarah said absent-mindedly, half turning to go.

'Huh,' Pamela replied. 'I don't think I know a *James* Parkinson. There used to be a Vince Parkinson who lived around here.'

'He was my father-in-law. Well, sort of. I never met him. He died before I married James. We were—'

Sarah interrupted herself because something had changed in Pamela's expression. She was now a person who had sat down to watch a cosy Sunday-night drama, only to accidentally switch on *Saw*.

'Huh,' Pamela repeated, although there was more of a punch second time around. '*James* Parkinson,' she added, though the name sounded harsher.

'You might know him as Abraham,' Sarah said, unsure what was going on. 'He goes by "James" though. He says it sounds more professional for his job...'

Pamela's mouth was open and she took a step backwards. It was as if they were having different conversations. Sarah thought clarifying her husband's name might sort things – except it had the opposite effect.

Pamela was stumbling: 'I suppose, um...'

'Is everything all right?' Sarah replied.

Another step backwards and Pamela almost slipped off the kerb. She glanced down and righted herself, before focusing back on Sarah.

'I just don't understand how you can be married to that man.'

Sarah stared back, unsure if she'd heard correctly. 'Which man?'

Pamela moved backwards once more, glancing over her shoulder before hoisting her bag higher.

'Don't you know what your husband did?' she asked.

TWO

Pamela had turned fully now, not wanting a reply. Sarah stood still, stunned at the events of the past minute or so. Pamela was spooked.

'What do you mean?' Sarah asked.

Except the other woman wasn't hanging around. She started to hurry away, glanced over her shoulder one final time towards Sarah, then disappeared around a corner.

Sarah was alone on the pavement, turning between the departed woman and the school, wondering what she'd missed. James had warned her that living in a village was going to be different than a city. 'Curtains twitch a lot more,' he'd said – but Sarah had shrugged it off. She'd grown up in a tower block with thin walls and ceilings. She was used to hearing others move around, of being generally aware what immediate neighbours were up to – but perhaps *this* was what he meant? Weird reactions from weird people.

Sarah considered chasing after Pamela to ask about the 'What your husband did?' comment – but she had things to do at the cottage. He'd probably knocked on her door when he was a child and run away. Perhaps this *was* the sort of place where grudges would hold for such goings-on.

Easy to ignore that stuff, when the view was so new and spectacular. Sarah had lived all her life surrounded by tower blocks and concrete but Carnington was a place with so much sky. So much blue. Nothing tall, nothing garish: everything surrounded by a lush blanket of green countryside.

Sarah had first visited James's home town six years before – and had fallen in love. She had pestered her husband since they'd met about making a trip back to the place in which he grew up. He'd resisted, saying it was too far to go for a day.

It had been, of course. They could have reached Scotland on the train in less time than it had taken to drive from London to Carnington. There had been country lanes and three separate tractors to get stuck behind. James had sighed his way into his home town but any of Sarah's own frustration had evaporated when she saw all the space. Even the air tasted different. She'd told James that day how she wanted to move. That village life had called and she wanted to leave behind the city.

Now, six years on, here they were.

Sarah shook off the encounter with Pamela, and enjoyed the September warmth on her skin as she walked. There were trees lining the high street, posters advertising some sort of amateur dramatics society, the historic old post office, with a blue plaque at the front because some poet had grown up there.

On through the centre and Sarah continued out through the other side, down the slope until she reached Puddlebrick Cottage. She didn't know from where the name had come, though she had been set on the place ever since it went up for sale. She figured there would be a charm to living in a house that sounded like it came from a fairy tale.

The cottage itself was nothing like a fairy tale – except maybe one of the Three Little Pigs' houses after the Big Bad Wolf had blown it down. The agency listing said it 'needed modernising', which was the only reason they'd been able to afford it. The previous owner had lived in it until she was ninety-six.

Sarah passed through the broken gate and opened the unlocked front door. Her 'hello' echoed along the warren of passages and was returned by her father's 'in here'.

When they'd viewed the cottage, James had said that there were more halls than rooms. He'd made it sound like a joke but there was definitely truth in the comment. Sarah told him it would mean more space for him to chase Oliver up and down because that's what he did on the stairs of their old apartment block anyway. There'd be more space for hide-and-seek, considering Oliver had quickly run out of places to conceal himself in their poky flat. James had smiled and conceded the point.

The house was a maze of corridors and Sarah traced her way to the kitchen. Her dad had unpacked the coffee machine and kettle. He was sitting at the large oak table with the back door open, looking out to the overgrown lawn and tangle of weeds beyond.

'How was Oliver?' he asked.

'He made instant friends,' Sarah replied.

'Not bad for day one. How many did you say are in his class?'

That had been one of the things Sarah made a point of emphasising when she was trying to convince James to move.

'Twenty-two,' Sarah said.

Oliver's old class had forty-one pupils, plus the Ofsted report said the city school 'required improvement', while this village school was 'outstanding'. Sarah had pushed and pushed, saying the move would be good for their son, knowing this would be the point on which James would relent.

Her father nodded along, though she wasn't sure if he was making a point. He was hard to read sometimes. She'd spent so long talking about class sizes to anyone who'd listen that she'd almost convinced herself that's why they'd moved. She knew it was more for her and suspected her dad knew that as well.

Everything had gone through a couple of days before the start of the new school year, with the only downside being that James was stuck working in New York.

Sarah's dad took a mouthful of his tea. 'Gonna be a bit of work to clear that,' he said, nodding towards the garden.

'James said he'd get started on it when he's back. One of his friends is a landscaper.'

'Long way to come from London for this...'

There was a hint of scepticism and Sarah knew her father was probably right. Despite her husband saying his friend might help, they all knew it was a long way to come for a day or two's work. Clearing the tangled web of branches and overgrown bushes from the edges of the garden was going to be on them.

'Kettle's still warm if you want one,' Sarah's father added.

She waved that away, hovering by the counter and eyeing the stack of boxes. With James away, her dad had said he'd help move them in – but she couldn't expect him to do all the unpacking. That was going to be on her.

As Sarah gazed at the boxes, she realised her father was watching her.

'You OK?' he asked.

She considered telling him about the weird woman at the school. The whole *what-your-husband-did*-thing – but it would be hard to explain and she wasn't sure she understood it herself.

Her father didn't wait for the answer anyway. 'Your mum always said we were never going to move again after we left the flat,' he said.

Sarah had long since left home by the time her parents had retired to the suburbs. Her mother had spent a lifetime talking about escaping the grind, and then been taken by cancer barely a year after managing it.

Her father seemed to realise what he'd said immediately

after coming out with it. He raised his mug and stood. 'I'm going to get on with the decorating upstairs,' he said. After initially going the wrong way out of the kitchen, Sarah watched him head back the other way and then listened to his footsteps on the stairs.

That was the other thing with Puddlebrick Cottage – Sarah thought of bungalows and cottages as being interchangeable. Both should only have one storey, except Puddlebrick had two. The estate agent had pointed out that there were loads of cottages with more than one floor, though it had felt odd to Sarah. Not that it had stopped her wanting to put in an offer for the place.

As her father got on with filling holes in the walls upstairs, Sarah unpacked more of the kitchen. James had packed the slow cooker, even though they hadn't used it in years. There were fridge magnets from old holidays, mugs with chips in the rim, random cutlery that had appeared over the years. They should have had more of a clear-out before packing – but Sarah wasn't about to have a big sort now. She shoved everything into drawers and cupboards.

Don't you know what your husband did?

What was Pamela talking about? Sarah knew she could text James to ask – but New York was five hours behind, so it would still be the early hours there. What would she ask anyway? 'What did you do?' was too open a question for a text. She'd have to wait until they next spoke.

Sarah spent the next hour and a bit pottering around the ground floor, unpacking boxes and filling bin bags. She was in the living room, deciding whether she should chuck a hideous flowery lampshade that had somehow survived the move, when Sarah spotted two women at the front of the house. They were dressed in shorts and hiking boots, as if they'd returned from a walk. One was pointing to the cottage, though both froze when they noticed Sarah in the window. Sarah waved but the gesture was unreturned. One of the women muttered something to the other, who nodded, then hurried off towards the village centre.

Sarah realised the first woman was her immediate neighbour. They'd met the day before, though Raina was now wearing a wide-brimmed hat and Sarah hadn't immediately recognised her.

Raina took an extra second, eyeing Sarah, before turning and heading towards her own cottage.

Hmmm.

It was an odd reaction, considering Raina had gone out of her way to knock on the door the evening before. She'd been welcoming then, saying she was always around if Sarah had any questions about the area.

But that did remind Sarah of one thing. She headed back to the kitchen and plucked the large Tupperware tub from the draining board. Her dad had folded a tea towel over the oven handle, so Sarah wiped the tub clean and fixed the lid. Moments later and she was back in the autumn sun, ringing her neighbour's doorbell. There was movement from inside, hurried footsteps, and then Raina opened the door. She had lost the hat and boots but was still in the shorts and light jacket. The woman blinked to take in Sarah, as if staring at a person she'd never seen before.

Sarah held up the tub. 'Just returning this,' she said. 'Thank you so much. The three of us had it for tea last night and Dad reckoned it was as good as anything Mum ever made. That's quite the compliment.'

Raina eyed the tub as she bit her bottom lip. She'd brought over a lasagne the afternoon before, welcoming them to the village and saying there was no rush to return the tub. At the time, Carnington had felt like the place Sarah always dreamed it would be. Neighbours helping one another and all that.

Except now...

Raina was staring in a way that felt so alien compared to the day before. There was no friendly smile now, no offers of help.

'Thanks,' she said flatly, taking the container.

Sarah hovered for a moment, trying to think of something to say. 'How was the walk?' she asked. Her chirpiness was forced but there was no reason for Raina to know that.

'Fine,' Raina replied.

'How far did you go?'

'I don't know.'

Raina's expression hadn't changed since the moment she'd opened the door. She was probably in her sixties, maybe a fraction older, though looking good for it. When she'd come by the previous day, it had been with that mumsy vibe of looking out for someone new. Now, there was apathy at best.

'I've got to go,' Raina said, already closing the door. A moment later and it clicked into place, leaving Sarah on the doorstep. She felt the older woman's stare through the eyehole and considered knocking again, perhaps even asking outright what was wrong.

Because something definitely was – and Sarah had the sense that it all looped back to whatever her husband had apparently done.

THREE

As soon as Sarah was back in the cottage, she texted James in New York. They'd had a back-and-forth through the previous day as he'd asked how the move had gone. Between the movers, Sarah, and her dad, they'd unpacked everything from the van by mid-afternoon – though that was barely the beginning. She'd told him that Oliver was excited to start school, while father and son had a few minutes on FaceTime before Oliver's bedtime.

It had all been normal, no hint of how things would be when Sarah mentioned his name to Pamela at the school gates.

Because it *really* felt as if that had been the moment everything had changed.

It was early in New York and, as Sarah scrolled through the previous messages with her husband, she couldn't quite bring herself to ask if he had any idea what was going on. He had a big day of meetings and, though Sarah didn't know why he couldn't do that on Zoom, it sounded important. She didn't want to put him off before any of that.

Besides, he was due to fly that night and should be at their new home in around twenty-six hours.

Not that she was counting.

Instead, Sarah messaged James to say that Oliver had got off to school with no problems. She wished him luck with his day, then waited for a reply that didn't come. According to the notification, he'd not even seen the message.

Sarah unpacked another living-room box, then stopped. She typed 'James Parkinson' into Google, along with 'Carnington', though nothing came up. His proper first name 'Abraham Parkinson' offered little more. If James had supposedly done something, there was no trace of it online. Of course, he'd left the town twenty-odd years before, back when the internet wasn't such a thing. At best, there were glitchy GeoCities and Lycos pages, nothing like the news offerings from the present day.

For a moment, Sarah wondered whether Pamela had been thinking of the wrong person – but then James's father was called Vince.

Hmm.

James had always been reluctant to move. That visit six years before had started Sarah's mind whirring, back when Oliver was only a year old. She'd pictured her son growing up in the village, as opposed to the hustle of the city. James had said it would be too far for his work – and it would have been, if not for the pandemic.

During Covid, he'd started working remotely – and he still was four days a week. Sarah had kept on about moving for long enough that he'd eventually given in. It would be better for Oliver overall, and if it's what she wanted, he would make the sacrifice.

Except he'd never been massively enthusiastic about returning to Carnington and Sarah was beginning to wonder whether there were reasons that went beyond his proximity to work.

If he'd truly done something terrible in the past, as Pamela seemed to think, he must have known it would come up again.

'You're not gonna get many vans down here.'

Sarah jumped at her father's voice. He'd appeared in the living room while making no noise. There were flecks of paint on his hand, more on his jeans. He nodded towards the front and Sarah followed her father's gaze. He was talking about the other big reason she'd given for wanting to leave the city. Oliver had almost been hit by a speeding van a year before and it had spooked Sarah to the point that she'd given her husband an ultimatum. She wanted to leave the city – and was going to do so with or without him.

It had got her what she wanted, even though the guilt hadn't quite left.

'Not speeding ones,' Sarah replied. The lane was too narrow for all that, with a bottleneck diagonally opposite that meant vehicles had to stop and give way. She blinked away from the front of the house and nodded upstairs. 'How's the plastering going?'

'Drying but I need to get more. Do you know if there's a hardware shop in town?'

Sarah didn't think so but checked Google Maps anyway, before relaying the bad news. 'There's a B&Q forty-five minutes away,' she said.

Her dad laughed, probably suspecting as much. 'I'll wash my hands and head out,' he said.

Sarah continued to unpack boxes, fighting the idea that she'd forgotten something that morning. The main job was to walk her son to school but there was a niggling sense she was supposed to do something else as well. Her dad soon reappeared, asking if she wanted anything else. He didn't do Google Maps or satnavs, instead asking which town was nearest the B&Q, then heading off in his car. He'd be a good four hours there and back by the time he'd stopped to ask enough people for directions.

There were times that Sarah loved the old-school nature of her dad, others she wished he'd take the easy option.

With the house to herself, Sarah unpacked two more boxes, then drifted into the kitchen, where she picked at the sausage rolls in the fridge. She checked her phone to see that James had read her messages, though not replied.

Whenever he said he was visiting New York, she pictured skyscrapers and honking taxis; giant pizza slices and steaming street vents. James always insisted the reality was poky studios, cramped meeting rooms, and traffic. She wondered where he was and why he hadn't replied.

Sarah was considering a second sausage roll when a knock echoed through the house. Her dad had taken the spare key, although she wouldn't be surprised if he couldn't find it. She hurried towards the front, still trying to get her bearings among the maze of passages, before opening the door.

It wasn't her father.

It was a man who was probably a similar age to her dad. He was tall, greying at the sides, wearing a fleece and chinos. Sunday-lunch-at-a-garden-centre stuff.

Sarah blinked at him. 'Hello...?'

The man cleared his throat while looking over her, into the house. 'Is Abraham home?' he asked.

It took Sarah a moment to remember her husband's actual first name. She called him James, everyone did, everyone she knew did.

'He's at work,' she replied. 'Can I help?'

A flicker of a frown creased the man's brow as he finally focused on Sarah. 'Do you know when he'll be back?'

Sarah almost replied 'tomorrow' but stopped herself. Quiet village or not, she didn't want to go around telling strangers she was temporarily alone.

'Who are you?' she asked instead.

'Martin Shearer,' the man replied immediately, with a tone

that made it sound as if she should already know. 'And when will Abraham be back?'

Sarah bristled at the name, even though it was technically correct. 'Why do you want to know?'

'I would like to speak to your husband.'

He had the knowing condescension that only men of a certain age could manage, as if about to tell a young woman they shouldn't get a tattoo.

'Do you know him?' Sarah asked.

'You could say that.'

'How?'

Martin's eyes narrowed as he scanned Sarah up and down. She shivered from the attention. 'Are you his wife?' he asked.

'Yes.'

A nod, because he already knew. 'Your husband killed my daughter.'

FOUR

Sarah stared, even as Martin glanced over her once more. It was as if he expected James to be in the house, despite what he'd been told.

'What do you mean?' Sarah managed.

Martin was ignoring her. He checked his chunky watch and took a step back. 'Tell him that Martin Shearer was looking for him.'

Sarah was about to ask whether James would know the name but didn't get a chance. Martin spun and strode along the path. He stepped around the open gate, then bounded into the shadows, towards the village centre. He'd spoken so quickly, and with such clipped authority, that Sarah hadn't thought to press further. Now, seconds later, she was filled by all the questions she should have asked.

Who was Martin's daughter? Why did he think James had killed her? How did he know James? How did he know they were back?

The final question, the how, had to be because of Pamela at the school gates. She was the only person Sarah had told about her husband coming from the village – and now, a handful of hours later, it felt as if everyone knew. That must have been where Raina next door had got it from.

Sarah returned inside, closed the door, then checked her phone. There were no replies from James but, regardless of time zones, she needed to speak to him. Sarah first tried FaceTiming, then calling – but neither attempt got a reply. She texted *Can you call me?* and considered adding an 'urgent', though decided against it. If she did that, James would think something bad had happened to their son. Regardless of anything, that wouldn't be fair.

Back in the living room, Sarah sank onto the armchair that faced the front window, half expecting Martin to have returned. She waited a moment and considered fully bolting the front door, before deciding against it.

Your husband killed my daughter.

It felt so... definitive. No 'I think', or anything like that. Did he mean recently? Or when James had been young, before he'd left Carnington as a teenager?

It didn't take long to find out who Martin Shearer was.

According to Google and various news articles, he was a councillor and local businessman. There were pieces about him sponsoring a local boys' football team and providing funding to set up a girls' side. There was an article about planning permission which said he owned a few houses in town that had been converted into flats.

Sarah scrolled on and on – because there was a *lot* about Martin out there. He'd organised a fun run for the local foodbank, where he'd won the seniors' race. He had been the first person in town to get a Covid vaccine, which involved being photographed with his sleeve rolled up while wearing a mask. He was the president of the amateur dramatics society and had taken the lead in some Gilbert and Sullivan thing the previous winter.

She could have kept reading but Sarah knew the sort. Every

town, every area, had a man of a similar age who was seemingly involved in everything. The heart and soul of a community, who'd end up with an OBE, a plaque on a bench, and a heart attack by the age of seventy.

The problem was, from everything Sarah read, Martin seemed like a nice guy. Sure, he had a whiff of somebody who calls rugby 'rugger' about him. A sense that he'd shot a few foxes over the years; that he went out of his way to make sure everyone knew he had black friends. All that.

But he wasn't *that* bad.

Sarah searched for 'Martin Shearer + daughter' but nothing came up. She tried Martin's name, plus James's, though there was nothing there either. Whatever had gone on between her husband and Martin – assuming it was something – had happened in the days before everything ended up on the internet.

James hadn't replied to Sarah's message. It was around eight a.m. in New York and she figured he'd be on the way to whatever meetings he had.

Sarah considered calling again, her thumb hovering over the green button before she decided against it.

James *couldn't* be a killer. She knew him too well for that. He was the guy who sobbed into his sleeve when the dog lay down outside the garage in *A Star Is Born*. He refused to watch *Planet Earth* because he'd heard something terrible happened to the seals. He even opened windows to let out flies and wasps.

He wasn't a killer.

But he *had* been reluctant to return home. It had been six years since they'd first visited Carnington as a couple, then five of Sarah niggling away to get him to agree. They'd spent the best part of another year looking for the right place until Puddlebrick had gone up for sale.

He'd caved for her, for Oliver, but Sarah never had the

sense this was what *he* wanted. She had pushed that aside, believing the move was right for their family.

But had James known moving back would get this reaction? Sarah so wanted to ask.

She had lived in more or less the same place her whole life, moving only a few miles at a time. It was partly why she'd been so keen for a big change – but James's experience was different. By the time he was twenty-one, he was at university and after university he'd found his way to the city. He'd never gone back to live in Carnington.

Sarah had known her husband for twelve years and they'd been married for seven. It wasn't a coincidence their son was the same age as their marriage. Everything about the start of their relationship had happened so quickly – although nothing felt rushed. It had gone from James giving her a piggyback home from the pub because her shoes made her feet sore; to moving in together within a few weeks. The pregnancy wasn't exactly planned but neither was it particularly unwanted. And they both felt slightly old-fashioned when it came to being married before actually giving birth. Then James had given up the weekly pub quizzes with his colleagues; the six-a-side evenings with his mates – all because he wanted to be home to read to their son each evening.

Whatever Martin thought James had done, it had to be some sort of mistaken identity. Sarah's husband wasn't that sort of person. He would be home from New York by lunch the next day and everything could be sorted.

That didn't stop Sarah desperately wanting to talk to him.

As she considered all that, she finished unpacking the living room as much as she could, then checked upstairs. Her dad had done a good job of patching the holes that speckled the landing, though he'd barely got through half. After the landing, there was a wall in the living room that needed work, plus the spare bedroom had a hole in the floorboards. The entire place needed painting but that would be an ongoing project. If they looked hard enough, Sarah figured they would never stop renovating the place.

Still, the house was theirs.

Sarah checked the time, wondering when her dad would be home. She could picture him on the side of a roundabout somewhere, asking for directions to the B&Q. She and James had both tried gifting him a satnav, then teaching him how to use Maps on his phone – but it wasn't for him. She'd long since concluded that he enjoyed a bit of chaos. If that meant getting lost on the way to a hardware store, then having to have a forty-five minute conversation with someone while asking for directions, all the better.

Meanwhile, it was ten a.m. in New York and James still hadn't responded. Sarah doubted she'd hear anything for at least another three hours, when he might stop for lunch. 'Might' was the key word. If not for that, she wouldn't get anything until after ten p.m. her time.

It was as Sarah was daydreaming of New York and absent husbands that she remembered it was time to pick up Oliver. She hurried downstairs, found her shoes, then locked the house. There was a weird double-click mechanism to the front door that the estate agent had shown them months before. If her dad got back while she was out, he'd have to use the spare key he'd definitely taken.

Despite the blue sky, there was an impending sense of dread as Sarah neared the school. She'd felt it that morning – and that was before she'd met anyone. That had been anticipation, this was reality. She'd spoken to precisely one person at the school gates that morning and it had led to her being shunned by a neighbour, then some bloke showing up at her door, saying her husband was a murderer.

It couldn't have gone much worse.

Sarah felt the stares even from a distance. She was

approaching from the corner, forcing a smile, even as she felt the daggers in return. The same group of women were there from the morning, plus that bloke with the beard. Pamela was with them now and, though Sarah was too far to hear anything, she saw their lips moving, saw the sideways glances.

When Sarah reached the circle, she was met with a series of small closed-lip, *leave-me-alone* smiles. All talk from before was silenced. Pamela was studiously avoiding any sort of eye contact, instead facing the school, arms folded.

The women were a collection of ages, everything from twenty or so up to Pamela in her seventies. Sarah considered saying hello, perhaps even introducing herself properly, though the words didn't come. What was she supposed to say?

Hi, you don't know me but, in case you're wondering, my husband didn't kill anyone.

She almost did it, before deciding to shut up. Instead, she folded her own arms and returned the closed-lip smiles with one of her own.

The awkwardness didn't last long as doors opened and children started to spill from the school. Moments later and Oliver was there. Sarah half expected him to be with the boy he'd been speaking with earlier – but he trailed by himself towards the back. By the time he passed through the gates, almost all the other parents and children had started to head home.

Oliver was scuffing his feet and only looked up to see where his mum was standing.

'How was school?' Sarah asked, trying to sound upbeat. If possible, she wanted to keep the madness away from her son.

'All right.'

They started walking towards the centre of the village, though Oliver had none of the enthusiasm from the morning.

'Are you sure?'

'Yeah.'

'Did something happen?'

'No.'

They were at the corner and Sarah paused, wondering if she should return to ask a teacher what had gone on. Something clearly had. It had only been hours before that Oliver had seemingly found himself some friends, now he had reverted to single syllables.

A car passed and they crossed the road together. In contrast to the morning, it was Oliver now lagging behind. Sarah waited for her son, making sure she was matching his pace.

'Is there something special you want for tea?' she asked, even as she knew the fridge and freezer were largely empty.

It was as if her son hadn't heard. 'When are we going home?' he asked.

'That's where we're going.'

Sarah could sense her son considering his reply, and then: 'I mean our *real* home.'

'The flat?'

'Yeah.'

'The cottage is our home now.'

They took another pace.

'Are you sure you're all right?' Sarah asked. This time, the only reply was a long, large sigh.

FIVE

It was a slow walk home in the September heat. Sarah again asked her son if everything was all right. Oliver told her it was, even though it clearly wasn't. She didn't know what else to do. She tried asking what he'd done at school, though she was met by a stunted 'nothing'. She might have expected such a thing from a grumpy teenager. He had been so excited that morning.

As they passed the poster for the amateur dramatics society, Sarah paid it better attention. This time, she noticed the upcoming play was directed by – and starring – Martin Shearer. There was even a picture of the man who'd stood on her doorstep. He was wearing a dinner suit in the image, with darkened, dyed hair. Things would have been a lot easier to dismiss if he was some loud-mouthed nutjob, not a pillar of the community.

Down the slope towards the cottage, and Sarah's father's car was back on the drive. The front door was unlocked and, as soon as they stepped inside, he called, 'How's my little star?' from the top of the stairs. Moments later and Oliver was grinning again. Somehow, Sarah's dad always managed to get a smile out of his grandson. It wasn't long until they were playing some sort of game that involved throwing a bouncy ball up the stairs and trying to catch it on the way down. It felt like the sort of thing of which Sarah should probably disapprove, although she couldn't think of a reason why. She watched them for a moment, enjoying how happy they were, before finally remembering the other thing she was supposed to have done that morning.

Find a supermarket.

The distraction of Pamela, Raina, then Martin had been too much.

Sarah left her father and son to their game, then headed along the passage into the kitchen. They had spent the past week in their old flat, eating desperate combinations of food in an attempt to whittle down what was in their fridge-freezer ahead of moving. Potato faces with refried beans and raspberry jam had been a particular low.

Now, what little they had in the new fridge was *very* middle class.

There were some out-of-date mini pita breads from the M&S near their flat, bought a few days before they'd moved; a half-eaten tub of hummus, four carrots, a tub of something called 'banana power boost' that was James's, plus some yoghurt that probably should've been binned before the move.

Sarah had spent so many hours moping around the house, worrying about other people, when she could have gone to the shops.

Back to the stairs, where Sarah's dad was still playing with Oliver. He caught her eye as she stood in the door frame and somehow knew what had happened. He didn't say anything, not at first, and there was no judgement – even though Sarah felt the failure herself. It was a constant push to try to be a good parent and she had been struggling to deal with the stress of the move, even before the village whispers came for her.

Somehow, her father saw all that.

'We should go out to eat,' he announced. 'Celebrate Oliver's first day at school.' He turned to his grandson. 'What would you like?'

Oliver was on the bottom step, bouncy ball firmly in his grip. He turned to his mum because they all knew takeaway night was Friday. This was a Tuesday. When he realised Sarah wasn't going to say no, the grin started to spread.

'KFC...?'

He spoke as if he couldn't quite believe his luck. Only he realised it was the wrong day and, if he said too much, someone else might realise.

At their old flat, there were two KFCs within walking distance, plus a Dixie Fried, Tennessee Fried and Alabama Fried Chicken. Sarah took a moment checking her phone. She'd been so used to having everything on the doorstep that planning ahead was going to take some adjustment. For Oliver, the immediacy of city life was all he'd ever known.

'The nearest one is out by that B&Q,' Sarah told her father. That was another forty-five minutes in the car. She tried Deliveroo but all that showed was a pizza shop in town, plus cans of pop and sweets from the petrol station.

'At least I know the way now,' her father replied. He might have winked at her, though Sarah wasn't sure, because he was already patting pockets, looking for his car keys.

As Oliver dashed upstairs to get changed, Sarah whispered to her dad that she could stay home, unpack a few more boxes. She felt the urge to do *something*, given her failure to refill the fridge across the entire day. He seemed to recognise the guilt, though didn't acknowledge it.

'Family celebration,' he insisted. 'James will be back tomorrow and it's not often you and I get to do something like this.'

Sarah hadn't sensed an edge – but he was right about that. When they usually did things as a family, it involved her, Oliver *and* James. This time was a gift, in a way. It was rare she spent much time with her father and not her husband.

Except the mention of James left Sarah forcing away a shiver.

Your husband killed my daughter.

Thundering footsteps banged down the stairs as Oliver reappeared. He jumped the final three, steadying himself and then turning as if to ask the adults why they weren't ready. His nervous feet scuffing from the walk home had been replaced by this new joy, which was something.

Sarah's father drove. There were narrow country lanes, high hedges, tight verges, tighter bends – and very little in the way of road signs. Oliver wanted to play I-spy and her father went with it, leaving Sarah to try to remember the positives of why they had moved. There was going to be much more open space for Oliver to play, far smaller class sizes, much better air quality, less pollution, nowhere near as much noise... all the stuff those studies endlessly insisted was essential for a happy life.

And yet...

Everything was so far away. They couldn't walk to the hardware shop, couldn't get food with the tap of an app, couldn't have same-day delivery from Amazon. Sarah wondered whether they needed all that stuff, or if it was simply that they'd become so used to it.

Your husband killed my daughter.

Sarah blinked the thought away as her phone buzzed. She hoped it was James on a break from work, messaging back to ask if everything was OK. He might even have ten minutes for a chat – except it wasn't him.

How are things? Is the cottage fab?!

Cara, from Cara and Richard fame, was one of James and Sarah's London friends. They lived a few streets from Sarah's old place, in a much larger flat. Their son, Harry, had been in Oliver's class until the big move. He was one of four Harrys in the same class. Give it a few years and every newborn would be Harry or Harriet.

In the final week before the big move, there had been vague talks of Cara, Richard and Harry visiting for a weekend. They could sleep in the spare room – a novel idea, given how cramped everything was for them all in the city. They would put the boys to bed and stay up drinking wine, maybe play some games or chat about how fantastic life in the countryside was. How everyone should escape the city, and so on.

It felt fanciful to Sarah now, given the spare room was nowhere near ready, the garden was a tangled mess, and the locals seemed to think James was a murderer.

Not that Sarah could say any of that.

It's fab! Everything's great! Can't believe how friendly everyone is! Can't wait for you to visit!!

Sarah regretted the text immediately after sending. One exclamation mark was overkill, two was unhinged, three was covering up an obvious lie, four was sectioning territory, and Sarah had gone with the full five.

Except what else was she supposed to say? That they were driving forty-odd minutes to get KFC because she'd forgotten to do a food shop? That Oliver was unhappy, though she wasn't sure why? That James was away, and some bloke reckoned he'd killed his daughter?

That would be *quite* the text.

Phone reception came and went as they slipped through the empty, dusty lanes until eventually emerging onto an A-road. There was ten minutes of a soulless dual carriageway and then, finally, signs of life. They passed a giant Asda, got on a ring road that took them past a sports arena, then Sarah's father pulled into a large retail park. It felt like a long way to come for a drive-thru, so it wasn't long before the three of them were sitting around a plasticky table in the KFC window.

Oliver seemed excited that the McDonald's they'd passed had a large outdoor play area, plus he'd seen a sign for a toy shop at the park entrance. With that, plus his actual food, he was happy enough asking his grandfather when they could come back.

That left Sarah scrolling her phone, thankful for the signal that didn't cut in and out. She was busy deleting emails when she realised her dad was talking to her.

'... I said how is the world of bookkeeping?' he repeated, nodding to the phone.

Sarah wondered how he knew she was going through her work emails. Her out-of-office was on, but that didn't mean much.

Oliver was wiping his greasy fingers on the colouring-in sheet they'd snagged from near the front door.

'Thrilling,' she told her dad, deadpan with a smile.

'Are your clients staying with you?'

'Most of them. It's probably enough for now but James said I could maybe go door to door with the businesses in town to see if they're after anyone. Either that, or there's probably a neighbourhood Facebook thing.'

Her dad nodded along, gaze unfocused, as she realised he'd asked to be polite. The idea of *actually* going door to door to drum up business was less appealing than clearing out those weeds from the back garden. As for the Facebook group, those local forums were only ever full of whack jobs arguing about whether a skateboarder might be a secret terrorist.

Oliver said he needed the toilet and Sarah watched as he headed off to the back of the restaurant. It had been a few months since he'd started insisting he was old enough to go by himself.

It was as Sarah glanced back to her phone that she realised she'd missed a message from her husband. James must have texted during the time they'd been driving, when reception had been intermittent. She'd not had a notification – but the reply had come more than half an hour before. She had spent all that time messing around with emails.

Everything OK? The team want to take me out later, so going from there straight to airport. Already checked out of hotel. Looking fwd to seeing you tomoz. Sent a vid for Ol – can you play it for him b4 bed?

Sarah read the message through twice, wondering if she could reply to the 'Everything OK?' bit by telling her husband that it wasn't – and that people were saying he'd killed someone. If she wasn't in a KFC, with her father sitting opposite, she'd have tried calling.

Instead, she replied with a meek:

Sounds great! Will show Oliver his video. Have a great night. See you tomorrow.

Sarah let the single exclamation mark go, then returned to not eating her food. She wasn't a fan of fried chicken at the best of times.

Oliver was back from the toilet and finished his colouring-in, while Sarah avoided the *Are you OK?* looks from her father. A melancholy had settled across them and Sarah didn't know how to break it. There had been so much stress ahead of the move, with solicitors, banks, deposits, moving companies, and hoping it would all be sorted before Oliver started the school term. That was before the practical stuff, such as the *actual* packing. Sarah had assumed that, once all that was done, everything else would fall into place.

And now… there was a creeping, niggling sense that she'd made a terrible mistake. Perhaps she'd be feeling that anyway – but the strangeness of people's reactions to her certainly hadn't helped, not to mention Oliver's apparent unhappiness from his first day at school.

As she considered that, Sarah's father helped clear the table, then they headed back to the car. It felt unfathomable that this sort of forty-minute-out, forty-minute-back journey could be the norm.

The drive back was similar to the one out: the soulless dual carriageway and then a bunch of hedges. Oliver's enthusiasm had given way to a doze in his booster seat, now he had a full belly. Sarah felt the sideways glances from her father as he drove – though he didn't outright ask if she was fine. He probably suspected doubts were creeping in.

The sky was beginning to turn purple as they finally emerged from the country lanes past the Welcome To Carnington sign. It had been a long day… a long *few* days, and Sarah was feeling it. She wanted to get Oliver to bed and maybe do the same herself. If she could only get a good night's sleep, she'd wake up to knowing James was on a flight home, then it would only be a few hours until everything was fixed.

Her dad took the turn for their lane and Sarah was impressed he'd remembered the route both ways. She was about to tell him as much, knowing he'd reply to say that's what every journey was like in his day, when he stopped, blocking the lane with the car.

Sarah was about to ask why – but then she saw it.

Sprayed onto the wall at the front of the house, in bright white paint, was a clear message for the new owners of Puddlebrick Cottage.

GO HOME

SIX

The air was cool as Sarah drifted through the cottage's front door, towards the front wall. Her dad was on the ground, scrubbing the paint, as a bucket's worth of soapy suds ran along the crumbling tarmac towards the drain.

'It's coming off,' he said, not turning from the wall.

There were no street lights and Sarah could only see him because of the gloomy white from the moon. She sat on the ground at her father's side and took the second scrubbing brush from the bucket.

'You don't have to do this,' her father said.

'*You* don't have to do this,' she replied. 'You don't even live here.'

'You're still my daughter.'

There was a simmering, seething anger below the surface that Sarah didn't want to poke. Her dad was furious on her behalf.

They scrubbed the wall together for a minute or so until he next spoke. 'How was Oliver?'

'He said he didn't want to sleep at the house.'

'Why?'

'I don't know. I think maybe the move is catching up to him. It's a lot in one go. New village, new house, new school.'

Somehow, that had all escaped Sarah ahead of the move. She was desperate to get everything through in time for Oliver to start the school year – except that meant there was more to overwhelm him.

She was *such* a bad mother... but at least he hadn't seen the graffiti.

'It's not you, love,' Sarah's father said, as if reading her mind once more. She appreciated the sentiment, except she worried it actually *was* her. Nobody had pushed for the move, aside from her.

'James sent a video, so I let Oliver watch that,' Sarah told her dad. 'He fell asleep during the third time round.'

James had filmed it with the backdrop of skyscrapers behind. He'd called Oliver his 'special little man' and said he was looking forward to seeing him. Sarah had listened to her kind, thoughtful husband, who adored their son, wondering how anyone could think he was a murderer.

It couldn't be possible... except at least one person with a paint can was presumably furious about the prospect of James's return to the village.

Sarah scrubbed a section of brickwork so hard that mortar began to crumble away. The O-M-E of the message was gone, leaving the first three letters. As her dad worked on the H, Sarah continued on the G.

'Why would someone do this?' Sarah's dad asked.

Sarah had known the question was going to come, even as she'd gone to put Oliver to bed while her father said he was heading outside. He was staying with her temporarily, to help with the move, and there was no way she could keep everything from him.

He listened as Sarah told him much of what had happened through the day. A woman at the school gates had been horrified when Sarah gave the name of her husband, then the immediate neighbour had a similar reaction. Lastly, someone named Martin came to the door and claimed James had killed his daughter. The graffiti was the icing on top.

James had always got on with Sarah's dad about as well as men did with fathers-in-law. They were from different generations, with little in common, but neither had ever had a bad word to say about the other – certainly not to her. She wondered if this might change things, though her dad was calm as he replied.

'Have you asked James about this?'

'Not yet. He's been busy in New York and I didn't think it was something I could text about. He's back tomorrow lunchtime anyway.'

'You never quite said why he was abroad...'

That was true, although it was something of a leading question. 'It was a work meeting,' Sarah said. 'He tried to move it, then asked if it could be remote, but his boss wanted it to be in person. It was a coincidence it happened the weekend before we were moving.'

Sarah's father didn't respond. He'd never quite come around to anyone working outside of a strict nine-to-five, Monday to Friday. It didn't help that James worked for a finance firm, managing investments, which had always sounded somewhat vague, even to Sarah.

'It was me who pushed to move here,' Sarah added, figuring her dad needed to know. 'James moved *for* me.' A pause. 'For Oliver. He wanted to make us happy. If it was up to him...'

Sarah tailed off because she knew the truth. James was a city guy. He liked the convenience of having everything on his doorstep, not to mention the underground commute, the theatres, the football stadiums, the stand-up nights, basement gigs in sweaty pubs.

He'd given all that up so Sarah could have what she wanted,

plus give Oliver what would likely be a better education. Were those the actions of a selfish killer?

'Did he ever say anything about any of this?' Sarah's father asked.

'Nothing.'

'Sounds like it's probably mistaken identity. Does he have a brother?'

'No, he's an only child.'

'Didn't his mum and dad die in a car crash? Maybe somebody's mixed them up...?'

Sarah and her father both thought on that for a moment as her father scrubbed away the final part of the graffiti.

'I'm sure it'll sort itself out,' he concluded – although Sarah wasn't sure that was ever true. Things didn't sort *themselves* out, there was always an external force. She hoped that James could be that force. That he had an answer for whatever was going on.

Inside, and the evening drifted by. Sarah's idea of an early night had been obliterated by the 'go home' message. She skimmed Facebook and some news websites, while her dad did the *Sunday Times* crossword. He'd been hanging onto it for two days, and always made sure his daughter knew he only bought the paper for the puzzles. He headed up to bed a little after ten. There was a mattress in the spare room, though Sarah and James had a vague plan to redecorate the room and get a proper bed.

When it came to the cottage, they had come up with a lot of vague plans since having an offer accepted.

Sarah was hoping to hear from her husband, before remembering that she hadn't asked any questions with her previous reply. Until he got to the airport in what would be the early hours for her, there was no need for him to message.

She headed up to bed herself, where much of the room was filled with boxes. The bed itself was the same from their flat, although there were yet more vague plans to get a king-size at some point. Sarah figured someone should have probably made a list of all the ideas, because she hadn't.

The bed felt empty without James, perhaps the entire house. Sarah was used to the creaks and quirks of their flat. The way the sun crept around the curtain in the morning, the sound of the clanking bin lorry at ten-past-six every Tuesday, the tippy-tap of their upstairs neighbour getting home from work when he was on late shifts. There was the groan of the lift from down the corridor, the squeak of their neighbour's shower, the way the rain started as a pitter but could become a roar.

But now, it was all so different. There was... nothing. Silence. *Actual* silence. It was so quiet that Sarah almost couldn't handle it. She needed the faint hum of traffic, or the squeals of the train when the wind blew in a certain direction. Plus, it was so dark. She hadn't got around to putting up their old curtains. The ones that came with the house were an ugly purple that left a big gap at the top – not that it mattered because there was no light to seep inside.

It was dark and it was silent.

This was what she wanted.

Wasn't it?

Sarah didn't remember falling asleep but her phone said it was a little before three in the morning. She reached across the mattress for James, then remembered he was in New York. He should have messaged to say he was at the airport, maybe even on the plane, but there was no reply since she'd told him to have a good evening.

Instead... there was something else.

Sarah put down her phone and sat up, listening to the creak from somewhere below. *Another* creak. She was certain the first is what had woken her. Was it pipes? A moaning radiator? Something like that.

EIGHT

The messages kept coming, one after the other. There was a thunderstorm in Dallas, which meant a plane that was supposed to be taking off from Texas hadn't made it to New York. The knock-on effect was that there was no plane to fly from New York to London, leaving James stranded at the airport. He was trying to rebook – but so was everyone.

He would have sent the messages expecting Sarah to be asleep – which was probably why he looked so surprised when he answered the FaceTime call. Well, surprised *and* tired. He was in a queue, trying to reach the airline information desk, holding the phone so close to his face that Sarah could make out individual nose hairs. She switched on the kitchen light, so he could see her better – but the bags under Sarah's eyes and the greyness of her skin shocked even her.

'Why are you up so early?' he asked.

'Noisy pipes,' Sarah replied, which was perhaps true. Better than admitting she might be hearing things.

'I don't think I'm getting on a flight anytime soon,' he said, before biting away a yawn. 'All the planes from the south are trapped because there's a massive storm. They're trying to move everything around but it'll be hours.'

He paused for a moment, listening to an echoing announcement that Sarah couldn't make out. James shunted forward in the line and offered a weak smile.

'What are you going to do?' she asked.

'Someone said they're giving out hotel vouchers, so maybe get a room? If not, I suppose I'm sleeping here.' He tapped something on the phone, changing to the outward camera and swinging the device around for Sarah to see what looked like a well-lit refugee camp. There were masses of people sitting and lying on floors and chairs, using bags as pillows. Others were standing in line, clutching luggage and fighting yawns. When he switched the camera back to himself, James offered a weak smile. 'Sorry,' he said.

'How was the meeting?'

'Same as last time. Don't know why it couldn't have been on Zoom.'

It had been a few months back that James had been on a similar work trip to New York. He'd been there for two nights, because of one morning meeting, then flown back again. It happened semi-regularly.

'Everything OK?' he added, which Sarah realised was in response to a sigh she hadn't meant to let out. She faked a yawn, which led to a real yawn. There was something about it being real love if you could yawn down a FaceTime call and show your tonsils to a partner.

His was such a loaded question. Things were definitely *not* OK – but Sarah couldn't tell James, not now, even if they were digitally face to face. Some conversations *had* to be in person – and asking your husband if they were a secret murderer had to be one of those.

'It's been a long couple of days,' Sarah said, which was true.

'I'm so sorry about all this. How was Oliver's first day?'

'He was quiet on the walk home but it's all new for him. He liked your video. Fell asleep watching it the third time.'

James broke into a smile. 'Day two will always be easier than day one...'

Sarah didn't reply because it sounded like something from a crappy inspirational poster. She loved her husband but, every now and then, he slipped down a live, laugh, love wormhole.

There was a garbled glitch on the call and then James was talking again: '... house like? Is your dad getting on well with everything?'

'He's about halfway through sorting out the repairs upstairs. He's waiting for the filler to dry.'

James was nodding but had the expression of a person who'd not heard what was said. He held up a finger as another announcement reverberated. Sarah still couldn't make out what had been said but suddenly James was speaking quickly.

'I've got to go. That was something to do with my flight. I'll text when I know what's going on. Love you.'

He didn't wait for a response, hanging up and leaving Sarah staring at the blank screen. She sat at the kitchen table and yawned once, then twice. If James had any concern that news of him being a murderer was to be exposed by returning to his home town, he hadn't said anything. He hadn't looked worried, just tired. Was that the response of someone with something to hide? It didn't seem like it.

Sarah googled 'America storms' – and there were already endless articles about the thunder and lightning rolling around Texas, Oklahoma, Arkansas and Louisiana. Hundreds of flights had been grounded, people were being advised not to travel, and there was a series of videos showing crackling forks of lightning flashing around the skies.

It didn't feel as if James would be home anytime soon.

Sarah did a bit of unpacking as quietly as she could in the living room, then returned to the kitchen where she made some coffee and read more about the U.S. storms. She yawned a lot and cursed herself for not going back to bed when she had the chance.

It was so quiet. No bin lorry, no distant chunter of traffic, nobody clumping down a corridor... just... *peace.*

Sarah put together a lunch of pitas, hummus, carrots and a yoghurt for her son, then hunted through the boxes until she found the breakfast cereal. There was milk at the back of the fridge that passed both the sniff and sip test.

As the sun started to come up, Sarah's father reappeared downstairs. He asked if she'd got back to sleep and Sarah pointed to the pot of coffee as an answer. It got a laugh, if nothing else. After that, she headed up to Oliver's room. She stood at the end of her son's bed for a minute or so, watching his covers rise and fall, hoping this move was going to be the right thing for him. His class size really *was* a lot smaller, the Ofsted report *was* so much better. She had to cling onto those things.

Sarah approached her son and gently placed a hand on his shoulder, rocking him steadily until his eyes fluttered open. He blinked and squinted until focusing on her, then yawning. She waited until he pushed himself up.

'Morning,' Sarah said. 'Did you sleep well?'

Oliver was still blinking but shook his head. 'Voices,' he said.

'Sorry if I was too loud.' Sarah opened the curtains fully, though the sun was on the other side of the house. 'I found the Coco Pops for you,' she said.

'Do I have to go to school?'

'Everyone has to go to school.'

'You don't.'

'Every *child* has to go to school. That's what you have to do if you want to grow up to be a juggler.'

Sarah just about kept a straight face. Juggling was her son's latest interest, though she doubted it would last much past the end of the month. For whatever reason, he'd got it into his head that juggling was his route to happiness, fame and fortune. With the move and everything, there seemed little point in dropping reality on him.

That more or less coaxed Oliver out of bed and it wasn't long until he was eating cereal at the kitchen table, while telling his granddad that his dad had promised him a trampoline now they had room.

Sarah had forgotten that. It was another in their long list of vague plans for the new house – albeit this one *wouldn't* be forgotten. Oliver wasn't going to let that happen.

Despite the reluctant way he'd scuffed his feet home the afternoon before, Oliver didn't make much fuss about getting ready for school. The sun was peeping over the top of the trees as they headed up the hill and, for a minute or so, he seemingly forgot himself as he reached for Sarah's hand. She clasped his in hers and they continued side by side until he realised what was happening and pulled away.

Sarah had been deliberately early the day before but she timed the walk so they reached the school gates at the exact time they opened. The mums were already dispersing as Sarah arrived with Oliver, meaning there were no awkward moments with Pamela or any of the others. A teacher was waiting near the gate and knew Oliver's name as she held the gate wide for him to enter. He mumbled what might have been a 'bye', then headed down the path towards the school.

'I'm Miss Callaghan,' the woman told Sarah. 'Oliver's in my class. I understand you just moved to the area...?'

She was one of those teachers who seemed impossibly young. Miss Callaghan smiled wide and Sarah wondered if she had lived in the village for long; whether she, too, knew that James had been accused of something he hadn't done.

'We only got the keys on Monday morning,' Sarah said. It looked as if Miss Callaghan was about to close the gate and head towards the school, so Sarah spoke quickly. 'Did something happen with Oliver yesterday? He was really quiet after school, even though he was excited in the morning.'

The teacher looked curiously at Sarah, then reopened the gate. 'Do you want to come inside for a minute?'

It felt ominous but Sarah trailed the younger woman along the path, across the playground, and through the main doors. There was a general sound of children chattering over one another nearby, though nobody else was visible in the reception area. Miss Callaghan told Sarah she'd be right back, then she disappeared into a corridor.

Sarah was alone in an entrance area, surrounded by memorabilia. There were ribbons over the door, celebrating what looked like a gymnastics competition win from a few years back, then another that might have been for majorettes. Sarah did a slow loop of the area, scanning a couple of the news articles that had been framed. There was one about a charity bake sale from the year before, another from a time when the primary schoolers had done a sponsored run around the playground.

On the wall opposite the articles were long rows of school photos. There were maybe fifty or sixty students assembled on benches, alongside half-a-dozen adults, everyone smiling into the sun.

The whole school photos looked so small.

When Sarah had been a similar age, there were over a hundred students in her year alone – let alone the entire school. This had been part of the pitch to James to convince him to move: smaller classes meant more direct attention for Oliver. It was so important at this primary school age.

But it really did look *small*.

There were probably more children living in the tower block next to their old flat.

Sarah moved along the line of photos, realising a full school photo had been taken once a year, every year, all the way back to 1981. There were lists of students and teachers printed underneath and Sarah found herself scanning through the 1990s and 1980s, searching for what might be there.

It didn't take her long to find it.

Abraham Parkinson was a little kid with big ears back in the late 1980s. The man she now knew as James had a number four all over back then and was beaming brightly to the camera. Her husband had the same smile now, even though his ears had – luckily – not grown with the rest of him. He had more hair, too.

Sarah used her phone to take a photo of the photo, figuring she'd send it to James and ask what was going on with his ears.

Except...

It wasn't only James in the photo. There were all the other children, too – and Sarah found herself running a finger along their names, passing Abraham Parkinson until she settled on the name of the girl at his side.

Martin Shearer had knocked on her door the day before, accusing James of killing his daughter.

And there, sitting next to Sarah's husband when they were barely eight years old, was little Lucy Shearer.

NINE

'Quite the collection, isn't it?'

Miss Callaghan had reappeared from the corridor and was standing a few paces from Sarah.

She nodded at the wall of photos, then pointed to one from the early 2000s. 'This is me.'

Sarah peered at a class photo which was eerily similar to the one from the 1980s. The children's uniforms were identical, with everyone sitting in tidy lines, the staff standing at the edges.

Miss Callaghan really *was* young. She was in the photo as an eight- or nine-year-old, grinning wildly.

'You came back to teach at your old school?' Sarah said.

'This is what I always wanted to do,' Miss Callaghan replied. 'Right back from when I was twelve or thirteen, I told my mum I wanted to be a primary school teacher. That was her job, too.'

Sarah nodded along. Perhaps this was what James had been trying to warn her about when he was reluctant to move? Carnington was the sort of place where the children of teachers became teachers, and went to work at the schools where they'd originally been taught. There was nothing wrong with that but it felt very circular. Very... um... incestuous.

Not that Miss Callaghan picked up on Sarah's needless unease. 'I don't think there was anything wrong with Oliver yesterday,' she said. 'I just checked on them and he was chatting away with one of the other boys.'

Sarah found it impossible not to show her relief. She let out a long breath that she hadn't realised she'd been holding.

'It's been such a busy time,' she said.

'Of course. I'll definitely keep an eye on him – and it's good to meet face to face. The only thing he did say yesterday was that he hadn't slept well. He said a woman had kept him awake...?'

It was phrased as a question, though Sarah stared blankly back at the teacher. 'I was the only woman in the house.' She paused, trying to think. 'Maybe I was talking in my sleep?'

It felt unlikely, even if Sarah's room did share a wall with Oliver's. When she had woken him earlier that morning, after their second night in the house, her son said something about 'voices' keeping him up. Sarah assumed it had been her whispering on the landing with her dad. But did that mean Oliver had been kept awake by voices *both* nights?

Miss Callaghan smiled. 'If you're certain. I just needed to check. I'm sure it's the stress of the move.' She angled towards the hall. 'I have to get back. I do need to lock the door behind you, so...'

Sarah allowed herself to be ushered towards the outside. Miss Callaghan offered another welcome to the area, then clicked the door closed. Sarah didn't bother hanging around and was barely out of the main gates before she'd googled 'Lucy Shearer Carnington'.

There wasn't a lot of information, though there was a short article saying Lucy had been declared legally dead in 2002. She had apparently gone missing seven years before, which explained why there was so little online about her. Carnington was a village in the back end of nowhere, and whatever happened with Lucy had occurred before the days of widespread internet.

It had been getting on for thirty years since Lucy had disappeared. James would have been around fifteen at the time, living in Carnington as 'Abraham'. Sarah re-read the piece – but it was focused on Lucy's formal 'dead' status rather than specifics. All it said was that she'd skipped school and gone missing as a teenager.

It wasn't only the article, though. There was a photo of a girl giving a thumbs-up to whoever was taking the picture. Fairly unremarkable for a nineties teenager: except for her smile. Even Sarah felt drawn to her, as if they had once been friends. She had to tell herself they were strangers.

No wonder people in the village hadn't forgotten her.

It had to be the same girl who was next to James in the school photo but was their placement an accident? Were they friends who chose to sit together?

As she was looking at the photo, Sarah realised James had messaged while she'd been inside the school. It was coming up to four in the morning in New York and he had checked into an airport hotel to try to get a few hours' sleep. The airline had booked him on a flight for eleven in the morning New York time, though he hadn't figured out what he was going to do when he arrived back in London. Sarah's mental maths worked out that he'd be flying at four o'clock in the afternoon her time, landing at around eleven p.m. There wouldn't be much in the way of public transport so late – let alone anything that could get him to Carnington.

He said he'd let her know when he had a clearer plan, then added a couple of kisses. Sarah wasn't sure how to reply. With everything that had happened the day before, she'd been relying on him getting home at lunchtime to clear everything up. It was now going to be another day at least.

Sarah considered asking if her husband knew Lucy Shearer but there would be no way to do that without inviting harsher questions over why she was asking. In the end, she opted for *Sleep well, have a safe journey X*, figuring she was going to have to wait for a better answer.

At least she had a name for this mystery daughter.

Sarah walked away from the school, wondering how she could find out more about Lucy without explicitly having to ask anyone. Surely if Lucy and James had some sort of connection, he'd have mentioned it. There was a big jump from Lucy's father saying James had killed her, to James saying nothing in the years Sarah had known him.

As Sarah made a slow walk back to the cottage, this time she remembered the need to pick up food. There was no big supermarket on the high street, but there was a small Spar with a sandwich board outside, advertising lottery tickets. Sarah continued past that, taking in 'Gem's Gems', which appeared to be some sort of dreamcatcher and crystal shop. Next to that was a bookshop, then a grocer.

Sarah bought some spinach, broccoli and carrots, then passed a fishmonger, gourmet deli and baker, before heading into Nixon And Son Butchers. After the fried chicken and chips of the day before, she could probably persuade Oliver to eat some greens if there were sausages to go with it.

An older man was behind the counter, wearing a dark apron over whites. As soon as the bell jingled above the door, the sound of a child crying seeped from a back room. He caught Sarah's eye and winced slightly.

'Can you hang on a minute?' the man asked.

'No problem.'

He disappeared into the back of the shop, leaving Sarah to browse the spacious meat counter. She was used to visiting the big Tesco at the end of her street, or, on occasion, the Waitrose at the other end. It was something of a novelty to have shop after shop of non-chains.

A minute or so passed and then the curtain swished. This time a new man appeared, younger than the first person, but also wearing an apron. The dark bags under his eyes made him look as tired as Sarah felt. He blinked himself awake and nodded towards the back room, where the crying child had gone quiet. 'That's my son,' he said. 'He's fine – promise – but he only goes quiet when his granddad holds him. My wife's ill, so I had to bring him in.'

Sarah gave a knowing smile. Oliver had gone through a stage as a baby in which he refused to be comforted by her. It was his father's arms, or an endless paddy. That was all well and good, except for the times his dad was at work.

'You must be the And Son,' she said.

The man frowned with initial confusion, before following her nod towards the Nixon And Son sign over the counter.

'Right!' he said. 'Well, technically no.' He pointed backwards. 'My dad's the "son", I'm the grandson.'

Sarah remembered Miss Callaghan, a teacher becoming a teacher because her mum was. 'A family business,' she said.

'Yeah – but don't let Dad start on about it. He'll be telling you about how six generations of Nixons have lived in Carnington. He's already talking about Naomi taking over from me, except I'm not in charge – and Naomi's only eighteen months old.'

There was a laugh but it felt loaded, as if he didn't find it as funny as he was making out.

'I've not seen you around before,' he added – and there was perhaps a loaded element to that, too. Sarah was used to a big city, millions of people, where a person could spend a lifetime living anonymously. She was going to have to get used to living in a place where everyone knew everyone else.

It wasn't only that. Telling people who she was, who she was married to, hadn't gone well so far.

Sarah stumbled with nervousness, before managing: 'I just moved here.'

The man was nodding along. 'Oh right! What made you pick this place? It's a bit out of the way, isn't it?'

'That's kind of why we chose it.'

Sarah wondered if he'd let it lie, except he continued to look at her expectantly. In the end, it felt as if she had no option other than to say it.

'My husband grew up here.'

The butcher was nodding, still waiting. 'Who is he?' he asked after an uncomfortable couple of seconds.

Sarah realised she'd folded her arms at some point. 'Um... *James* Parkinson,' she said, emphasising the 'James' part.

The frown told her so much more than Sarah wanted to know.

'I used to know an Abe Parkinson,' the man said.

'That's him,' Sarah replied, wishing she didn't feel the need for honesty. 'James is his middle name and he uses that now.'

The man was nodding, though his eyebrows had dipped with... something. Confusion, maybe? Then he let out a long, low puff of breath.

'Huh,' he said. 'Abraham used to be my best friend.'

TEN

'Your... um... *best* friend...?'

Sarah had repeated things without meaning to. She realised she didn't know the man's name but he was staring at her curiously and she wondered if she'd pulled some sort of expression.

'Are you OK?' he asked.

It took a moment for Sarah to compose herself. She forced herself to uncross her arms, then tugged at a strand of hair. It had hit her all at once that this was now her life. It wasn't a few days away in the countryside, Carnington wasn't a holiday, it was *her life*. She couldn't live with all these new people staring when she mentioned her husband's name. She couldn't be somewhere that had graffiti telling her to leave. There was a rushing, bludgeoning sense of falling and then Sarah found herself blinking rapidly at the man as she found herself blurting out what had been happening to her.

'A man visited the house yesterday,' she said, stuttering. 'He was looking for my husband, saying James had killed his daughter. Then someone graffitied "Go home" on the wall last night. James is in New York. It's all been a bit...'

She tailed off and found herself slumping onto a single

chair near the door. It felt as if the ceiling was grunting its way slowly towards her, closing in, trapping her, giving her no space.

Then, from nowhere, the man was at her side. He rested a warm hand on her shoulder. 'Are you sure you're OK?' he asked.

There was crying from the back room, though Sarah couldn't remember when it had started again. Perhaps it had never stopped?

'Look,' the man said. 'My name's Dean. I'm going to walk Naomi around the park to see if it tires her out. Why don't you come?'

Sarah gulped away what felt like possible tears. She needed to get herself together. 'Sure,' she said.

Like so many things in Carnington, the park was like something from a period drama. There was a duck pond in the middle, with a gravel track around the outside, all of which was surrounded by a few acres of manicured lawn. A play area was near the entrance, a roundabout, swings and climbing wall surrounded by soft rubber matting. No broken equipment here, no scorch marks on the grass from where someone had tried to start a fire, no tyre tracks from a dirt biker doing wheelies. That was the park closest to where Sarah and James used to live in London.

She carried her bag for life walking next to Dean, as he pushed a buggy along the outside path of the park. The sky was blue again, the sun warm on her arms as they moved in and out of the shadows of the whispering trees.

Baby Naomi was quiet in the buggy, seemingly asleep, as Dean had spent the short walk from shop to park cooing at his daughter. By the time they passed through the gates, things were quiet once more. More importantly, Sarah had got a hold on herself. That rushing, crushing sensation had lifted as soon as she'd got outside.

Now, she was ready to talk. Or, more to the point, listen.

'There's only the one primary school here,' Dean said, which was something Sarah already knew. 'Abe and I – *James* and I – were in the same class all the way back to when we started.'

'When you were five?'

'Something like that. Maybe even four? Everyone goes to the same primary school and a lot of the other villages have their own. Then, when it's time to go to big school, everyone from the villages get bussed in and out. That's on the far side of town.'

Sarah knew that, too. She'd seen that as a positive but was now wondering whether it was.

'You said James was your best friend...?'

Dean slowed to bump the buggy over a ridge that took them onto a bridge over the pond. The wheels *chik-chakked* across the ruts until they reached the other side. Dean stopped to check – but Naomi hadn't stirred, so they continued on a new loop.

'We were at times,' he said. 'Mainly at primary school. There was always Lucy as well.'

Sarah shivered at the mention of the other girl's name. She said, 'Lucy Shearer,' without quite meaning to.

'You've heard of her then?' Dean asked, not sounding surprised.

'A bit,' Sarah said, which was probably a lie. She couldn't say she'd known nothing of Lucy until seeing her name in that school photo.

Dean didn't pick up on any hesitation. 'Boys and girls were separated for most things back then,' he said. 'James and me would be in the football team, and had PE together, that sort of thing. But then, when we were in mixed classes, it was always him and Lucy. We were sort of best friends – but not all the time.'

'Were they an... *item*?'

It didn't quite come out as Sarah meant and, from the way Dean slowed and glanced sideways to her, he'd clearly taken it as some sort of jealousy thing. She was more worried about what Martin had said the day before, with James killing his daughter. Until now, Sarah had no idea Lucy might have been an ex-girlfriend of her husband. She'd known him for twelve years. Twelve! She didn't think the name 'Lucy' had ever come up, even though they'd had those talks about exes, firsts, and the like.

Dean paused, perhaps choosing his words. 'I don't know if they were ever together like that,' he said. 'Everyone assumed they were but they might've just been friends.'

Sarah couldn't work out if he genuinely wasn't sure, or if he was trying to protect her in some way. If they were talking solely about some ancient relationship her husband might have had two-and-a-bit decades back, she didn't mind. Those couples who obsessed over exes were baffling to her.

Perhaps sensing that, Dean continued, 'I actually think Lucy might've had a boyfriend near the end. Eric-something. I didn't really know him. It was a long time ago. I'm sure he still lives in town.'

They were back at the park gates where they'd started. The serenity of the morning had seemingly calmed both the baby and Sarah herself. She wasn't sure what had happened back in the butcher's shop.

Dean paused at the gates. 'I'm going to do another lap...?'

He phrased it as a question and Sarah nodded her head. 'I'm not in a rush.'

It was technically true, although there was still a lot to do at the house and she'd only given herself a week away from her accounting. Either way, they started another lap of the park. In the time since they'd arrived, a pair of mums had set out blankets on the green and were busy sipping coffees. That's what Sarah had always thought Carnington would be: blankets in the park, morning coffees with friends.

'Lucy and Abe were the naughty kids,' Dean added. 'That was maybe the other reason me and him weren't such good friends after primary school.'

It didn't sound as if he'd said it to cause trouble, more a statement of fact. 'How do you mean "naughty"?' Sarah asked.

'Oh, you know: teenage stuff. He and Lucy used to skip school quite a bit. There was a small fire that got blamed on them. That kind of thing. Harmless really. I stayed out of it though.' He gave a wry smile. 'Wasn't as cool as them.'

Sarah wasn't sure what to say. Was a fire 'harmless', regardless of its size? When she'd met James, he'd worked in the city and was the sort who never let an insurance policy expire. He made sure the council tax was paid on the first day it *could* be, not the final day it *had* to be. They joked about how he was a rule-follower who kept things organised. The idea of him being a naughty kid who skipped school was baffling.

Dean slowed again, slipping a sideways glance towards Sarah. 'Lucy disappeared when we were about fifteen, sixteen. A lot of people round here thought Abe might've...'

He tailed off and returned to facing the path. The implication was clear, though.

'What happened to her?' Sarah asked.

'I don't know. I'm not sure anyone does. One day she skipped school and never made it home. Martin always said Abe was involved. I think Abe was the last person to be seen with her. He might've been off school, too.' He paused, then added, 'They declared her dead in the end...'

Sarah knew that much – but it was a lot of new information. Her husband had once been good friends with a girl who went missing. He was the last person seen with her.

Dean and Sarah walked quietly for a short while, reaching the bridge once more and passing across the water. A young boy was feeding oats to the ducks. Dean knew the mother and they stopped for a minute or so as the parents made small talk. There was something about the mother ordering a joint of lamb from the butcher, though Sarah wasn't really listening.

This was the first she had heard of *any* of this. There couldn't be two people from Carnington who'd once been called Abraham Parkinson. This was her husband. Perhaps everything with Lucy *was* the reason he'd started using his middle name? He'd never been quite clear over why, other than to say he thought James sounded more professional.

By the time they were walking again, Sarah was wavering for the first time. Her husband couldn't be a killer, he just couldn't, and yet...

'I always felt sorry for Martin,' Dean said, from nothing. 'He's a good bloke. I lived in one of his flats for a while after leaving home. He never once raised the rent. He lives on a farm up the hill and let me kip in the spare room one time when he was sorting out a bit of damp in the flat.'

As he spoke, he pointed up towards the hill in the distance. There was a lot of green, as well as a dot that might well have been a farm.

The way he was describing Martin Shearer was slightly different to the man who'd turned up on Sarah's doorstep the day before.

'He renovated the whole place up there,' Dean continued, oblivious to Sarah's unease. 'He ran a mini zoo for a few years. Nothing dangerous, just goats and that, for the kids. When the shop nearly went under during Covid, he put in a massive order for us to cater a barbecue he was hosting. That kept us going when we needed it.' A pause. 'Lucy was his only daughter...'

Sarah wasn't sure what to say. She hadn't known Lucy and was feeling as if there was a large chunk of her husband's life she didn't know, either. She thought of Oliver at the school and how protective she'd been the day before when it seemed like something might have happened to him. If Martin truly believed James had killed his only child, no wonder he'd turned up angrily on their doorstep.

Dean was still going. 'Martin's wife died from Covid, so it's just him now. He couldn't even have a funeral for her. Dad dropped a meat pack up for him because we didn't know what else to do. Lots of people lit candles...'

The sentence ebbed away and Sarah still didn't know what to say. A part of her was starting to wonder if she'd misread things the previous day. Martin was a man who seemingly did a lot for the people of the town. His wife had died at a time when it was hard to mourn – and that all came after his only child had disappeared. It was easy to see why he might hold a grudge against the last person to see her.

None of that meant James was a killer.

They were back at the gate for a second time and the shopping bag was starting to feel heavy on Sarah's shoulder. She was also in a conversation she no longer wanted to have. It was too much to hear when James wasn't there to say what had actually happened.

They waited at the gates, Dean angling one way, Sarah the other.

'Did you say Abe— James was in New York?' Dean asked.

'He works for a finance firm. He has to go out for meetings two or three times a year.'

Dean pouted a lip, though nodded along. 'Huh. Maybe, um... when he gets in, tell him where I am? We can have a catch-up, something like that?'

He didn't sound particularly keen, more one of those things people say to be polite. Sarah said she'd pass on the message – and then turned and headed towards the slope that would lead down to her cottage, wondering exactly who she was married to.

ELEVEN

After arriving home, Sarah put the food away and then spent a couple of minutes sitting in the kitchen, searching the name 'Lucy' in her messages from her husband. She couldn't ever remember a conversation with James in which he'd mentioned her and, though it was a long shot, there were also no messages in which he'd used the name.

Everything Dean had said made it sound as if they'd been talking about different people. Sarah simply couldn't picture her husband being responsible for 'a small fire', as Dean had said.

Except the things with which she couldn't see him being involved in were really building up.

There had been no further messages from James since he'd said he was checking into a hotel. It was still the early hours on the East Coast, though Sarah considered calling her husband anyway. She desperately wanted to ask about the situation in which she was finding herself. Who was Lucy and what had happened to her?

After deciding not to call, Sarah headed upstairs, to where the filling in on the landing was largely done. Her dad was sitting on the floor, scraping a final smear into the dimpled wall, before stopping to take her in.

'It looks really good,' Sarah said. 'Thank you.'

'It's no worry. How was Oliver?'

'I think he was all right. I spoke to his teacher, who said he was a bit tired yesterday. She hadn't noticed anything else that was odd.'

That got a nod. 'What about the other stuff?'

By that, Sarah assumed her father meant the graffiti and reception from the other mums. 'It was fine,' she said, not wanting to get into everything Dean had said. She wasn't sure she understood it herself.

Her dad wiped his hands on his front and stifled a yawn. 'I was going to do that last bit of filling in, then some painting downstairs, before heading home.'

Sarah was nodding. It was what they'd agreed when he said he'd help her move. He'd crack on with the most important jobs around the house in the way dads seemingly always did. It would take a day or two, then he'd return to his own place. Sarah had known it was going to happen, yet that was when she thought James would be back.

'Thanks for the help.'

He perhaps sensed some unease. 'I'm only an hour and a half away if you need me.'

Her father said it to be comforting – but those ninety minutes suddenly seemed like a long ol' way.

'I can stay another night if you want...?'

It was the sort of thing her father would definitely offer to do. Sarah was his only child and he was another who'd lost his wife. She could see the parallel from him to Martin Shearer. One still had their daughter, the other...

'It's fine,' Sarah said, even though it wasn't. 'I'll cook us dinner one Sunday soon. You'll have to come back.'

He grinned. 'Is that your way of scaring me off?'

She laughed at the gentle dig. Despite his help the past couple of days, her father had his own life. He played golf a couple of times a week with his friends, and was a member of a lawn bowling society. He played poker for what he called 'beer money' with his friends. There were times when she had a morning free and asked if he wanted a catch-up, only to discover he was booked up for weeks on end.

Sarah did a little more unpacking, more or less finishing off the downstairs, as her father did the painting he'd mentioned, then cleaned up. She listened to him repack his small bag – and then he was at the front door. He again offered to stay another day but Sarah said no. It was as he drove away that she felt a gentle stab of something in her chest. This was supposed to have been part of an amazing life-changing dream. They had a perfect little family, in a perfect village, with their perfect home.

And yet... none of this was what she thought it would be. A part of her, perhaps the biggest part, wanted to go back to London. Yes, their flat was small, the area was noisy, and all the other things... but she'd not had any of these new worries back then.

As if to emphasise the point, Sarah's phone started to ring. The screen had the name of Oliver's primary school, which only made those stabbing pains worse.

'Is that Mrs Parkinson?' a woman's voice asked.

'It is.'

'We were wondering if you could come into the school as soon as possible? There's a problem with Oliver.'

TWELVE

Miss Callaghan was waiting at the main door as Sarah approached. It was only a few hours before that she'd locked it but now the teacher held it wide for Sarah to head inside. They stood together in the reception area, surrounded by the wall of school photos.

'Oliver didn't want to go back to class after lunch,' Miss Callaghan said. 'I've been keeping an eye on him this morning but didn't notice anything strange. Then, when it was time to sit back down, he wouldn't go inside. He kept asking for you. He's in the office.'

She angled towards a pair of steps and led the way towards double doors. She knocked on one, then opened it. Inside, Oliver was being swallowed by a large chair. He was staring at the floor, though glanced up briefly to take in his mum, before returning his gaze to the ground.

'I'll wait out here,' Miss Callaghan said, nodding to a separate pair of chairs in the hall. 'Someone's watching the class, so I've got a few minutes.'

Sarah continued into the office and closed the door. She took the seat next to her son. 'What happened?' she asked.

'Wanna go home.'

'We can do that – but you have to come to school each day. Did something happen?'

'Wanna go to our *real* home.'

Sarah struggled not to sigh. It would probably be easier to take if she was enamoured with the new town. Instead, she was feeling the same pangs of regret about the move.

'*This* is our home now,' she said, trying to convince herself as much as Oliver.

'Don't like it.'

'What don't you like?'

There was a long pause. Oliver was swinging his legs restlessly, aimlessly, and didn't look up from the floor.

'Is this about the voices from last night?'

Sarah was watching her son, wondering if she had accidentally woken him up the past couple of nights.

There was a gentle shake of the head and then a soft, 'No.'

'What is it then?'

The reply did come, though not until Oliver stopped swinging his legs. 'Shark,' he said.

It was so quiet that Sarah wasn't sure she'd heard correctly.

'Did you say "shark"?'

The nod was minimal, though just about there. At least this explained one thing.

Sarah told her son she'd be back, then headed out to where Miss Callaghan was sitting in the corridor, tapping something into her phone.

'Is he OK?' she asked, looking up.

'Is there a shark in the class?' Sarah asked.

The teacher stared for a second, momentarily confused. 'There's a big marine poster on one of the walls.'

Sarah laughed humourlessly. She should have anticipated this and might have done if there weren't so many other things going on. 'Oliver's scared of sharks,' she said. 'It started with the big one in *Finding Nemo* but then his class read a book last year and there was something about a shark in that, too. He was having nightmares and didn't want to go to the beach last summer. My husband tried assuring him that we don't have sharks here but it was all a bit much.'

A weight had lifted and Sarah found herself smiling. She could deal with phobias that a child would grow out of.

Miss Callaghan was nodding. 'Oh! No wonder he didn't want to say anything in front of the others. We can definitely take down the poster.'

'I think it's probably all enhanced because his dad's away, it's a new school and new town. He's not used to any of this.'

'The poor thing. It's nap time at the moment, so I'll take down the poster while they're resting.' She pointed towards the office. 'Do you want me to talk to him?'

It felt odd for Sarah to accept parenting help from a relative stranger – especially one so young – but she took the offer.

Together, they returned to the office, where Miss Callaghan told Oliver she was going to take down the poster. She said she used to be scared of cats when she was his age, which Oliver found baffling. Miss Callaghan asked Sarah to wait, then she returned Oliver to the class. Minutes later and she was back with a rolled-up poster in her hand.

'I think we're good,' she said. 'Thanks for coming in.'

Sarah said it was no trouble, then they were in a short cycle of thanking one another. It wasn't long until the teacher acknowledged something that had gone unsaid.

'I know it's hard coming to a place like this,' she said. 'I think you picked a good time to start him. They all make friends at this age, then go up to the big school together.'

Sarah glanced towards the school photo in which she knew James and Lucy were sitting side by side. They had been primary school friends who'd gone to the secondary school together.

'Did you go there?' Sarah asked, knowing the answer.

Miss Callaghan nodded. 'It's a great school. There was the same head, Mr Horlock, for about thirty years until Covid. I've heard the new one is good, too.'

Sarah almost brought up the outstanding Ofsted report, though figured teachers might not be so keen on such things.

'Thirty years is a long time,' she said instead.

'Right – but time flies. He lives in the old post office in town. I see him most mornings. He gave me a reference for this place. I think he'd still be teaching if it wasn't for the stress of when things went remote.' She took a breath and turned back to the corridor. 'I've got to get back. I'll keep an eye on Oliver and we'll call if anything else comes up. I'll ask around the staffroom later to see if anyone else has sharks on their walls.'

Sarah thanked her again and then the teacher showed her out.

She was halfway home when her phone buzzed once more.

It was good news, at last.

James had checked in for his flight, which was due to take off on time. His company were going to pay for a car to take him home from the airport, meaning he should get in at around three to four in the morning, depending on how long it took to get his bags.

Sarah hovered over a reply, wondering how she could sum up the past few hours. In the end, she opted for: *Great news! Can't wait to see you* – both of which were true.

Except, what James didn't know was that they were fourteen to fifteen hours away from the biggest reckoning of their marriage.

THIRTEEN

Back at the cottage, Sarah continued to unpack more of the upstairs boxes, including all of Oliver's clothes and toys. She scrubbed the bath and shower, then put away some of her own clothes. The house felt empty – and the quiet was beginning to sting to the point that she put on the radio, simply to have another voice in the background.

It wasn't long until she had to head back to the school for the third time that day. Sarah was nervous of those sideways looks from the other mums, perhaps even another confrontation with Pamela. She slowed as she turned the corner and had timed the journey badly enough that there was no way to avoid waiting at the gates.

Rather than engage with the other parents, Sarah took out her phone and stood to the side. She felt the weight of being watched, even as she did her best to ignore the attention. Not everyone had ignored her.

'Are you Sarah?'

A woman was standing between Sarah and the other mums. She was around Sarah's age, clutching a tote bag that had 'Tough Mudder Finisher' on the side.

'I'm Bonnie,' she added. 'My daughter's Georgia. She just started reception.'

Sarah wondered if there was some sort of follow-up. Bonnie knew James from back in the day and wanted to say that he tortured badgers, something like that.

Nothing came.

'I just moved here,' Sarah replied, nervously, though she figured Bonnie already knew that. 'My son's in Miss Callaghan's class.'

Bonnie was smiling. 'Welcome to the area.' She took a step closer, then lowered her voice. 'Look, you probably noticed a lot of the others are talking about you...'

Her lips barely moved, though she flicked her eyes upwards, indicating the women behind. Sarah couldn't see them through Bonnie, though she didn't doubt her name was being mentioned.

'It's hard to miss,' Sarah replied.

'Don't let them get to you,' Bonnie said, still whispering. 'There's always something new with the coven. My husband killed himself last year. He'd had mental health issues all his life but that lot were desperate to say it was my fault.'

Considering how appalling that sounded, Bonnie spoke with assured confidence.

'That's terrible,' Sarah said – and it was.

'It's not all of them,' Bonnie whispered. 'Just three or four. I think people get bored around here. There's no real drama, so people have to create it.' She took a breath, then shifted away slightly, adding, 'Anyway... what brings you here? We're a bit out of the way.'

Sarah wondered how much Bonnie already knew. It felt as if news of her arrival, plus the identity of her husband, was out there.

'My husband grew up here,' Sarah said, taking the question

at face value. 'James Parkinson. People around here tend to know him as Abraham.'

It got a blank look, though Bonnie was nodding as if Sarah had said any name. It didn't feel as if she knew him. She nodded backwards. 'It's a lovely area once you get past this nonsense. We moved here around seven, eight years back. We wanted somewhere with more room for when we had kids. It's great for that, plus the Ofsted reports are incredible.'

There was a moment where they made eye contact in which Sarah felt a connection that she thought the other woman shared. They were both the type to sit on a laptop, hunting down Ofsted reports. Both the sort to know it shouldn't matter, even though it sort of did.

There was movement from the side and Bonnie glanced to where the children were starting to leave the main doors of the school.

'If you want to ask anything, or sneak a coffee and a digestive, I run the bookshop in town.'

'How about a chocolate digestive?' Sarah replied, with a smile that felt like the first genuine one in days.

Bonnie laughed. 'I can probably do that.'

The school gate was opened by one of the teachers and children started heading for their parents. Oliver was near the front, not scuffing his feet this time, almost bouncing as he reached his mum. Sarah said her goodbye to Bonnie – and would've thanked her more for the kindness if Bonnie's own daughter hadn't emerged at the same time. They each gave a hectic 'bye', then headed off in separate directions.

'How was the afternoon?' Sarah asked her son, as they walked to the corner.

'Nora doesn't like sharks either,' he said happily.

'Is Nora in your class?'

'Yeah – she thinks sharks are rubbish.'

Sarah laughed at the description and they walked side by

side through the village centre as Oliver talked about his new friend. Back in London, he'd been smitten with a girl named Victoria for a few months, as they bonded over the fact they both liked *Bluey*. Sarah vaguely remembered being a similar age and having strong friendships that might only survive a few weeks.

Still, Oliver's happiness bled into Sarah's own mood. It had been a dark day until the conversation with Bonnie and now this. Suddenly, Carnington didn't feel like such a terrible idea. Perhaps all that initial research *was* correct and it *would* be all right.

They were at the bottom of the slope, almost home, when Sarah noticed the man sitting on the wall of the house. He was on top of where the graffiti had been the night before. For a moment, from a distance, Sarah thought it was her husband. James had somehow got an earlier flight, an earlier car. He was home and—

It wasn't James. This man was older and, from what Sarah had seen, harsher.

It was Martin Shearer.

FOURTEEN

Oliver was apparently drawn to Martin. He stood in front of the man, staring up to him.

'Hello,' Martin said, using the full chirpy voice adults do when talking to children who aren't their own. 'Who do we have here?'

'I'm Oliver.'

Sarah interrupted before either could say any more. 'What have we said about talking to strangers?' she asked.

Oliver looked between Martin and his mum. 'Um... Don't talk to them.'

'And who's this?'

'I dunno.'

'What do we call people we don't know?'

'A stranger.'

Sarah widened her eyes as her son mumbled something that might have been a 'sorry'. She took him to the door and unlocked it, then told Oliver to go inside, change out of his uniform, and wash his hands. She watched him head for the stairs, then closed the door and turned back towards where

Martin had stepped down from the wall. He was standing a little outside the gate, slightly off her property. Sarah moved along the path towards him.

'What do you want?' she asked.

Martin nodded towards the wall. 'I came to apologise for what happened last night. It's not who we are in this town. The person who did it has been dealt with – but I'm happy to take it to the police with you, if you prefer.'

Sarah stared at him, trying to figure out whether he was being genuine. He was speaking like some sort of Godfather, whose minions were out of control.

'Who did it?' Sarah asked.

She expected some sort of excuse but Martin held out his hands, palms up. 'It's a long story but the short version is that it was the son of someone I play squash with. Me and his father were talking about other things yesterday, then the topic of Abraham came up. The son overheard and...' He nodded towards the wall. 'I can tell you the name if you want but I doubt it'll mean anything to you. He's only thirteen but anyone would understand your decision. I really *am* happy to call the police if you prefer. I play golf with the chief constable.'

It felt as if he was saying two separate things at the same time. Yeah, she *could* set the police on a thirteen-year-old – but everyone would know she'd done so. And, hey, Martin was mates with the chief constable anyway, so none of the power was with her. Sarah had no choice, only the illusion of it – and they both knew it. Somehow, despite being a victim, she felt threatened.

Sarah tried not to show it, pushing herself up fractionally on her heels. 'How did you know what he'd done?' she asked.

Martin ran his tongue across his top teeth. 'Word goes around town pretty quickly.'

Sarah had already figured that, considering she mentioned

James's name to one person at the school gates, then, within minutes, it felt as if everyone knew. She was still focused on the way Martin had said 'topic of Abraham'. Her husband was a topic, apparently.

'He's not called Abraham,' Sarah said. 'It's James.'

That got a nod, though nothing more in acknowledgement. It felt as if the conversation was Martin's to dictate and that Sarah was there to listen, not take part.

'I also wanted to apologise for coming over yesterday,' Martin added. 'I was shocked to hear of Abra— your husband being back in town.'

It didn't *sound* like an apology.

'Why do you think James killed your daughter?' Sarah asked. 'I read that she was missing...?'

There was the merest, gentlest, hint of a smirk from the man, as Sarah realised he'd *wanted* her to go away and do the research. Perhaps he'd *known* James wasn't at home and had visited the previous day to take advantage of that. Whatever was happening between Martin, James, and her, Sarah felt a step behind.

The leer was gone almost the moment it appeared. 'Lucy was missing,' Martin said coolly. 'She skipped school and the last person she was with was Abra— Was James. He was the person she was with the most often. He never had much of an explanation for where he was when she disappeared, though wanted everyone to believe it was nothing to do with him.'

Sarah was torn. She was certain she'd seen that momentary sneer and yet, now, Martin spoke like a broken man pining for a daughter who'd been taken from him.

Who was he? A grieving father, desperate for justice? Or some manipulative lunatic obsessed with revenge on the wrong people?

'You said he killed her...?' Sarah replied.

A nod. 'That's what I believe.'

'Some people believe the earth is flat. That doesn't make it true.'

Something twitched around Martin's eye as he pressed his lips together. 'Your husband killed my daughter,' he replied flatly, decisively. 'But, look, that's not all he did. He started a fire at one of my offices. He stole my car when he was only sixteen, not even old enough to drive. They found my racing-green Mini burned out near the quarry. He constantly skipped school and took my daughter with him. He—'

'How do you know he did any of that?'

It felt as if Martin had been building to a crescendo. He didn't seem like the sort who was used to being interrupted and he stared at Sarah, eye twitching again. To Sarah, it felt like a reasonable question.

Martin took a moment, though his gaze never left Sarah. 'Lucy was perfectly happy,' he said, calmer now. 'She was doing well at school until they ended up in the same class.'

'But you said he started a fire. He stole your car. Didn't you call the police...?'

From nowhere, Sarah knew the answer. If her husband *had* been involved in those things, then it had been alongside Lucy. When Martin said James had stolen his car, what he'd missed out was that his daughter had – at the absolute least – been there as well. It could have been her entirely.

That was what Sarah told herself anyway.

It felt as if Martin was about to say more – but there was a bump from the house. Sarah looked round, though the front door was still closed.

'I have to go,' she said, turning back to Martin. She almost left it there, except there was something more, something instinctive that surprised even her. 'You're not welcome here,' she said firmly. 'I don't want you coming back.'

Martin eyed her, his gaze a fiery steel. For the second time in as many minutes, he felt like the sort of man who wasn't used to being told what to do.

And then, with a steady nod of his head, it was over. 'As you wish,' he replied – and then he turned to walk away.

FIFTEEN

Sarah kept herself busy through the evening. James's flight was on time, he'd land later that night, would get home in the early hours, and things would be explained.

She cooked for Oliver, who was a lot happier than the day before. He played on his Nintendo for a bit, then read in the living room with her. He talked a lot about his new friend, Nora – though predominantly over how she didn't like sharks either. At least he had bonded over something.

As it reached the point of Oliver's bedtime, Sarah was yawning herself. If she could only force herself to sleep, even at such an early time, she could wake up when James got home.

Once he was in bed, she read Oliver another chapter of his book, fighting back those yawns, then tucked him in. He was on his side, eyes barely open when he spoke.

'Can I sleep in your bed tonight?'

It had been around a year since Oliver had been allowed in his parents' bed. He was probably too old for it then but had been ill for a couple of days with a stomach complaint. Either Sarah or James had been getting up with him anyway.

This time, Sarah almost said yes again. Part of her craved

company, even if it was from her seven-year-old son. But she said no.

'You need to get used to your own room.'

'It's not my room.'

'It is. This is your room, your bed.'

She remembered him saying voices had woken him up. Miss Callaghan had repeated a similar story.

'I'll be quieter tonight,' Sarah told her son.

Oliver huffed with annoyance but was too tired to argue. He let out a frustrated, 'OK,' then closed his eyes.

Sarah pushed herself up, then put down the book and pulled the curtains. A slim sliver of light crept around the edges of the door but the room was otherwise dark. Sarah was about to leave when her son's voice wavered through the gloom.

'I don't want to sleep in here,' he said.

'Why not?'

There was no reply at first and Sarah wondered if Oliver had fallen asleep in the second it had taken to reply. He occasionally talked in his sleep.

But then the room was suddenly cold as the response sent a chill skidding along Sarah's back.

'The woman under the bed keeps talking to me.'

SIXTEEN

Oliver had always been a boy full of imagination, ready to make up stories, or draw creatures and scenes. Sarah knew that children could sometimes have imaginary friends – but that hadn't yet been true of Oliver. This felt like something else. In a roundabout way, he'd told both his mum and his teacher that he'd been hearing voices on the two nights he'd slept in his new room.

'Shall we look together?' Sarah said. She didn't want to outright say there was no woman under the bed, even though she knew there wasn't.

Oliver didn't reply, but Sarah fumbled across the darkened room and switched on the bedside lamp. A glum orange shone a halo on the ceiling and across the floor. Sarah crouched next to the bed, untucking her son and letting him clamber onto her lap.

For a moment, just a moment, he was a baby once more, desperate for his mother. Sarah held him, craving the love, before letting him go. She swished the bedsheets up and onto the bed, revealing a large nearly empty space under the bed.

There was only an unpacked box, mainly full of Lego, that she slid forward to reveal the clear carpet and wall beyond.

'Is that all right?' Sarah asked.

Oliver peeped underneath and then sat up.

'I can put this box in another room if that helps...?'

There was a slow 'OK', though Oliver didn't sound sure.

Sarah helped him back into bed and re-tucked the covers. She said to call if there was a problem, though the only reply was a mumble. Sarah carried the box out of the room and left it in the hall, before heading into her room.

It was a new house to them, full of quirks, creaks and ticks. She was sure she'd heard someone moving around in the early hours – but there had been nobody there. There was every chance her son had heard something similar.

Except, now she was in her own room, hoping for an early night, Sarah was no longer tired. She tried to force a yawn, wondering if it might bring on a real one – but there was nothing. The mini drama had woken her up.

Their bedroom was the last with much left to unpack, so Sarah quietly went about unloading the boxes. There was James's guitar, which she'd have happily lost on the journey down. He'd been learning for years, though barely seemed to get past a couple of basic chords. Sarah didn't have the heart to tell her husband, but James had the voice of a stepped-on dog. He'd made vague statements about starting a band with 'the guys from work' that had thankfully not come to anything. Plus—

It had been a minute in which Sarah had forgotten the other stuff about her husband. That he'd once been Abraham, and was apparently good friends with a girl named Lucy who had disappeared. A girl whose father insisted she was dead at the hands of Sarah's husband.

All that, and he'd somehow never mentioned Lucy to her.

There was a box in the corner of the bedroom with 'James' on the side. Sarah had figured she'd leave it for him to unpack, yet was now drawn to it. Their marriage had never felt like it was filled with secrets, yet here they were. Perhaps there was a gigantic one that had been left unanswered all this time?

The flaps of the box had been concertinaed into one another. Sarah pulled them apart to find a stack of shoes, and a couple of game controllers from a PlayStation that Sarah didn't think they had any longer. The mangle of cables that all men seemed to own was wedged between some coasters which had been packed away years back because they had rude words written on them. They'd been a joke gift that neither of them had felt able to get rid of. For some reason, James had packed rubber bands and paperclips. There were pens and a whiteboard eraser, even though they didn't own a whiteboard. James had also kept inner tubes, despite selling his bike three years back as he didn't use it. So much stuff that shouldn't have made the move. It was a wonder they'd had space for it in their old flat.

Sarah continued unpacking, piling things onto the bed until she was at the bottom of the box. There was a crimson National Record of Achievement folder, filled with certificates. Sarah had lost hers at some point in the past. Every student in her school had been given one, with the insinuation that their entire career would hinge on filling the folder with as many qualifications as possible. In reality, landfills had ended up full of the things.

James still had his. There was a swimming certificate, his official GCSE one, plus bits and pieces from university. Everything had been kept meticulously pristine. The GCSE certificate had the name of his senior school at the bottom.

The idea seemed bizarre that he'd endlessly skipped school, and not particularly bothered with education, only to end up proudly keeping the results for so many years. It was so difficult to reconcile the man she knew, the one she'd married, versus the person who'd been described by both his supposed best friend, Dean, and the father of the girl he'd allegedly killed.

Sarah started to refill the box with James's things when she realised she'd missed a couple of items at the bottom. The thin card was tattered but the red-on-yellow Kodak logo was clear enough on the small wallets. Sarah picked out the packets of photos, remembering her own from years back. They'd all disappeared over time, not necessarily thrown out, yet not surviving various moves. There had been photos of her with friends from the old days, probably even some with her mum. Memories that would be forever lost because the photos were gone.

James had two bulging wallets filled with old six by fours – and Sarah grinned as she thumbed through them. Almost all were slightly out of focus, likely taken with those disposable junk cameras. There was James in his uni days, topless and downing a yard of ale, another of him sleeping with his toes sticking out of a blanket. One had him wearing a giant novelty Guinness hat, presumably for St Patrick's Day. He was running some sort of race, in a vest that was too big, then yelling in terror on a rollercoaster.

Sarah felt a pang that she hadn't kept many of her own old photos.

She was returning James's to the wallets when a photo unstuck itself from one of the others. It was slightly smaller than the rest, the quality grainier. James was younger in the photo, skinny with tanned skin and what his teenage self clearly thought was a smouldering look. All youngsters had a similar photo, in which they thought they were giving a red-carpet stare that was actually a Carpet World grimace.

But it wasn't James who interested her so much. It was the car he was posing alongside.

A racing-green Mini.

The one Martin had said was found burned out near a quarry.

SEVENTEEN

THURSDAY

The front door sounded at eighteen minutes past four in the morning. Sarah had heard a car outside, which wouldn't have disturbed her back in the city. Lots of trundling engines at all hours back there. Here, in the middle of nowhere, cars didn't idle at such a time.

It wasn't as if Sarah had slept anyway. She hadn't even tried. She had been sitting in the living room. Maybe there was a five-minute doze here, ten minutes there – but she'd been awake. She'd been waiting.

And now James was home.

There was a scrabbling at the lock. James hadn't been there to pick up the keys but she'd messaged to say she'd left one hidden underneath the doormat. There was more scratching and then a waft of cool air breezed through the ground floor. Sarah pulled her cardigan tighter and waited.

The door closed and there was a whump of a suitcase on the ground. Footsteps bumbled along the hall and then a door opened. James hadn't been in the house since they'd viewed it months before and Sarah heard the cupboard open, presumably by mistake, before it was closed.

Then he was in the kitchen. A light switch sounded, then the fridge door. Sarah got up from the sofa and followed the hallways until she was in the door frame of the kitchen. James was standing at the back at the room, staring through the closed door towards their garden. He was drinking a can of Diet Coke that he must have picked up from the airport.

When he turned, he let out a high-pitched, 'Oh!'

Sarah smiled thinly through the gloom to her husband. He was unshaven, his hair sticking out to the side as if he'd been leaning on it.

'I didn't expect you to be up,' he said.

Sarah took a breath and then: 'Who's Lucy Shearer?'

EIGHTEEN

The can of Coke had been halfway towards James's mouth when he froze. He lowered his arm and stared across the kitchen towards Sarah.

'How do you know that name?' he asked.

No denial. That's what Sarah wanted. She wanted him to say 'Who?' To insist he'd never heard of such a person. But he *did* know her.

'Because people around here know *your* name,' Sarah replied. 'Well, not *your* name. They know Abraham.'

James frowned but then downed the rest of the can, before placing it on the side. 'Is there a recycling box?' he asked – and Sarah almost laughed.

Almost.

'Under the sink,' she replied flatly.

James opened the cupboard and dropped the can into the blue box. She felt him tense slightly. On another day, another lifetime, they'd have a mini disagreement over whether the cupboard was an appropriate place for the recycling. James would want it closer to the front door.

But this wasn't another day, and Sarah only had one lifetime.

'What's happened?' James asked, as he sat at the kitchen table. It felt like neither of them were going to sleep.

'A lot,' Sarah replied, and then, quickly after: 'People are saying you killed Lucy Shearer.'

No instant denial.

'Which people?' James asked instead. He didn't wait long, before adding: 'Her dad?'

'And others.'

James was drumming his fingers on the table, staring at the surface, though Sarah didn't know whether he was deliberately avoiding eye contact. 'I can't believe this is still a thing. I thought it was dealt with back then.'

He sighed and continued to stare at the table. Sarah waited. It was hard to know which of the thousand questions to throw at him first.

'Is this why you didn't want to move back?' she asked.

'No.' The reply came too quickly and he knew it. 'I mean... not really. It's not like I have loads of happy memories from here. I told you that. We lived in a small flat when I was growing up, there was damp and mould. I left when I could and didn't come back.' He caught her eye. 'None of this is new. *You* wanted this.'

That was true. Sarah knew James had grown up poor within a village where most people weren't.

'I didn't want *this*,' Sarah countered. 'I wanted to get away from the city, for Oliver to have some space. I didn't want people whispering about us because they think you killed someone.'

That got an exasperated shake of the head. 'I didn't kill *anyone*.'

'Why didn't you tell me about Lucy?'

There was a shrug that had a guilty edge. 'Have you told me about every friend you've ever had?'

'I would've told you if I'd been accused of killing one of them.'

That got another huff, louder this time. 'I didn't kill anyone! This is so ridiculous. Is this why you waited up?'

Sarah thought of the photo of James with the racing-green Mini that she'd returned to his box. Martin said that exact car was stolen. If Martin was telling the truth about the car, was the same true of what had happened to his daughter?

James mumbled something that might've been 'sod this' and then stood. He filled the kettle, flicked it on, then started opening cupboards.

Sarah knew what he was after and said, 'The one by the back door.' Her husband found the tub and filled the French press with coffee, before placing it on the side.

They definitely weren't going to bed.

'I'm sorry you've had to deal with whatever this is,' he said. 'It's so overblown. It was then. Lucy and me were friends. We skipped school a few times together, got the bus to the seaside, stuff like that.'

He scratched his head, sat, stood again. Sarah wasn't used to seeing her husband so agitated. When the house sale was going through, there was a time in which it looked like they might be technically homeless for a week. While Sarah had panicked, James had found a storage place that could hold their things, along with a nearby hotel. That was the James she knew.

'Lucy's dad never liked me,' he said.

'Martin.'

A nod. 'He was this rich guy, big house, all that. My family weren't. We lived in one of *his* flats actually. He had these big houses that he'd converted and we were on the middle floor. He didn't like me and Lucy hanging around with each other and tried to blame pretty much anything that went wrong with her on me.' He shrugged. 'It would've been the same for anyone she was friends with. He wanted her to go to Oxford, because he had. He couldn't accept that she didn't want that.'

The kettle boiled and James filled the French press two-thirds of the way, before adding cool water from the tap. He gave it a swirl and then carried it to the table, along with a pair of mugs.

Sarah was certain of everything James said. She'd seen something in Martin that made it easy to believe he didn't want his daughter hanging around with some poor kid.

'What happened when Lucy disappeared? Martin said you were there?'

James's eyebrows almost met in the middle as lines deepened on his forehead. 'He spoke to you?'

'He came to the house.'

James didn't speak for a moment. His mouth was open and she figured he probably had questions too.

'He told me you were there when Lucy disappeared.'

'I wasn't.'

'But he must have a reason for thinking that...? If you were home with your parents, at football, something like that, people would be able to say where you were.'

That got a long sigh that only stopped when James pressed the coffee granules to the bottom of the glass. He filled one mug, then motioned to the other.

'Not yet,' Sarah said and then: 'What happened?'

James yawned, stretched, then yawned again. She should tell him the caffeine was a bad idea, but he was old enough to figure that out himself.

'We were sixteen,' he said. 'Well, I was. Lucy was a couple of months older than me. A bunch of us used to hang around at this place outside town. You follow the train tracks, then end up at an abandoned quarry. People called it The Den for some reason. There were loads of rocks at the top, then a big pool of water at the bottom. In the summer, people would sunbathe at the top, then jump off the cliff to cool off. You'd climb back up, then go again.'

He stopped to sip the coffee.

'People would bring beer to The Den,' he said. 'Actually, it was usually cider – but you could smoke and there'd be a bit of weed around. Nobody ever bothered us. I think I've told you this.'

He seemed unsure but, as soon as he mentioned it, Sarah realised that they *had* been over such things. When they were getting to know one another there'd been a time when they'd spoken about things they'd done in their youths. They'd both tried weed and Sarah had an Ecstasy pill, that she hadn't enjoyed. James had smoked for around a year. She'd not thought much of any of it at the time. Everyone was entitled to a past, after all.

She was still fairly sure Lucy's name hadn't come up.

James tipped the remains of the milk into his mug and sipped the coffee. 'Lucy and me were supposed to be at school but we went to The Den instead,' he said. 'We did that fairly often – not just me and her but people from our year, or maybe the one above. If it was dry, there could be twenty people bunking off school in the same place.'

'Was it busy the day she went missing?'

'I don't think so. I think it might have rained a bit in the morning. I don't remember. We'd have gone out at around lunchtime.'

'What did you do?'

That got a bit of a laugh. 'Who knows? D'you ever wonder what we used to do before phones? Maybe we read a magazine? She had a Discman with plug-in speakers, so we might've listened to a CD? I don't know.'

Sarah took the point. She was more or less the same age and struggled to remember anything she'd done with her friends when they'd been teenagers. Now, it was phones and Bluetooth speakers. Back then... time somehow passed. It was impossible to explain to someone born after around 2000 that there was an age when kids hung around and sort of... didn't do anything.

'I'd told my dad I'd help him put up a shed for one of his mates when I finished school,' James added. 'I had to leave The Den at about half-three? Four? Something like that. Lucy didn't want to go.'

'You left her?'

A shrug. 'It wasn't weird. We were mates and she had a boyfriend at that point anyway. She didn't want to go – and I had to. So I left her.'

It felt blunt to Sarah, yet perhaps she was seeing things through modern eyes? Was one friend leaving another at their usual social hang-out a big deal, even if one of them was female?

'That was the last time you saw her?'

A nod. 'I assumed she'd gone home after a bit. It wasn't the only time I'd gone one way and she'd gone another. Sometimes she'd be out there with other friends, and so would I. We weren't joined together. I didn't know she was missing until the next day. We always met on the same corner to catch the bus to school but that day she wasn't at that corner. It was before phones and it's not like I could text her. Then at school a teacher said her parents had reported her missing the night before. The police came and talked to me. I told them more or less what I just told you – but I probably remembered it a bit better then. I didn't even know I was the last person to see her until later.'

He stopped for another drink of the coffee and, this time, Sarah reached to fill her own mug. She was going to need more than one to get through the rest of the day.

In the hours she'd been waiting for James to get home, Sarah had pictured more of an inquisition. She couldn't believe her husband had never mentioned Lucy and yet, the more they spoke, the more she understood. She'd once been at a house party when she was around sixteen or seventeen. One of the girls from her year had been sexually assaulted in a toilet and the police had interviewed everyone to ask what they'd seen. Sarah barely knew the two people involved and had said as much. The memory had largely dissipated but it was suddenly with her again. She'd not known anything had happened until almost two days after the party, when the police had come to the school.

It was so hard to explain to young people how different everything was, even a generation before. No phones, nobody with a camera to record every waking moment. People *did* get left behind, people *did* head out with the general hope they might run into friends, while not knowing entirely who was going to be where.

Sarah could see one friend leaving another at a spot where others hung out, because they had to rush home to help a parent. She could see someone waiting around to see if more mates were going to join. Similar things had happened to her.

Except Lucy and James had genuinely been friends – and she had disappeared. That must have haunted him ever since – but apparently not enough to mention it to his wife, even when they were planning to move back to the town where it had happened.

It felt… *odd*.

'Were you and Lucy more than friends?' Sarah asked, adding quickly, 'It doesn't matter if you were.'

It got a shake of the head – and James was unusually firm as he spoke. 'Not like that.' He sighed, scratched his head, likely anticipating what was next. 'They checked the water at the quarry for a body but never found her. Her dad blamed me but I blamed him. He was the reason she didn't want to go home. Except he owned half the town. He was telling everyone I killed his daughter.'

Sarah believed her husband, except she had the niggling sense he wasn't telling her everything. It was hard to judge, largely because they were both so tired. Not only that, she'd spent hours thinking and overthinking everything. Of all the dark, dangerous ideas that had passed through her, James's explanation was probably the mildest.

She yawned and, against her better judgement, chugged half the mug of coffee. The choice would be regretted by lunchtime when her body wanted to drop.

'What else did he say?' James asked.

'Martin?'

A nod.

'Something about a fire at one of his offices.'

James shuffled slightly, barely there, until he corrected himself. 'I don't know anything about that.'

Sarah watched her husband for a moment and, for the first time since he'd got home, she wasn't sure whether she believed him.

'He said you stole his car.'

'Which car?'

'Did you steal more than one?'

That got a snort, though it didn't feel entirely good-natured. 'I've never stolen a car.'

'He said something about a green Mini...?'

There was a micro pause and then James picked up his mug and pressed it to his lips. 'I don't know anything about a Mini,' he said.

'You've never been in one?'

It felt like a question too far, that perhaps he'd guess she'd seen the photo, but James shook his head. 'Never.'

Something had shifted in the air. Sarah was certain he was lying and perhaps he realised it.

He stood somewhat unexpectedly and finished the mug of coffee. 'I know I've just had that,' he said, offering up the mug, 'but I'm going to see if I can get a couple of hours' sleep. Oliver will be up soon.'

He yawned, then rinsed out the mug in the sink, before leaving it upside-down on the draining board.

'How's Oliver been sleeping?' James asked, when he turned.

'Not great. There was a shark on a poster at the school. The teacher's taken it down now.'

'That shark thing again...' James crossed the kitchen and crouched to peck Sarah on the head. 'Are you coming up for a bit?'

'No,' Sarah said, even though she knew she should. She needed the sleep as much as her husband – but there was too much on her mind.

If James was lying about the green car, what else was he lying about?

NINETEEN

Sarah did get some sleep, sort of. She dozed on the sofa but never for more than fifteen minutes at a time. She had used her phone to take a photo of that picture showing James with that green Mini. A part of her wanted to demand her husband explain it. Did he know Martin still lived in town before they chose to move? That he still owned a bunch of things? That his wife had died? When they'd visited for that single day six years before, James could have come and gone with nobody knowing who he was. He'd battled with Sarah on and off ever since then about moving to the town – but had he done that for his benefit, or hers?

So Sarah slept.

Sort of.

James came downstairs around two hours after he'd headed up. He yawned his way into the living room, stretching high.

'The landing looks great,' he said. 'Your dad did a great job.'

'He said he'll come back the weekend after next if we want more help.'

James was yawning again, mirroring how Sarah felt. Neither of them were particularly practical when it came to household stuff. Her dad was one of those men of a certain age who could seemingly do anything. Sure, he'd overload one socket with six extension cords and three plug blocks – but when the fuses blew, he'd know how to fix it.

Any further conversation was cut off by a pitter-patter overhead. James broke into a wide grin that was impossible to fake. The love was written on his face.

Oliver stumbled his way downstairs. He called a curious, 'Mum?' and, when James put a finger to his lips, indicating he didn't want to spoil things, Sarah replied with, 'In here.' Moments later, Oliver entered the living room. He started to ask what was for breakfast, before noticing the other person in the room.

'Dad!'

The pair of them leapt at one another, as James scooped their son off the ground and spun him around. In the old days, it would have been effortless but there was a grunt as he hoisted their seven-year-old into the air.

When he was back on the ground, Oliver turned to his mum. 'Dad's home.'

'I wondered who that was.'

'How's your room?' James asked enthusiastically. 'How's the house? How's school?'

It was too many questions in one go and there was brief puzzlement on Oliver's face until his father tried again.

'Did you sleep well?'

That got a slow shake of the head. 'No.'

'Oh! Why not?'

'The woman keeps talking to me.'

James glanced to Sarah, who stared back blankly. 'Your mum?' he asked.

'No.'

'Which woman?'

'Dunno.'

The next time James looked up, Sarah added, 'We did check under the bed, didn't we?'

Oliver nodded reluctantly as Sarah offered her husband a slight raise of the eyebrows to say they'd talk about it later. She didn't know *what* they'd talk about, given it was apparently three nights in a row that their son had been hearing voices. Was it a series of dreams? Nightmares? Was he creating an imaginary friend? Although he didn't seem happy about the woman talking to him.

James said he'd sort out some breakfast, then took Oliver through to the kitchen. The next forty-five minutes wasn't too different from their lives before the move. One of them sorted breakfast for Oliver, while the other used the bathroom. They swapped in time for Sarah to put together a lunch for Oliver and then met again near the stairs.

'Are you walking him in?' James asked. He spoke with a half-yawn, in a way that made it sound more like a request than a general enquiry. 'I've got a bit of work to do,' he added. 'Plus I was going to unpack the rest of the office.' He clearly didn't like the look Sarah was giving him, feeling the need to clarify. 'It's probably only four or five hours, then a few calls.'

'You are off this weekend, though?'

'Yes. Promise.'

It didn't *sound* like a promise, even as he said it. Through the summer leading up to the move, James had been working far more than Sarah was used to. There had been days he'd disappeared into his office before seven in the morning, not to emerge until after nine in the evening. On the days he was in the office, he could be gone for even longer. He always said his work went in cycles.

'Are you still going back on Monday?' he asked, talking about her work. Sarah had taken a week away from her bookkeeping to help with the move and try to get Oliver settled with school. James said he would take time off – but it couldn't be *this* week. He had too much on.

Which meant, despite the move, despite everything that had happened, they were back where they were.

'We'll see,' Sarah replied, unsure because it was so difficult to plan. James nodded an acceptance, then headed off to the spare room, which was going to be his office. Sarah likely wouldn't see him until some point much later in the afternoon. The upside of that was consistency for Oliver. He was used to this sort of thing and cheerily said goodbye to his dad, before heading out the door with his mum.

The talk of a mystery woman keeping him awake was gone as Oliver almost skipped his way up the slope towards town. He asked what time his dad had got in, and how long the flight had been. He asked if he could go to New York one day and then moved onto the important issue of when he could get the trampoline he'd been promised as a moving-in present. With their new garden, with space to play, that was the thing he was looking forward to most. Sarah placated Oliver by saying she'd talk about it with his dad – and it wasn't long before they arrived at school.

The gates had just opened, with youngsters starting to pass inside, which felt like a small relief to Sarah. She was far too tired to deal with any further nonsense. She wouldn't have minded a friendly face in Bonnie but there was no sign of the bookshop owner from the afternoon before.

This time, there was no reluctance for Oliver to head inside. Miss Callaghan held the gate wide and he gave her a high-five as he passed, before the teacher exchanged a smile with Sarah.

That was it.

Very little traffic, no long waits at pelican crossings, no snarling police cars racing through city streets, sirens blaring. No needles on the street, no drug addicts screaming at invisible nightmares. The school drop-off had gone from a daily build-up of stress to something that should – in theory – be the easiest part of a morning.

This was what Sarah had wanted.

Oliver turned and waved and Sarah waited until he was out of sight before turning to head home. A drop-off could have taken forty minutes on a bad day in the city, this was barely ten. Sarah was thinking of bed and maybe getting some sleep when she almost walked directly into Pamela. The older woman held up both hands defensively as Sarah stepped back.

'I wanted to say sorry,' Pamela said quickly. 'About everything with your husband. I told a couple of the mums and didn't realise it would go around like it did. I was so sorry to hear about what happened to your wall.'

It took a second for Sarah to realise she meant the graffiti. News really *did* travel fast in Carnington. She'd not told James about that yet.

'It's fine,' Sarah replied tersely, not wanting a conversation. She stepped to the side, ready to go around the other woman, but Pamela wasn't done.

'I didn't mean anything by it. It's not just about Martin and Lucy. I suppose I was annoyed about what your husband did to my son.'

Sarah sighed, not bothering to hide it. She'd had enough insinuation for a lifetime. 'I'm not interested,' Sarah said, too tired to pretend otherwise. 'Lucy went missing. It's sad, but it was nothing to do with James. I don't know anything about your son.'

She stepped to the side again but Pamela moved once more. The other woman had planned this ambush, probably even rehearsed what she was going to say.

'My son's Christopher,' she said. 'He was in the same year as Abraham and Lucy. He was the one who saw Abraham on the afternoon Lucy went missing. He was the one who told everyone there was blood on Abraham's trousers.'

TWENTY

Sarah had taken another sidestep but stopped and stared at the older woman. 'Blood...?'

It was such an evocative word. Impossible to hear and not think of red.

'Christopher told the police what he'd seen but didn't feel like he was listened to,' Pamela added, relishing the moment. 'Nothing really came of it. We were friends with Martin and his wife. We'd sometimes have them over for dinner. Then Lucy disappeared and everything changed. Martin wasn't the same after that. Everyone was so worried about the poor girl.'

It had taken Sarah a few moments to catch herself. 'I don't know why you're telling me.'

She *did* know: it was antagonising. Hoping for a reaction that could be fed back to the other gossipers. The coven, as Bonnie had called them.

'Christopher moved away not long after,' Pamela continued, barely missing a beat, still sounding rehearsed. 'He went to South America on some sort of backpacking thing but didn't come back.'

This time, she glanced up, waiting for Sarah to catch her eye.

'He's still out there?' Sarah asked, wishing she hadn't.

'He was shot in a bar.'

'Oh... Wow. I... I'm so sorry.'

Sarah didn't know what else to say. There probably *was* a degree of agitating in what Pamela was saying – but she *had* lost a son. It sounded as if she thought the only reason Christopher had gone to South America was because the police hadn't taken him seriously. In a way it didn't matter if it was true: she believed it.

Ripples.

James was at the centre of something that had sent divisions spinning through a community. None of it had gone away, not really, even after a quarter of a century and more. Even after he'd changed his name.

'Why wouldn't the police have done something?' Sarah asked, not sure she believed the other woman.

Pamela was past the stage of being rehearsed. 'I don't know,' she replied dismissively. 'That's a question for them. I don't think they ever found Abraham's trousers and he told the police he was wearing shorts.'

Things were starting to make sense, in a roundabout kind of way.

'Your son told Lucy's dad about the blood...?'

Sarah asked it as a question, even though she knew the answer. It was why Lucy's dad was so certain James was responsible for whatever had happened to his daughter. The police hadn't found her and he'd heard about there being blood on James. He *had* to believe it was true because he had no other explanation. It also meant it was likely Pamela had gone directly to Martin after their first chat at the school gates. No wonder it had gone around the community so quickly.

Pamela didn't deny it. 'When the police didn't do much, Christopher felt he had to say something.'

Sarah didn't react, not outwardly anyway. She didn't know what to think. If there *had* been blood on James's trousers not long after Lucy went missing, it was a big deal. If Oliver disappeared and one of his friends was seen not long after with blood on his clothes, she'd assume the worst as well.

'Christopher might've been wrong,' Sarah said, partially talking to herself, definitely not sounding convinced.

There was no easy way of knowing considering the one witness to this was apparently shot in a foreign country.

Pamela acknowledged the point with a 'Maybe' that made it sound as if she had long since made up her mind. 'Jealousy does terrible things to people,' Pamela added, back into her rehearsed mode.

Sarah wanted to leave but couldn't resist the bait. The other woman had dangled it so tantalisingly.

'What do you mean by that?'

'Haven't you heard?' Pamela added airily, as if talking about the weather. Definitely wanting a reaction.

When Sarah felt as if she'd finally had enough and stepped around Pamela, ready to head home, the other woman moved backwards and started speaking quickly.

'Lucy had a newish boyfriend back then,' she said. 'That was the thing. Everyone was saying it. Abraham was smitten with her but she never saw him in such a way. She was seeing a boy named Eric. He works at the garage on the high street. You've probably seen him around. Anyway, Christopher always thought that's what happened with them all. You do hear about these things, don't you? Love triangles, all that...?'

She'd said it in a not-saying-it kind of way. The implication was clear that Pamela thought James had killed Lucy because she didn't see him as a romantic partner. Or perhaps she didn't *really* think that, not after so many years, she simply wanted the reaction.

That was the news cycle nowadays. Do or say something knowing it will get a response, endlessly repeat and report on the response, then keep repeating and reporting on the response to the response. It was a non-stop circle that had bled into real life.

Sarah knew she had to be careful. Any anger, any wavering of support for her husband, would quickly, and gleefully, be fed back.

'What do you want me to say?' Sarah asked, trying to sound calm.

There was a shrug. 'Nothing really. I suppose I just want you to know the truth. I'm sure you want your son to be safe...?'

Oh, there it was.

Sarah felt the blood rush. This was how to get to her. Tingles rippled along her spine and the base of her neck. She knew she couldn't rise to it – and yet every part of her wanted to tell Pamela where to go.

And she just, *just*, kept control of herself. 'We *are* safe,' she insisted, before moving around the other woman and hurrying off towards the centre.

TWENTY-ONE

Sarah fumed as she walked. She deliberately dug her nails into her palms, letting it spike and sting because the alternative was marching back to Pamela and poking a finger in her face, demanding to know just who she thought she was.

But that would be the reaction Pamela wanted.

Sarah wanted to go home, *real* home, their flat in the city, not this village with its spiteful coven of whispering agitators. What was it Bonnie had said? There was no real drama around, so people had to manufacture it? Something like that.

Pamela had picked her moment – and yet, as calculated as it felt, Sarah didn't have the sense she was outright lying. Her son probably *had* said he'd seen blood on James's clothes. He might have made it up, and wasn't around to answer any questions now, but other people believed him.

Sarah felt the red mist diluting to orange as she continued through the centre. A couple was sitting outside the café, both in matching shorts, shirts and walking boots. A pair of hiking poles were leaning against the window as they munched croissants and sipped cappuccinos. Before they'd moved, Sarah had visions of her and James spending their weekends with nature. They'd become one of those couples who took family photos at the tops of hills, with blankets of green stretching into the distance. They'd post hashtags like #familygoals or #countrylife to let everyone in the city know how fantastic it was.

It felt such a long way away now.

She continued towards the slope at the end that would lead to the cottage but noticed for the first time properly that there was a garage off to the side. She'd passed it a good dozen times since moving, paying the forecourt little attention. There was a stack of tyres off to the side and the faintest sound of a radio from somewhere within the actual workshop. Two cars were parked outside, with another inside on a raised platform. A woman was standing by one of the cars as a man in dark overalls pumped air into a front tyre. There was a pop and a hiss and then he gave a thumbs-up. 'You should be good,' he said.

'How much?' the woman asked.

'It's fine.'

Sarah realised she'd slowed to a near stop as she watched the woman drive off with the newly inflated tyres. A day before and she'd have paid it no attention – but now both Dean and Pamela had said that Lucy was seeing a boy named Eric at the time she'd disappeared. Pamela had even planted the seed to say he worked at the garage on the high street. She'd obviously done it deliberately, but Sarah found it impossible to ignore. She had so many questions.

The mechanic was around the right age, in his early forties and broadly athletic. He gave a slight flinch as he stood straighter. Those forty-year-old joints weren't getting any looser, something Sarah knew all too well.

Probably because she was staring, the man gave a small wave, which Sarah returned. It felt like the sort of thing that probably happened in a village like this.

Sarah continued walking a few steps but then stopped and called across to him. 'Are you Eric?'

The man seemed somewhat amused by the question, even as Sarah regretted asking. She couldn't help herself.

'How'd you know that?' he replied.

Sarah moved across the forecourt until she was near the air compressor, a few paces away from the man. There was grease on his chin. 'I heard your name in passing the other day,' Sarah said. 'I'm new to town.'

It was such a bad choice of words and Eric grimaced. 'You heard *good* stuff in passing...?'

Every word Sarah spoke was another one deeper down the hole. She shouldn't have bothered talking to Pamela and definitely should have kept walking past the garage. It was too late now.

'I heard you were Lucy Shearer's boyfriend...?'

Eric's features darkened. 'Why would someone tell you that?'

'My husband is James Parkinson.' The reaction was almost nothing, until she remembered the crucial part. 'He used to be Abraham Parkinson.'

Then it clicked. She saw the light bulb. 'Abe's back?' Eric was stunned. 'I didn't think I'd ever see him again. How is he?'

It sounded like a genuine question.

'He's good,' Sarah replied, which was probably true. 'It's just a lot of people in town seem to have opinions about him. It's hard to know what to believe.'

There was a pause now. Eric chewed the corner of his mouth, accidentally spreading the grease onto his lip. 'I can see that.' He thought for a moment more and then nodded towards the garage itself. 'Do you want a cup of tea?'

Sarah wondered if more information was a good idea. The fact Eric had *specifically* asked whether James was OK probably meant he wasn't as prejudiced as someone like Pamela or Martin.

'As long as it won't get you in trouble with your boss...?' Sarah replied.

'This is my place.'

He took no offence, breaking into a grin and nodding her towards the small reception area at the side of the garage. He washed his hands in the sink and filled a kettle, before grabbing two teabags from a giant bag on the counter. He took a glass bottle of milk from the mini fridge and sloshed half a mugful into his cup, alongside four heaped sugars. His drink was going to be around thirty per cent tea. After checking what Sarah wanted, they ended up sitting across from one another on plasticky school-style chairs.

'How long have you been in town?' he asked.

'Since Monday.'

'Oh! Really recently. Where are you living?'

'People call it Puddlebrick Cottage.'

That got a laugh. 'It's nice down there, backs onto the woods. Have you seen a fox yet?'

'No, I think my son would love that.'

'How old is he?'

'Seven.'

That got a nod.

There were foxes in London, though Sarah had never seen one. Every now and then, someone from the Facebook group that covered their housing block would post a photo – but it was always a fox going through the bins. Creatures living in the countryside seemed more romanticised, but maybe that was just her.

He didn't reply, so Sarah added a hopeful, 'I suppose I'm curious about Lucy. Ever since I moved here, I keep hearing about her – but I never knew anything about her before...?'

Eric took a breath, glanced towards the poster of the sports car on the wall, and then back to Sarah. For a moment, it felt as if he might clam up but, instead, he smiled wistfully.

'There was a woman found in the river in the 1940s. There's almost nobody still alive who remembers her – but people still speculate about what happened. Nothing ever goes away. Not here.'

'Like with Lucy?'

That got a slow nod. 'It doesn't help that her dad's Martin...'

It felt loaded and Sarah wondered how far she should push, if at all. Martin seemed like one of those beloved types, for whom nobody ever had a bad word. Sarah had thought she was the outlier in being suspicious of him.

Eric nodded through the window, towards a large house on the other side of the road. 'He owns that.'

'Martin?'

A nod. 'He converted it into flats. There are more around town. I lived in one for about six months after leaving home.'

Sarah almost told him that Dean had said the same thing to her the day before. Even James had lived in a flat owned by Martin Shearer when he'd been growing up. It felt as if everyone in Carnington went through such a thing, as if it was a rite of passage.

'It sounds like he owns quite a lot,' Sarah replied.

'Someone said he has a stake in the coffee place. I think he might have made some mortgage payments for the bakery during Covid...? Maybe the butcher's? I don't know. People talk a lot but you don't know what's real.'

So much was beginning to make sense. No wonder someone felt the need to graffiti 'go home' on Sarah's wall. No wonder people like Pamela felt the urge to stick up for him. Not only did he sponsor clubs and events around the village, not only did he run societies, it seemed like he owned a decent amount as well.

Eric didn't seem particularly cowed by any of that.

'People are saying James killed Lucy,' Sarah said.

Eric nodded along, though he was still staring aimlessly through the window, cradling his tea. 'Did you ask him about it?'

'Of course.'

'What did he say?'

Sarah took a moment, then held up her hands. How was she supposed to respond? He'd obviously said it wasn't him. And yet...

Eric got it.

'I suppose you wouldn't be asking me if you liked what you heard.' He sipped his tea and glanced to his poster again. The edges were crisp and curling. It looked as if it had been on the wall for years.

'I don't want to get involved in a domestic,' he said.

'It's not a domestic.'

Sarah felt Eric's gaze flicker across her, weighing up whether this was going to be worth it.

'I was going out with Lucy at the end,' he said. 'I was seventeen at the time and she was my first proper girlfriend – but it was always a bit strange between the three of us. She and Abe had been friends for years and spent loads of time together. I don't think anyone was really sure if they were actually a thing. Most people at school assumed they were. Even when me and her were together, she talked about him a lot.' He waited a moment, then added, 'I'm assuming you know most of this?'

'James said the same thing.'

That got a shrug of sorts. 'So, I'm not saying anything different. If they were together, I never saw it. I know he was the last person to see her.'

Eric caught Sarah's eye.

'That doesn't mean he killed her,' she said.

'I know. We always got on all right and I never said he did.

But Chris said he saw blood on Abe that afternoon – and lots of people went with it.'

'Didn't the police look into it?'

Eric's eyes narrowed a fraction as he realised she already knew this part. 'I assume so. They definitely talked to him but they talked to me, too – more than once. They talked to everyone. I didn't see anything that afternoon – I was in lessons – but people believed Chris about the blood.' He held up his hands. 'I guess all this means they still do.'

Considering the conflicting allegations swimming around the village, there was a surprising amount of consistency in what everyone was saying.

'Nobody knows what happened to Lucy,' Eric said. 'Well, one person might.'

He caught her eye once more.

'If you really want to know, if you can't let it go, your husband is the only person who knows how Lucy was when he left her.'

'He said it was normal that he left her. She sometimes met other friends, and he had somewhere else to go. But that it was fine.'

Eric didn't reply, though he didn't need to. If Sarah had been happy with the explanation, if she had a hundred per cent faith in her husband, she wouldn't be sitting in the reception of the garage, asking questions.

Sarah hadn't touched her tea. She apologised for that but stood and moved towards the door. 'Thanks for the talk,' she said.

'Any time,' Eric replied. 'And if your husband's up for a catch-up, it'd be great to see him. There really are no hard feelings at my end. It might take a bit of time getting used to calling him "James", though.'

Sarah said she would pass on the message, then headed back onto the street. She knew Eric was right in the sense that only James knew how Lucy had been when he left her – and it felt as if she was going to have to make a choice about whether she believed him. If it wasn't for that photo of him with the green Mini and the sense that he'd lied to her, it wouldn't have been a question. Except a large part of her felt as if neither James nor Martin was being honest about everything.

It didn't help that the one witness to the supposed blood from that afternoon was also dead.

Sarah stopped to check her phone, in case there was something from the school. There were some new emails, though they could be dealt with at home. She was about to continue down the slope when what sounded like a muted scream came from the other side of the road. It was the sort of sound somebody might make when coming to bed in the dark, stubbing a toe, and desperately trying not to wake a partner.

It was hard to work out whether it had come from a man or woman and, for a moment, Sarah considered ignoring it. Somebody probably *had* dropped something. She waited a second, two, then decided it couldn't do any harm to check. Sarah looked both ways, even though there was barely any traffic at any time, then crossed. She was outside the big, old house Eric said was owned by Martin. The one converted to flats. A giant metal wheelie bin was on the pavement and Sarah headed around it, through the gateposts onto a crumbling path. There was a tree on one side, with a muddy flower bed on the other.

The noise was louder now, not a scream but what sounded like very heavy breathing. Sarah followed it around the front of the house, towards the side, where a smaller bin was almost blocking the way.

A woman was there, wide-eyed and staring as she spun to take in Sarah. She had one hand on her chest, wheezing as if mid-asthma attack.

Because there, on the ground a few paces away, a man was

on his side, not moving, blood seeping from a gaping head wound.

'I think he's dead,' the woman managed.

Sarah hadn't moved towards him but it was hard to argue. She also knew who it was. The same man who'd knocked on her door two days before to call her husband a killer.

Martin Shearer was on the floor, soaked by his own blood.

TWENTY-TWO

The woman turned between Sarah and Martin, still breathing heavily, apparently unable to speak. Sarah scrambled for her phone, struggled to unlock it because Face ID wasn't working, then managed to dial 999. The handler asked which service she wanted and Sarah said ambulance and probably the police. The truth was, she didn't know.

She told the woman on the other end of the call that a man was covered in blood and was asked whether he was breathing.

Sarah wasn't sure. She'd stepped ahead of the other woman, with Martin now at her feet. The only dead body Sarah had ever seen was her mother's in the morgue a few years ago. That was after the mortician had done his thing, meaning she looked peaceful, almost asleep. Sarah had still hated it and spent almost no time in the room – yet this... was something else.

It was a man Sarah barely knew and, from her few interactions with him, hadn't particularly liked, and yet... there was so much blood.

'... are you still there?'

Sarah blinked back to the side of the house. She'd been lost for a moment. A trickle of Martin's blood was nudging the edge of her shoe and she stared at the red.

'I'm here,' Sarah replied, stumbling over the words.

'Can you see whether he's breathing?'

Sarah sidestepped around the body and crouched, picking up Martin's limp arm. There was no resistance and she held a finger to his wrist, where there should be a pulse. She couldn't feel anything, so shifted her finger around, hoping. His chest wasn't rising, his nostrils weren't flaring. He hadn't moved.

'Is he dead?' the woman at the corner of the house asked.

Sarah looked up to the stranger. She'd forgotten the other woman was there but nodded.

'He's dead,' she said, speaking as much to the woman as she was the call handler.

Sarah was struggling to remember the past minute or so. The handler asked for the address. She wondered if she'd already given it but realised she couldn't have because she didn't know it. She might have said Carnington's high street, something like that.

At the new request, Sarah stood and headed back around the house to the front. She read the number to the handler, who said an ambulance was on its way. Sarah looked over the road, to where a couple were cautiously heading towards her. She wondered if the scream had been louder than she thought.

'Is everything all right?' a woman asked. 'I'm a nurse.'

Sarah pointed at the woman to the side of the house, though knew it was a bit late for medical care. Meanwhile, the call handler asked if Sarah wanted to stay live while waiting for the ambulance. Sarah thanked her and said she was all right, before hanging up.

How long would an ambulance take in a village like Carnington? Back in her old flat, there would be sirens throughout the day and night. She'd found them annoying most of the time but, now, the convenience of having the emergency services so close felt like a blessing.

A handful more people had drifted onto the street, though it was hard to know how or why they knew there was an issue. Sarah ignored them and returned to the corner of the house, where the nurse was now on the ground, checking on Martin. The woman who'd found him hadn't moved.

'Is he...?'

The nurse glanced up to catch Sarah's eye. 'He's got a *really* soft pulse. We need an ambulance.'

Sarah couldn't stop the surprised 'Oh' escaping her mouth. She'd made a mistake in thinking he was dead.

'There's one coming,' Sarah said.

It was then that the woman on the corner started speaking. 'I was coming out of the house and found him there,' she said.

'Do you live inside?' the nurse asked.

'I'm on the second floor. I thought I heard a bang but couldn't see anything out the window. I almost ignored it but figured I might as well check. When I got down here...'

The nurse had no idea of the man's identity. 'Do you know him?' she asked.

'It's Martin. He owns the building. He comes by every Thursday to clear the noticeboard and check the fire alarms.'

The gentlest howl of a siren was on the breeze. It could still be a mile or more away. There were three women now standing around Martin's bloodied body, though a scuffing of feet from the path behind made it sound like more were on their way.

And then the woman said what Sarah had been thinking. 'It looks like someone hit him over the head.'

TWENTY-THREE

The sound of a click-clacking computer keyboard trickled around the landing as Sarah reached the top of the cottage stairs. She waited a moment, then slipped into the bathroom to check herself in the mirror. She looked tired, which wasn't a surprise. There was no blood on her hands, despite touching Martin's body. A part of her had wondered if some might have got on her fingers, then her face – but she was clear.

Sarah washed her hands and stared at herself once more. It might be the light and the way it kissed the mirror, but she looked washed out. The rings around her eyes were reaching panda levels. She washed her face and dried it, then sat on the toilet, staring at the wall.

She couldn't stop picturing Martin's body. All that blood.

It took a few minutes to compose herself and then Sarah went to the other end of the landing, where she knocked gently on the door. There was a sound of footsteps and the door swung inwards. James was wearing jogging bottoms and slippers, with a smart shirt – which meant he'd been on a Zoom call while she was out.

'How's the office?' Sarah asked.

He held the door wider for her to head inside. While he'd been away, Sarah had unpacked most of the other rooms – but the office was his. Since Sarah had last seen the space, James had covered the floor with rugs, unpacked his books onto a set of shelves, set up his computer, and aligned his various certificates across the wall – largely to cover the small holes. There was still a spare box under the window – but it was a lot better than his cramped corner back in their old flat.

'It's nice to have some space,' he said.

Sarah had wondered if the prospect of having his own office was the biggest reason why her husband had agreed to move. He'd certainly listened to the arguments around Oliver's schooling, Ofsted, and the class sizes – but, really, the times when they both worked from home were frustrating for the pair of them. James would be in one corner of the living room on his computer, trying to have a Zoom call, while Sarah would be in the bedroom, attempting to do her own work.

'Are you all right?'

Sarah had been staring into the room, focusing on the dash of red from a tie that was looped over a chest of drawers in the corner.

'Did you hear the sirens?' she asked.

James stared blankly at her. 'What sirens?'

Something felt off, though Sarah wasn't sure what. She didn't think James had blinked and his expression hadn't changed.

'It looks like someone attacked Martin Shearer,' Sarah said.

She looked for the reaction, anticipated one, except James didn't flinch. 'How do you mean?' he asked.

'I'm not sure. He was bleeding from his head. It looked like someone might have hit him. We thought he was dead for a few minutes.'

James still didn't react. He was back on his chair, half-turned between Sarah and his screen.

'But he's not?'

'There was a nurse who checked him. He was in a serious way and they rushed him to the hospital.'

'Bit of a longer journey here than the city.'

It was true, but not what Sarah expected. She'd thought there would be surprise at the very least – and definitely interest. Instead, James was drumming his fingers on the desk.

'Did Oliver get off OK?' he asked.

It was such an abrupt change of subject that Sarah needed a moment to remember the reason she'd been outside was to drop off their son at school.

'Um... yes, I think so.'

'What was the thing with the woman keeping him awake?'

'I don't know. He said it the night before. I wondered if I was talking in my sleep but I didn't even get to bed last night.'

Saying it out loud made Sarah yawn. For now, there was so much going on that they could leave it another night to figure out if Oliver had invented an imaginary friend for the new house.

'We need to sort out the trampoline by the weekend,' she said instead. 'Oliver's not forgotten that we promised.'

James spun back on his chair and grinned. 'Shame he can't remember to brush his teeth but he *can* remember a promise made once almost six months ago.'

Sarah didn't laugh. She was still thinking about Martin and how fast James had changed the subject. It was such a strange reaction.

Her husband rocked slightly on the chair, wanting to get back to his computer. Except, when he swung back towards the screen, the light caught something. Sarah had taken a step towards the door but shifted back, standing over her husband as she took his hand.

'What's that?' she asked, pointing to an unmistakeable brown-red smear on his skin.

James held his hand up to the light, then rubbed it hard on his jogging pants.

'I had a nosebleed earlier,' he said, before almost immediately starting to type on the keyboard.

'Was it a bad one?'

'What?'

'The nosebleed.'

'Oh, I guess... not really. Probably the dry air from the plane and airport.' He spun and gave a thin smile. 'I've got to get back,' he added. 'I don't want to be a dick about things but can you close the door?'

TWENTY-FOUR

Sarah spent over an hour working her way through emails. The out-of-office remained on but she didn't mind taking some time to let her clients know she wasn't off the grid. As James continued working upstairs, she reassembled a cheap coffee table they'd had in the flat and had talked about using in the back garden of the new house. They would buy some garden furniture eventually, but it would work as a temporary thing.

That done, she began to fold down the miniature city of cardboard they'd amassed over the past few months. They'd had a post on the community Facebook page asking for spare boxes and taken everything offered – except now they had no need of the card.

In better times, Sarah might have registered for the town Facebook page and put up a post asking if anyone needed it. With the way everything had gone, she dreaded the possible replies. Instead, she dragged the boxes into the front garden and started stamping them flat. She'd have to check to see when the recycling was due for pickup.

It was as she worked on the fifth box that someone caught Sarah's attention. She'd met Raina – the neighbour who'd kindly given them food on day one, only to blank her on day two – but she'd not run into the people on the other side.

A very-pregnant woman was standing at the fence, waving to catch Sarah's attention. She was slightly angling away, cradling her back.

'Are you Sarah?' she asked.

Sarah half-expected her to want to talk about things from decades before but figured there was little point in deliberately picking an argument with a new neighbour.

'That's me,' she replied, trying to offer some degree of enthusiasm. 'We just moved in. I was going to come over and introduce myself at some point but we've had so much on.'

The woman returned the smile, which was something of a relief given many of Sarah's interactions from the past few days.

'I took this in for you,' she said, lifting a box over the fence. 'The Parcelforce man said no one was in. I was on the toilet.' She pointed to her belly. 'Happens a lot at the moment.'

Sarah laughed and took the parcel. Her name was on the front and it was heavier than it looked. From the way the weight shifted from side to side, it felt like someone had sent a bottle of something.

'He said he left one of those delivery cards,' the woman added. 'I'm Trish, by the way.'

Sarah introduced herself and said that her husband was James – not bothering to give their last names. She wasn't in the mood for anything that might come. 'I didn't see a card,' she added. 'I was dropping off my son at school.'

Trish nodded towards her house. 'My husband works at the dairy, so we always have free milk if that's your thing. Just give us a knock.'

Sarah thanked the woman for her kindness, figuring this was more the sort of community life she'd envisioned. They said their goodbyes and then Sarah carried the parcel to the house. When she opened the front door, she realised there *was* a delivery card. It had somehow tucked itself almost entirely under the welcome mat, with only a red triangle of the corner poking out.

She carried everything through to the kitchen, then used a knife to open the package. It wasn't a complete surprise to find two bottles of wine inside – alongside a *lot* of bubble wrap, and a card.

Don't drink it all before we come to visit, you greedy cow!

Sarah laughed as she flipped the card to see Cara's name on the back. It was definitely the sort of thing her best friend from London would write.

She took out her phone and started a text thanking her for the gift, though stopped halfway through. She wanted Cara and Richard to visit – and yet, with everything going on, it was far from the best time. She tried to think of a way to say, 'Can't wait to see you' while not making it sound like an invitation.

That was when she took proper notice of the Parcelforce card.

The delivery driver had written 'next door' on the top of the card, with a time directly underneath. He might have rounded up or down by five or ten minutes – but the time listed was almost an hour before. That was when Sarah had been talking to Eric at the garage, the same time that someone had attacked Martin.

Sarah put down her phone and picked up the card, checking it again for further information.

If the delivery driver had knocked, or rung the bell, why hadn't James answered?

Sarah picked up one of the bottles and headed upstairs. She tapped gently on the door of James's office, not waiting for a reply before opening it and heading in. He turned from his monitor as she offered him the bottle.

'What's this?' he asked.

'Present from Cara.'

'Oh, that's nice of her.'

He motioned to turn back to the screen but Sarah wasn't done. 'Did you go out earlier?' she asked.

'No. Why?'

'Because next door took in the parcel for us. The driver left a card because nobody answered the door.'

James had frozen, one hand on the keyboard, not typing. 'Oh... um... I guess I didn't hear the door. Are you sure the bell works?'

Sarah realised she hadn't tried. She took back the bottle, closed the door, and headed downstairs. After opening the front door, she stretched to press the button – which immediately sent a loud *ding-dong* echoing through the house.

She closed the door and stood alone in the hall, listening to the echo.

James didn't say he'd been on a call, unable to answer – he'd said he hadn't heard it. But there was no way the sound could have been missed.

Which left only one explanation.

If her husband hadn't answered the door... it was because he wasn't in.

TWENTY-FIVE

Sarah returned to the kitchen. She put the wine in the cupboard and picked up the mail card again. The time was unmistakable. Martin Shearer had been attacked at almost the exact moment the delivery driver had tried to drop off the parcel.

James *must* have been out.

And there was a brown-red smear on his hand. It might have been a nosebleed, as he'd said, but Sarah hadn't known him to have them.

For the first time, perhaps ever, Sarah was wondering if she could trust her husband. She'd been unsure in the early hours, especially considering there was a photograph of him next to a car he claimed to know nothing about. The same one Martin said he'd stolen.

Could James *really* have left the house to attack Martin Shearer? How could he have known where he was?

Sarah couldn't believe it, *didn't* believe it. Except... maybe she did.

Had James *really* killed Lucy all those years ago? Surely not? Surely it wasn't possible?

And yet, there were so many questions unanswered. How

was she supposed to get answers for something nobody had witnessed and that had happened decades before?

Sarah was sitting at the table and considered opening one of the wine bottles. If ever she needed a drink, it was now – except downing glasses of wine by herself at lunchtime on a random Thursday was not going to solve anything.

She steadied herself enough to send a message of thanks to Cara, before an almost immediate reply came back.

How's the house? How's the peace? Not jealous at all!

Where to begin? Sarah had spent so long telling her friend how excited she was to move, she couldn't bring herself to explain that it was all falling apart. That the man upstairs, the person to whom she was married, suddenly felt like a stranger.

It's brilliant. Loving it so far. Still unpacking but it's coming along.

Sarah muted the message thread to stop herself replying to anything else. She was one more piece of bad news away from revealing the lot.

There were still bits and pieces of work to do around the house but Sarah couldn't bring herself to pretend everything was fine. She loaded Facebook – never a good sign – and searched for a page relating to the town. There was something named 'Carnington Friends And Family', which had a little over a thousand members. Sarah joined the page – and wasn't surprised to see that news of the attack on Martin was spreading. There was shock, with a mix of people asking how he was, combined with others asking the rhetorical question of who would do such a thing.

Sarah scrolled through the comments and was relieved to see that nobody had mentioned the names of James or Abraham. The drama Pamela had started seemingly hadn't made it online, though it felt as if it was only a matter of time.

What was the stain on James's hand?

Actually, Sarah *knew* what the stain was – he'd even told her. It was definitely blood. But was it his?

Sarah thought about James's explanation for missing the parcel and how bad it was. He could've said he was wearing his noise-cancelling headphones to focus on his work. He could have said he nipped into the back garden and missed the doorbell. He could've said he was in the shower, or on the toilet. Any number of far better explanations than simply not hearing it.

Did that mean he was telling the truth? Or had he simply failed to realise he was going to be questioned, and was not great at thinking on the spot?

Sarah had no idea.

Late morning became early afternoon and then there was the sound of a flushing toilet. A few minutes later, there were footsteps on the stairs and James yawned his way into the kitchen. Sarah watched her husband potter around, looking for any sign that he was behaving unusually. If a person really *had* battered someone into a coma, would they be making themselves Marmite on toast a couple of hours later?

And, if so, could that person *really* be her husband?

James was yawning and Sarah found herself joining in. She covered her mouth and they caught one another's eye, both breaking into a smile.

'Why don't you go back to bed?' James said. 'You can get a few hours.'

'What about picking up Oliver?'

'I was thinking it would be nice for me to get him anyway. Get away from the laptop for a bit – plus it's been a while since I walked around town.'

Sarah was second-guessing herself, probably him as well, wondering if there was another meaning. If there was, she couldn't think of one. The part of her that had been so keen on the move craved this sort of thing. Even if they were both working from home, it would be nice to take twenty minutes or so to walk and collect their son together.

'Let's both go,' Sarah replied. 'It'll be nice.'

It was as James pointed to a bedding shop and said, 'It used to be a video rental place,' that Sarah temporarily forgot herself. She'd pictured this life of them walking side by side in the sun, her husband telling stories of how the village used to be. She'd wanted to have lunch together outside one of the cafés, or sneak a cake from the bakery. They were a partnership and living here would bring them together.

They passed another shop that appeared to sell outdoor furniture – and James nodded towards it. 'That was a newsagent,' he said. 'I used to get *Shoot* from there.'

'Is that a football magazine?'

'Yeah, and I'd collect all the stickers, too.'

That was how things continued as they reached the other end of town, rounding the corner to head towards the school gates. Parents were crowding and Sarah felt their stares. She wasn't sure whether it was better or worse to have James at her side. It was him they'd been gossiping about, after all.

As it was, they didn't make it all the way to the gates. Bonnie was standing a little away from the crowd. She was scrolling her phone but looked up as Sarah neared, then broke into a smile.

'Good to see you again!' she said.

Sarah made the introductions between her and James and they said their own hellos. She felt her husband's interest wane as the topic turned to Georgia and how Bonnie's daughter was getting on in reception class. James was busy looking over them, towards the other women who were pretending not to be watching him. Sarah wondered if any of them *really* knew him from back in the day, or if all they had was the gossip.

Meanwhile, Sarah listened and nodded along. Bonnie's daughter was doing half days at the school, and it was mainly playtime. The children did a lot of painting.

'It's always better when someone else cleans up after,' Bonnie said with a laugh.

Sarah didn't get a chance to reply because, from nowhere, a fourth person joined their circle. It had been a few hours since Sarah had last seen Pamela, when she'd tried to stir things up. Now, there was something manic about the older woman. She didn't bother with either Bonnie or Sarah, instead jabbing an angry finger towards James.

'Was it you?' she said.

Sarah watched her husband look down quizzically on the woman. 'Was *what* me?'

'I know you. Christopher knew what you were like, too.'

There was a beat where Sarah watched her husband realise who was in front of him. Another light bulb going off, not that he got a chance to say anything.

'I remember you, Abraham Parkinson—'

'That's not my name.'

'It is, though. Everyone knows who you *really* are. So was this you?'

'Was *what* me?'

'Was it you who hit Martin over the head?'

Pamela was still poking a finger, mind already made up.

James continued to frown over her. 'I've been at home all day,' he said.

Pamela snorted at this. 'As if!'

Sarah wasn't convinced her husband *had* been at home all day, but she also wasn't prepared to stay quiet.

'You're mad,' she said, wedging herself between Pamela and James. 'What are you doing?'

Pamela backed away, though not by much.

Sarah risked a glance past her to see every other parent watching the entertainment. At least none of them were filming.

'You don't know anything about me,' James said firmly. 'About us.'

'I know you attacked Martin once before.'

The back of Sarah's head was pressed to her husband's chest and she felt him breathe in.

'No I didn't,' he said.

That got another snort. 'So you're definitely a liar.'

'I've never attacked anyone?'

'Really? Because there's a video of it on Facebook.'

TWENTY-SIX

The room at the back of Bonnie's bookshop was almost irresistibly cosy. There was a rocking chair, two regular seats, a tray with a teapot, cups and saucers, an almost finished packet of digestives, plus – as promised – a recently opened packet of *chocolate* digestives.

Oliver was sitting on the floor, building Lego with Bonnie's daughter, Georgia. They were being supervised by the shop spaniel, Gary – which Sarah thought was a hilarious name for a dog, if only she was able to appreciate such a thing.

As it was, she was in the rocking chair, nibbling a chocolate biscuit. Bonnie came through from the main shop with a swish of the curtain. It was one of those where dangly bits of cork and wood tinkled into one another.

'Feeling any better?' Bonnie asked, standing over the rocking chair.

'I think so. I just need an hour away.'

Bonnie's hands were on her hips. *I'm a little teapot.* 'What's James going to do?'

Sarah checked her phone, where there were no messages. Back at the school, just as Pamela had claimed to have video of

James attacking someone, it had felt as if things could get ugly. But then the gates had opened, children had started to spill out, and everything had calmed. Bonnie had suggested bringing Oliver to the shop to give everyone a bit of time – and Sarah had gone with it. James hadn't argued. He'd said hello to Oliver, then said he had to head home for work. Everyone had watched as he'd hurried away, including Sarah.

She lowered her voice, not wanting Oliver to hear her talking about his dad. 'Do you think I humiliated him by letting him go home by himself?'

Bonnie smiled kindly. 'Sometimes, it's OK to make something about you. It's OK to take an hour.'

It felt like good advice – and the biscuits were helping.

'Pamela has a right mouth on her,' Bonnie said. 'She's a proper battleaxe. I wouldn't worry too much.'

'She told me her son was shot in a bar on a backpacking trip. I think she's just... I don't know... *sad*.' Sarah glanced towards Oliver in the corner, who was handing Georgia a grey Lego tower. 'I think I'd be the same.'

'No reason to take it out on the rest of the village. Especially someone who's just moved here.'

Sarah didn't disagree – but then she realised Bonnie was likely talking about herself.

'What happened with your husband?' Sarah asked. Bonnie had spilled a little the day before, saying he'd killed himself and that some of the villagers hadn't been too kind – but Sarah had been too absorbed in her own world to ask for more. 'You don't have to say,' Sarah added. Perhaps it was too personal?

Bonnie slipped into one of the chairs and picked a non-chocolate digestive from the pack. She glanced towards the children and their Lego, smiling sadly.

'Lance had depression when he was younger, before he met me. He was on various antidepressants his whole life. I know that makes it sound like he had some big problem but, for the most part, nobody would've known. *I* didn't know for the first few months we were together. His medication worked and he was a normal, happy, fun guy.'

Sarah sensed the 'but', though didn't push. She had another small bite of the biscuit, giving Bonnie time.

'Then his sister broke up with her husband. She came to live with us for a while and it was fine for the most part – but Lance needed his routine. He always ate at the same time, always went to bed at the same time. When his sister was with us, everything was off. Even when she moved out, something was different. I wanted him to go back to his doctor, and he said he had.' She sighed, glanced towards Georgia in the corner. 'He hadn't – but I didn't know that 'til later. He hanged himself. I got home from the shop and he was just... there.'

Bonnie had been getting quieter and her final word was barely spoken. She was staring at the floor and Sarah could almost see the nightmare. The opening of the front door, the calling out to say you were home, and then... a hanging, swaying body.

'I'm so sorry,' Sarah said.

Bonnie clicked her tongue, shrugged a fraction. 'I try to talk about it when anyone asks. He'd actually done the nursery run that morning, dropping off Georgia, then driving home. I was here and he texted to say she was at daycare safely. I think that was the last thing he did.'

Sarah didn't know what to say, so let it sit. It felt as if Bonnie wanted to talk, and Sarah didn't mind. She'd spent a large part of the past few days wrestling with her own issues.

'They say things happen for a reason,' Bonnie added. 'It's been a tough year with Georgia. She was acting up a lot and I didn't think she'd be able to start school. She refused to spend any time away from me but calmed a bit over the summer. It's still a day at a time.'

She paused and they watched the children with the Lego.

Neither Georgia nor Oliver were saying much but they had an understanding in what they were doing. It looked as if they were trying to build some sort of castle.

'It was my dream to run a bookshop,' Bonnie said, from nothing. She'd taken another biscuit and bitten a large chunk. 'I practically lived in the library when I was a kid. Then, about a year after we moved to Carnington, the man who owned this place wanted to sell and retire. He didn't have any takers and it looked like it was going to close at one point. Lance and I scrabbled together some savings and I took out a loan. We bought it together but the shop was always for me.'

Sarah felt like there was an obvious question, that she was reluctant to ask. It was a small village, with little in the way of passing trade, especially outside the summer. It was hard to know how any of the businesses kept going, let alone a non-essential one.

Bonnie likely sensed it, answering even though Sarah hadn't asked. 'It's fine in the summer,' she said. 'People come to town to hike the trails, then they stop and have a wander. I've also been putting some of the rarer items online, so a few sales come in from that. In the winter, it costs a lot to heat everything. There's a cellar downstairs full of books – and it has to be kept warm to stop mould getting in. It more or less works out.'

She sounded less sure with the final part but her pride was impossible to ignore – even if Sarah had been in the shop for half an hour or so, while no customers had come through the doors.

'It's a lovely place,' Sarah said, meaning it. She'd never been a voracious reader but there was something irresistible about the smell and atmosphere of a bookshop.

'Sometimes, when there's no customers, I sit here reading,' Bonnie said. 'I honestly don't think I'd rather be anywhere else.'

The only sound was the gentle *tick-tack* of Lego bricks – and Sarah couldn't disagree. She set the chair rocking slightly, then realised Bonnie's gaze was focused on the computer towards the back of the alcove.

'Do you want to look for it?' Bonnie asked.

Sarah knew she was talking about the video Pamela had mentioned. Where James had apparently attacked Martin. Pamela had added no further detail, though the 'once before' made it sound like it was from when he'd first lived in the town.

'No,' Sarah replied, before adding an almost instant, 'OK.'

She *didn't* want to see her husband attacking anyone, even if it was a different him from decades before. And yet... she knew she had to.

Sarah flicked a glance towards the children, who were in their own world. 'Maybe with the sound off,' she added.

Bonnie had shifted so she was sitting at the computer. The case was bulky, the monitor one of the earlier 'flat' screens that was an inch thick and weighed as much as a brick. The web browser took a while to load the village Facebook page. A circle spun as it jumbled into view, bringing back memories of the old days and *eeeeeeeeeee-urrrrrrrrrr* modems.

The video didn't take much finding. It was on the same post Sarah had seen earlier and was now the highest-liked comment. Someone had written 'Remember this?', then attached a grainy video. It was the sort that would've been recorded on an old camcorder from the late 1990s or early 2000s. From before the days that everyone had a phone.

Bonnie clicked to play and the circle spun once more. An agonising few seconds passed as Sarah waited for the content. She was standing behind Bonnie and shuffled sideways, making sure the view from the other side of the room would be blocked and Oliver couldn't see by accident.

On screen, the video was shaking from side to side, making it hard to make out what was going on. Bonnie whispered, 'Like *Blair Witch*,' which was definitely a way to discover who was a teenager in 1999.

And then it was there.

The camera almost missed it because of the shaking but a man was on the ground, with someone angled over the top. The figure launched one, two, three punches, all into the man's side, before reeling back and aiming a wild kick towards his head. It might have missed, though it was hard to tell. The intent had been there.

The next time the image was clear, there was a girl pulling back the person who'd dealt the blows. It was clearer who they were now. The man on the ground was older, perhaps early- to mid-forties. The other pair were teenagers – with the girl shouting what was clearly 'Stop!', even with the sound off.

They disappeared out of shot as the video focused on the man, who was picking himself up. He was in some sort of dusty park, with patchy yellow grass – and there was a moment of déjà vu for Sarah as she watched crimson spill from the man's head.

It was definitely Martin Shearer. He had darker hair then, plus more of it. Sarah knew his face and, even decades younger, it was him. He put a hand to his head and stared at the blood, before the camera zipped away to focus on the huffing, puffing, furious face of a young man.

He was fifteen or sixteen, his top ripped, dirt on his face. So different, yet exactly the same. He had the face of the man Sarah had looked into thousands of times before. Tens of thousands.

'Is that James?' Bonnie asked.

The teenage boy was snarling and spitting, needing the girl to keep him from launching at Martin once more. He aimed another kick, though this was entirely at the air.

'It's James,' Sarah replied.

TWENTY-SEVEN

The video continued, zooming out to show Martin on one side of a grassy patch, James on the other. The girl was presumably Lucy, though Sarah didn't know for sure. She had a hand on James's shoulder as he shouted something to Martin, who was still transfixed at his own blood. James's T-shirt was hanging around his waist, a large rip through the side.

'I guess that's her dad,' Bonnie said – which was the first time Sarah had realised it. Lucy on the video was trying to stop her friend from attacking her father.

Sarah had seen enough and turned towards the children who were still – and thankfully – oblivious in the corner. Gary the spaniel was sitting at Oliver's side and he was stroking the dog, watching Georgia build.

'I didn't expect that,' Bonnie said, easing herself away from the computer desk. The video had stopped. 'It was so much more violent. He was really laying into him on the ground.'

Sarah didn't know what to say. She had never seen her husband show any aggression, let alone anything similar to what was in the video. He'd never told stories of youthful fights or gangs. If anything, he was a mediator. A year or so before, there had been a fight in the park nearest their flat. It was a Facebook Marketplace deal that had gone wrong, with one man threatening to give another a right kicking. James had got in the middle, de-escalating to the point that everyone shook hands. Sarah had never once felt threatened in his presence.

And yet, it was undeniably him who had rattled those punches into the side of a man already on the ground. It felt impossible to square.

'They've disabled comments,' Bonnie said, pointing to the screen.

Sarah didn't reply. She felt shell-shocked by what she'd seen. Perhaps it was no wonder Pamela had accused James of the recent attack on Martin, given the clear evidence of the same thing happening so many years before.

And he'd denied it to Pamela's face. She was right that he was a liar.

Plus there was blood on his hand earlier.

Sarah had seen too much blood for one day.

'How did you meet?' Bonnie asked.

Sarah almost missed it because she'd been lost in thought, wondering if James had really left the house that morning. Wondering whether she'd seen his blood, or Martin's, on her husband's hand.

She'd returned to the rocking chair and tea. Bonnie was trying to change the subject and Sarah let her.

'It's kind of old-fashioned,' she said. 'I was in a pub on a Saturday night. It was the summer of the Olympics and I'd been living in this horrible flat. I used to go out as much as possible to avoid being there, but didn't have much money, so tried to make everything last.'

'I think we've all lived in a place like that,' Bonnie said. 'I was once in a place where the landlord borrowed his friend's cat to try to deal with the mice.'

Sarah shivered at the ick. 'Mine wasn't *quite* that bad,' she said. 'It was just mouldy. But I was out that night, like most nights, and there was athletics on the big screen. Then there was this guy who'd come in with his mate. He was looking for the toilet and walked into a door frame, then turned to see if anyone had noticed. I think it was only me, and we caught each other's eye.'

'That was James?'

'Right. A bit later, we were at the bar at the same time and things kinda went from there.'

'That *is* old-fashioned.' Bonnie laughed kindly, though Sarah didn't feel in the mood after watching the video.

'He worked in the city,' she added. 'It's funny, I'm still not a hundred per cent sure what he does but it's something to do with predicting insurance trends.'

Sarah glanced to Bonnie, who was pulling a face as if to say it didn't sound like a real job. That got a genuine smile from Sarah.

'I know,' she said. 'But it's good money and the hours aren't terrible. He works from home three or four days a week. I'm a freelance bookkeeper and at home five days. Back in the flat, in London, it meant we were on top of each other all the time.' A pause as she caught Bonnie's mischievous eye again. 'Not like that.'

They stopped a moment, watching the children and the dog. Oliver was smitten by the spaniel, who was resting his head on the boy's lap and enjoying the chin scritches. Sarah knew it wouldn't be long before her son was asking for a dog. Back in the flat, they'd have said there wasn't enough room – but that wasn't true now. There would be plenty of room in the back garden, then there were acres of woods and fields. There was no better place for a boy and his dog.

'He grew up here...?' Bonnie asked, obviously knowing the answer.

'You know when you first meet someone you like, and you

stay up and have that talk about everything? James told me he came from a village, then left for uni and hadn't really gone back. A long time later, after we'd been together a while, I convinced him to bring me here one weekend, just so I could see the place.'

'And you liked it...?'

Sarah laughed a little. She could still feel the warmth of that day, picture the endless blue of the sky, breathe the purity of the air. She'd fallen in love.

'I've always lived in a city,' Sarah said. 'I couldn't believe how quiet it was here. Then, with Oliver, I thought it would be a better life for him, better school, all that.'

'It was the same with Georgia. It draws you in, doesn't it?'

Sarah didn't say anything, though she didn't need to. She felt the connection that they had both moved to this village, thinking it was best for their child.

'James didn't want to come back,' Sarah said. 'We talked about other villages or towns, but he wasn't into those either. Plus I pretty much had my heart set on here. But then it was Covid and we were stuck in the flat all the time, with a toddler. Then Oliver was nearly run over.'

'What?! By a car?'

'It was on our street – a delivery van going too fast. He was supposed to be holding my hand but he pulled away, just for a second. He knows to look both ways but... I don't know. He just stepped out. I saw it happening and it was like slow motion. A combination of Oliver not looking properly and the driver going too fast. He swerved at the last second, just missed Oliver and hit a bollard.'

'Oh my God! That sounds terrible.'

Sarah was watching the children and felt Bonnie doing the same. Hard for her to hear such a thing and not see Georgia in front of the van. Impossible for Sarah not to talk of it and relive the entire incident. She'd felt so helpless as Oliver froze in the van's path. She still wasn't sure how the vehicle had missed. It was as if it had teleported around her son, ending up embedded in the bollard.

'It was my fault,' Sarah said. 'But I told James that night we had to move – and, for the first time, he didn't argue. I started looking for houses here the next morning.'

Bonnie was quiet for a moment, probably still putting Georgia in the same position Oliver had been. People talked about a parent's worst nightmare – but there were so many of them.

'Was James happy to come back here by then…?'

Sarah needed a moment. She'd gone from seeing that ancient video of her husband's twisted features, back to picturing that van millimetres from her son. Now she was thinking of the video once more. It had almost certainly been filmed somewhere close to Carnington, if not in the village itself.

'Not really,' Sarah said. 'He agreed to return for me and Oliver.'

She sighed, not meaning to, understanding for the first time properly why James didn't want to live in the place he'd grown up. Even without whatever had happened to Lucy, he had his ghosts. Everyone probably did – but something had happened here many years before that felt bigger than anything Sarah could have imagined. Perhaps it was even larger than James believed because, had he known any of this would happen, surely he'd have flat-out refused to move.

As Sarah thought on that, she wondered if she'd been even more insistent than she thought. Had she given an ultimatum that they move? She didn't think so but it was impossible to know how another person interpreted things. She'd made it so clear, over such a long period, that her heart was set on this village. James's reluctance had seemed like something for her to work on; something for her to reassure and persuade him on.

Not something that would genuinely have stopped them coming.

'I'm going to have to talk to him about the video,' Sarah said, more talking to herself, although it wasn't a surprise that Bonnie thought it was directed to her.

'Are you OK?'

'I guess so. But we've not even lived here a week – and so much has happened. I don't think I can have another week like this.'

Bonnie tapped Sarah on the shoulder. It was the briefest of touches, though it still felt comforting.

Before either of them could say something, a bell jangled from the front of the shop and Bonnie said, 'Customer.' She quickly rounded the rocking chair and disappeared through the curtain, leaving Sarah with the children.

'Georgia's got *so much* Lego,' Oliver said.

'It used to be my dad's,' she said proudly. 'Mum says Santa will get me a new set every Christmas, as long as I'm not naughty.'

Sarah raised an eyebrow to her son. He'd reached the age where he'd started to question Father Christmas – but he knew enough not to say so in front of a true believer.

'What else do you like?' Sarah asked, talking to Georgia.

'Dressing up. They take my picture.'

Sarah assumed she was talking about Bonnie. If the other woman's camera roll was anything like Sarah's, there'd be ten thousand photos of her child, none of which were ever looked at. Not that Sarah could delete any of Oliver. She figured there'd come a day, probably when he'd moved out, that she went through them all.

Georgia had been stacking Lego bricks into another wall for the castle but she stopped and looked up to Sarah. Her voice was clear and inquisitive. 'Who's the woman that wakes up Oliver?'

TWENTY-EIGHT

Sarah looked from Georgia to her son. He had an embarrassed look, as if a big secret had been revealed.

'What woman?' Sarah asked, talking to them both.

Oliver nudged Georgia with his elbow. 'I said not to say.'

'He said she talks to him,' Georgia added.

'Who talks to you?' Sarah asked.

'No one.'

Sarah stared for a moment, making a mental note to google imaginary friends when she got home. Was there an age that children started making them? An age where they left them behind? She didn't know if it was healthy, or something that should be discouraged. Either way, there definitely wasn't a woman in Oliver's room at night.

Oliver was still stroking Gary the spaniel and Sarah decided not to push things. He was embarrassed at Georgia raising it, so Sarah figured there was little point in making it worse.

Besides, the curtain was tinkling again, as Bonnie pulled it to the side. Beyond her, a woman was standing near the counter in a police uniform. For a moment a chill ran through Sarah. Was this about James?

'I'm going to have to close early,' Bonnie said.

Sarah made a point of looking towards the police officer and Bonnie added quickly, 'It's nothing big. We should do this again.'

Not about James, then... Phew.

There was little choice for Sarah other than to pick herself up. She told Oliver to make sure he had his things, then they said goodbye to Georgia and the dog. At the door, Bonnie again told Sarah to come by another time – and then Sarah was back outside. She hadn't noticed it on the walk to school, and perhaps it was new, but in the distance, opposite the garage, a police car was parked by the house where Martin had been found outside. White and blue tape fluttered in the breeze, ringing the gates at the front.

Not that Oliver noticed. 'Can we come back tomorrow?' he asked, probably thinking about the giant box of Lego.

'Maybe,' Sarah told him.

James was out of his work shirt, fully in his lounging gear as Sarah and Oliver arrived home. He'd made a jacket potato for Oliver's tea, saying he'd given it a head start in the microwave, and they left their son eating in the kitchen. Sarah and James sat a little outside the back door, facing the messy lawn and garbled web of branches and bushes.

They both knew they needed to talk.

'I think Oliver might have an imaginary friend,' Sarah said first. 'He was telling Bonnie's daughter about a woman who speaks to him at night.'

James seemed to think for a moment. 'Oh... Is it a problem?'

'Google says no and that it can even help develop social skills – but then he's *specifically* talking about a woman, not a child, so I'm not sure.'

'I can't imagine what parents did before Google. Did they just go to the doctor all the time?'

Sarah snorted a little at that. It was no wonder her mum had told her that swallowed chewing gum would stick in her stomach, that sitting too close to the TV would damage her eyes. Parents learned from each other – and all it took was for one to come up with some old nonsense, and they were all spouting it.

Not that the internet was nonsense-free, of course.

'We could call NHS Direct?' James suggested.

Sarah thought on that. It wasn't a bad idea, though did remind her she'd have to register them all at the local surgery. If nothing else, even when things went perfectly, moving really was a pain in the arse.

'Maybe give it a week?' she said. 'If it's keeping him awake at night, it might be a problem?'

'Did you google the night thing, too?'

'I'm worried about googling too much. If you keep adding symptoms, it eventually tells you it's cancer.'

It was James's turn to snigger. 'Sore ankle: cancer. Eyesight not as good as it once was: cancer.'

They sat quietly for a few seconds, listening to the sound of Oliver's knife and fork scraping the plate from the kitchen behind. In their old flat, he'd have been eating in the same room as his dad would have been working. The same room as the television and the sofa. Now, they at least had their own space to talk when things were serious.

And things definitely were.

'Did you watch the video?' Sarah asked.

The moment of lightness was gone – but it was some relief they could still share those.

'No,' James said quietly. 'But I know what's in it. I can't believe it's online. It must be nearly thirty years old.'

'What happened?'

Sarah wasn't sure she'd get an answer.

Her husband slumped forward in the seat, resting his head in his hands and almost speaking to the ground. 'I dunno. I was young and an idiot. A rush of blood.'

'But why? You must have hit him for a reason?'

James shuffled back, ran a hand through his hair, tugged at his clothes. 'I don't remember.'

It felt like a lie.

'Was that Lucy holding you back on the video?'

'Yes.'

There was still a gentle scraping from behind. Oliver would be finished before long and Sarah needed to ask her questions before then.

'Did you leave the house this morning?' she asked.

There was a pause. A *long* pause.

'I needed to get outside,' James said eventually. 'Clear my head from the jet lag. I spent ages in airports and on planes. I did a run around the block. Only about two miles or so. They must've tried to deliver the parcel then – but I don't know how I missed the card.'

Sarah didn't know whether to be relieved he'd admitted to his earlier lie, or dismayed that he'd fibbed in the first place.

He knew what she was going to ask next, getting the explanation in first. 'When you said he'd been attacked, I panicked. I figured no one would know I'd left the house, so I said I was home. I didn't know there was a parcel.'

Sarah listened, figuring it might be true. Except, when she'd questioned him that morning, he hadn't flinched. She was also a little unnerved by the 'he', instead of Martin's name.

With one lie revealed, Sarah pushed against what felt like another. 'You've still not said why you were hitting him years ago. You must remember.'

James shook his head a fraction. He'd barely stopped fidgeting since she first asked. 'It was a different time. I was a different person.'

'That's not an answer.'

'I just—'

They were interrupted by a loud *clank* from the kitchen. James was on his feet immediately, uttering a quick, 'I'll get it,' and rushing away.

Sarah turned and watched as James fussed around their son, mopping the blackcurrant squash that had been dropped on the floor, wiping their son's front, then making him another drink.

'Is everything OK?' Oliver asked. If nothing else, he was perceptive. There were times when Sarah and James had silent but full-flung arguments over silly things. It was all raised eyebrows and short sentences to get a point across. Oliver always seemed to know when they weren't getting on – and had likely picked up on something again.

'Of course,' James said. 'There's just a lot going on with the move. How was the bookshop?'

It was an expert changing of the subject, one their son was too young to notice. Sarah couldn't quite see his face around the door frame, but she heard the change in Oliver's tone.

'Georgia has so much Lego!' he said. 'Can I go again?'

'I'm sure Georgia's mum won't mind having you over.'

Sarah heard a knife scratching a plate and a slow, 'Um...' It was what always came before a question Oliver wasn't sure how to ask. 'Can I get a dog?' he asked.

Sarah had to stop herself from laughing. She'd known it was going to come at some point – though she'd not had time to tell her husband about Gary the spaniel.

'A dog?' James replied. 'Um... I dunno about that. We'll have to see. Don't you want a trampoline?'

'Can I have a trampoline *and* a dog?'

'I'll have to talk to your mum...'

That was inevitable. It also meant Oliver would give it an hour, if that, and then ask Sarah if she'd personally come to a decision over the dog. He definitely wasn't going to forget.

'Time to finish your tea,' James said.

A few moments later and he was back in the door frame, making no attempt to sit.

'A dropped drink,' James said, angling back towards the inside of the house.

Sarah wasn't ready to let things go. 'What happened with you and Martin in the video?' she asked – for the third time.

James eyed her for a moment, then turned away. 'Can we leave it? It was so long ago.'

'He's just been beaten into a coma – and then somebody posted that video. It all happened days after we moved back. Everyone's going to think it was you.'

James opened his mouth, closed it again, licked his lips. He knew all that. 'I don't really want to get into everything again. I told you what happened with Lucy. I bet you did stuff as a kid that you'd rather forget.'

'I never punched someone's dad.'

He started with an 'I—' but then interrupted himself. 'Can you let it go?' he asked.

Sarah didn't think she could – but there was only so many times she could say the same thing. 'Who filmed it?' she asked.

It was such an abrupt change that James answered, apparently without thinking. 'A friend of ours: Dean. He might still live around here, actually.' He waited a beat, then added, 'Can we drop it?'

No, Sarah thought. They definitely could *not* drop it – but at least she now knew who to ask about what had happened.

'OK,' she replied.

TWENTY-NINE

James and Sarah's first evening together in the new house had a degree of normality. Oliver went to bed at the usual time. His dad read him a story and returned downstairs not long after, saying their son had been asleep within minutes.

They moved a few things around the living room, then half-watched part of a wildlife show on iPlayer. Half-watched, because neither of them put down their phones. Sarah didn't know what her husband was looking at – but she was scanning the town's Facebook page, looking for an update on Martin that wasn't there. The last she knew, he'd been taken away in an ambulance, unconscious but alive.

Just.

Sarah tried to stop herself from watching her husband too much. She couldn't look at him without seeing the young man angled over a younger Martin, walloping those punches into him.

Then there was the admission that he *had* been out of the house that morning – except, since he'd told her, Sarah wondered if that, too, was a lie. Had he been sweating when she got in? Were there dirty clothes? Was there any way to check whether he'd *actually* been running?

The only thing Sarah knew for certain was that there had been blood on James's hand.

On screen, there were a pair of alligators having what looked like some seriously angry copulation, not that Sarah was paying them much attention.

I bet you did stuff as a kid that you'd rather forget, James had said – and he was right of course. Everyone had said or done something their adult self definitely wouldn't have done. Making idiotic mistakes and not doing it a second time was an important part of growing up. There was a time Sarah had told her parents she was going to be at a friend's house, and instead went to the pub, even though she was eighteen months too young. She would have got away with it, had her mum not tripped and broken her ankle. Her parents contacted the mum of the girl Sarah said she was with – only to find out she had no idea where Sarah was.

That stuck in Sarah's mind as something to regret – and yet Sarah found it hard to get past the deranged look on her husband's young face. Something must have happened that made him not just punch Martin – but to hit him so many times while he was on the ground.

Not only that, it had happened *in front of Martin's daughter*.

James must have had some idea this sort of thing would come up when they moved to Carnington. Sarah was torn between being amazed he hadn't warned her, while wondering if this was proof there was nothing serious in James's past. If he *genuinely* thought he'd done nothing wrong, there was no reason to say anything.

For now, as they sat at opposite ends of the sofa, both swiping and tapping, Sarah felt certain Carnington held more secrets – but she didn't think any of them would be revealed by her husband.

Time passed. The alligators had been replaced on screen by a baby raccoon. It looked cute but had some serious teeth.

There was a creak from the stairs. Sarah and James both stopped fiddling with their phones and looked to each other. Moments later, Oliver was creeping into the living room, still in his pyjamas.

'Can I sleep in your room?' he asked.

Sarah and James were on their feet but Sarah reached their son first. She crouched, so they were eye to sleepy eye. 'What's wrong?' she asked.

'The woman keeps talking to me.'

THIRTY

It was a good job they hadn't finished unpacking. Sarah had found the camping mattress the day before and left it in a pile in their room. The pile was loosely a stack of things she would take to the charity shop, if it was solely up to her. The mattress had only been used once, back in the days when they'd naïvely booked festival tickets. They thought it would be a fun break, forgetting the fact they were well into their thirties. They'd spent a weekend feeling like grandparents, standing in a muddy field, surrounded by children smoking weed. Add that to the fact that Sarah enjoyed such simplicities as a roof and a bed, and she didn't think they'd be getting much use from the mattress.

Except she was now.

Sarah was on her side, underneath a duvet, sleeping on the floor of Oliver's room. It wasn't ideal, but she'd suggested this, instead of having him sleep with them. The thinking was that they wanted him used to his own room. The reality was that Sarah needed a night of not being next to her husband. She needed to think.

Oliver had fallen back to sleep almost immediately after

Sarah had put him back to bed, then settled on the floor. Her body ached with tiredness and yet it wouldn't let her fall asleep. There was too much going on, too many swirling thoughts.

Too many doubts.

It wasn't a question of whether she believed everything her husband was telling her, it was figuring out the bits she thought were definitely lies.

She stared at the ceiling, her eyes adjusted to the dark as she followed the dimples of the plaster.

She blinked.

According to the clock by the door, seventeen minutes had gone – and Sarah realised she must have fallen asleep. She rolled over until she was facing Oliver, watching for a moment while he breathed in, long and low, held it, then breathed out.

Another blink.

Helllllooooooo...

Sarah jumped into a sitting position. She looked to the clock, where thirty-eight more minutes had passed. She must have fallen asleep again – but something had woken her. Sarah was facing her son but he was still on his side, slowly breathing in.

Silence.

Sarah listened, wondering if she'd been dreaming. If not that, was it the creaks and groans of an elderly house? At the flat, she'd been so used to the undercurrent of the road outside, people in the corridor, all that, that she could almost tune it out. This was all new. No traffic, no people, just the waning, swaying old cottage.

Sarah closed her eyes again but she was alert now, listening, listening...

And then it was there: A woman's voice, as clear as if next to her ear.

Helllllooooooo...

THIRTY-ONE

Sarah leapt from the covers. Oliver hadn't moved but the voice had been so sharp and precise. The lights were off, though Sarah turned in a circle, groping her hands into the empty air, searching for the woman.

It was silent again.

Sarah was standing, trying not to wake her son as she stumbled towards the door and fumbled around the wall.

Hellllloooooo...

Sarah yelped. It was impossible not to. It felt as if the woman's voice was all around her, repeating the same word in the same tone. She'd read a story a while back about a woman who discovered a person living in her attic. He'd been there for almost nine months before he was found. The woman had noticed food going missing and had blamed her children.

That was all Sarah could think about as she finally reached the switch. She blinked at the wrong time, and swam in greeny stars as light filled the room.

There was nobody there.

Sarah dropped to her knees to look under the bed, even though she knew there was only an empty space. She moved to the other corner, opening a box that was far too small for a person. There was nothing inside but toys.

She'd definitely heard a voice and yet...

Sarah moved towards her son and, as she stepped around the camp bed, the woman's voice croaked once more.

Hellllloooooo...

This time, Sarah remained quiet and still. She gradually rocked her foot back into the position it had been, feeling the floorboard dip spongily from her weight.

Hellllloooooo...

The voice was coming from directly underneath Sarah's foot. She was above the living room, but the voice was too clear to be downstairs.

Sarah moved from the spot and glanced to her son, who hadn't shifted, despite the light and noise. Sarah could feel her heart *whumping*. She thought about getting James, though worried that she'd return with him, only to find the noise had gone.

Instead, she moved to the edge of the room, lifted the carpet and hauled it towards the camping mattress. It was heavier than she thought and Sarah felt sure Oliver would wake. But as she dumped the folded carpet back in on itself, she looked across to see her son still dozing.

Another of their vague plans was to replace all the carpets in the house – and, from the blackened, semi-rotted state of the floorboards, it felt as if they might need to consider a bigger job.

But the damaged floorboards wasn't the only thing Sarah could see.

There was some sort of mucky white... *sphere* sitting in the spot where Sarah's foot had been, almost entirely embedded in the wood. She squatted next to it, peering closer at what now looked like a plant bulb. It was more of an opal shape than she first thought, around the size of a shallot.

When Sarah touched it, the familiar *Hellllloooooo* croaked

from the shape. For the first time, Oliver started to stir. Sarah carefully picked up the object. It was a dirty cream, slightly spongy to the touch but more solid underneath. She folded the carpet back into place, wincing as it thumped into the floor, then quickly switched off the light and took the bulb to the bathroom.

Sarah sat on the toilet, the lid down, gently twisting the object, until accidentally making the voice speak once more. It felt quieter away from the floorboards. Less ominous in the light.

Hellllloooooo.

Sarah couldn't work out what it was – but, not for the first time since they'd moved, Google did its thing.

The woman who'd been waking up their son wasn't a woman at all, nor was it an imaginary friend. The bulb was apparently a speech module that would usually sit inside a doll or teddy. Sarah pressed it again, as if to confirm, and the same voice echoed out.

Sarah allowed herself a laugh, even a sigh of relief. In a week of mysteries and curiosities, finally – *finally* – she'd solved one.

THIRTY-TWO

FRIDAY

Bonnie was waiting a little away from the school gates, ready to intercept Sarah as she dropped off Oliver the next morning. It was good to see a friendly face, even as the other parents – the coven – wittered in their circle. Sarah ignored them, focusing on the one person who was actually being nice to her.

'How's it been?' Bonnie asked, though it was unclear if she was asking about James and the video, or the fact that Sarah had immediately launched into a yawn. The yawn became a laughing acknowledgement that she was exhausted.

Oliver was talking with Georgia, as Sarah handed Bonnie the speech module she'd found under the bedroom carpet.

'This was keeping Oliver awake,' she said. 'I found it last night.'

Bonnie touched it, setting off the *Hellllloooooooo*, and leaving her with a curious look on her face.

'What is it?' she asked.

'It's from a toy. It somehow got stuck under the carpet and then was setting itself off somehow. Oliver thought a woman was talking to him.'

Bonnie returned the bulb and Sarah put it in her bag. She

liked having it around for some reason, perhaps because working out what had been disturbing Oliver was her single success since moving.

'It's creepy,' Bonnie said, which was hard to argue with.

'Was everything all right with the police yesterday?' Sarah asked.

'It was nothing really,' Bonnie replied quickly. 'There were a couple of break-ins a week or so back, so they wanted to talk me through a few security measures.'

'Oh... it doesn't seem like the place for that sort of thing.'

Sarah was used to hearing about petty crime in the city – but it felt out of place in the village, especially for a bookshop. How much could there be to steal?

'I think it was more preventative,' Bonnie replied. She flicked her eyes upwards, indicating they were being watched, without having to say so. Sarah nodded fractionally, though didn't turn around. Let the coven talk.

'Have you heard anything about Martin?' Sarah asked, which was – admittedly – a dangerous question considering at least some of the parents standing behind her thought James was responsible.

'Last I heard, he was in intensive care,' Bonnie replied. 'It sounded serious. Something about bleeding on the brain.'

That was more than anyone had posted on the Facebook group – and it definitely *sounded* serious.

There was a noise of footsteps and then the gates opened. Oliver said his goodbyes as Bonnie led Georgia towards her teacher. The other children filed in and, as parents started to drift away, Bonnie returned to where Sarah was standing.

'Come by the shop after school again, if you want. Georgia's on a half-day but she'll probably have a nap this afternoon and then be full of energy for a while. She couldn't stop talking about Oliver after you went. I think she has a bit of a crush.'

Sarah smiled at that. There was a couple of years between the children but it wasn't a big enough gap to be an issue.

'Oliver had fun too – but he also enjoyed meeting Gary.'

It was Bonnie's turn for a giggle. 'Everyone loves Gary.'

'He wants a dog now. He asked his dad last night, then he was talking about it this morning. He's definitely not going to let it drop.'

'Sorry about that.'

It felt as if Bonnie might ask if Sarah wanted to do something in the moment. They hovered on the corner for a short while, before Bonnie said she had to get to the shop. Sarah said goodbye and watched her go. With James working at home in the office, she had her own plans for the morning.

Sarah waited until Bonnie was out of sight – then followed in the same direction. When she reached the centre of the village, she continued past the bookshop, into the butcher's shop. She'd known what she was going to do from the moment James had mentioned Dean's name the night before.

James's old friend was behind the counter, in the same apron as the day before. He looked up at the sound of the door and smiled curiously. 'How have you been?' he asked. The last time they'd seen one another was when they'd done two laps of the park. He'd been the first to tell her Lucy and James were friends.

'It's been a long week,' Sarah said. She'd not planned to say it – but even she heard the exhaustion in her voice. She wasn't usually so honest with strangers.

'Is Abe— James back?'

A nod. 'He got in yesterday.' A pause. Sarah couldn't think of a better way to ask, so simply came out with it. 'He said you shot the video that's going around...?'

Dean stared for a moment, eyes narrowing, before he glanced towards the curtain that led to the back room. There was no baby crying this time. When he looked back, he nodded an acknowledgement.

'I got a little Sharp Viewcam for Christmas one year. I was a United fan and they used to advertise it on the shirts. It was second-hand and I think Dad got it from the pawnshop. I used to take it to school in my bag, then film us playing football. Everyone wanted to see replays of their goals, and it was like we were on *Match of the Day*.'

He grinned and Sarah understood why. It was hard to explain to young people that there was a time in which, once things happened, they were gone. People had memories but they would fade and perspectives would shift. Actually being able to watch back something like a playground goal was a novelty.

'But you happened to film James...?' Sarah asked.

A nod. 'Right place at the right time.' He bit his lip. 'Maybe wrong place, I suppose.'

'Where was it?'

Dean pointed past the window, towards the school and whatever was beyond. 'Martin and Lucy used to live in the house that overlooked the canal. You follow the train tracks and there's an intersection. If you keep going, you end up at the quarry. It was on the towpath there.'

It more or less matched everything James had said about the train track and what he called The Den. It sounded like people needed to pass near Martin's house while heading there.

'It's all history,' Dean added. 'They used to get stone from the quarry, then transport it to the canal on the tracks. That was the main industry here until the eighties.'

Sarah considered that for a moment. There was a black and white photo of a train on the wall and it felt like this might be one of Dean's passions. She didn't want a long conversation about such things.

'Why did you keep the videos for so long?' she asked.

Dean had been about to say something else but stopped. 'I found the tapes a few years ago. There's hours of us playing football on the playground and the fields. I digitised quite a few of them and sent them to mates. The one with James...' He tailed off a moment, probably choosing his words. 'I probably shouldn't have done that one. I'd forgotten about it until a year or so back. It was on a tape with a load of football. I ended up showing it to my wife. I didn't know she was going to share it with a WhatsApp group. Someone from there must've put it on Facebook.'

He sounded disappointed, perhaps. It was hard to know.

'Everyone's worried about Martin,' he added. 'Sorry I didn't tell you about the video the other day. I didn't think you'd want to know. If it wasn't for what happened, I don't think it would have ever come out.'

That felt likely to Sarah as well. She didn't blame Dean for trying to spare her feelings. If Martin wasn't attacked in the present day, that video would have likely stayed on a hard drive.

'What does James think about all this?' Dean asked. Sarah had been lost in her thoughts and didn't want to say that she'd not passed on any messages to her husband about a potential catch-up.

'He says it was all in the past,' Sarah replied. 'Different times.'

Dean nodded along. 'That's true. I'm kinda glad I only really filmed football stuff. I got up to all sorts of nonsense as a kid.'

There was a shadow as somebody walked past the front window. For a moment, Sarah thought they were going to come inside and spoil the privacy – but they kept moving past the door and along the high street.

Sarah had been thinking of a good way to ask but, with the absence of a better idea, just went for it.

'Why did James attack Martin?' she asked.

Dean screwed his lips into one another. 'I don't know. Martin never liked James and Lucy being friends – everyone knew that. He reckoned James was getting her into trouble. I guess it was linked to that.'

'*Was* he getting her into trouble?'

Sarah wasn't sure why it mattered. They were talking about something from decades before. Teenagers grew into adults who could be very different.

The answer came as Dean looked to the side. 'I mean... yeah. But it's not like he was forcing her to do anything. I skipped school with them sometimes.'

It felt like the end of a conversation. Sarah wasn't sure she'd learned anything, especially as Dean also didn't know why there'd been a fight. She considered buying something, more to thank him for his time than because they needed anything. Then she realised there was something more to ask.

'Are there any other videos of James?' Sarah asked. 'Not football ones.'

The answer came in the same way the previous one had. Dean looked to the side, avoiding her gaze.

'I was worried you'd ask,' he said.

THIRTY-THREE

Sarah was standing on the towpath that lined the canal. She had followed the train tracks away from the town, as Dean had said, until reaching the crossroads. The house where the Shearer family had lived was a decent five-minute walk from the track. It was run-down now, with boards on the windows, tiles missing from the roof, and a mesh fence around the outside. Sarah walked around the perimeter, unsure what she was looking for, then retraced the route back to where James had beaten up Martin many years before.

She rewatched the Facebook video, while sitting a short distance from where the attack had happened. The train tracks would have been just out of shot, while the bushes in the background were vastly overgrown compared to how they had been decades before.

It was still unmistakably the right place.

The video was playing a second loop as Sarah's phone dinged with a WhatsApp alert. The 07 number wasn't in her contacts but three messages came through, one after the other.

Dean had promised he'd find the other movie files when he was on his break – and here they were.

Sarah almost didn't want to watch. Dean had said he couldn't remember what was in the videos, though he was likely sparing her feelings. She was sitting on a log, surrounded by silence, as she pressed to watch the first.

There was a moment of motion sickness as Dean went full *Blair Witch* again, then the video was focused on a circle of people sitting in what looked like a cramped living room. There were a couple of beanbags but it mainly seemed as if they were mostly sitting on the floor, knee to knee. It was such a throw-back to see ashtrays on the carpet, with a spiralling haze of smoke hanging in the air. That was the thing whenever a TV show or movie tried to imitate the past. There might be allusions to smoking – but the sheer scale of the bluey-grey fug was rarely recreated. Every social situation from the time was experienced through a murky cloud and series of gentle coughs. Sarah only knew the very back end of it.

The first few seconds of the video were hard to make out, partly because of the smoke, partly because Dean couldn't keep his hand still, partly because everyone was talking over everyone else. There must have been ten or eleven teenagers crammed into the space. There was a girl sitting on a boy's lap, another with her head resting on someone's shoulder. Lucy was sitting next to James – but it was only as the frame settled that Sarah realised James had his arm around a different girl. She had short, dark hair and Sarah had no idea who she was.

The camera juddered once more and then a boy's voice off-screen asked, 'Truth or dare?' A couple were kissing at the side of the image, oblivious to what was happening around them, as the camera focused on James. He drank from a bottle of lager – and looked impossibly young. Undoubtedly Sarah's husband but with a thinner face and none of the lines around his eyes that made him the person she knew. His head wasn't quite shaved – but the cut was so much shorter than anything he'd had since she met him.

'Truth,' he said, between swigs.

'Who do you love the most? Lucy or Gemma?'

There was slurred amusement in the voice asking the question. The person speaking knew they were instigating trouble.

James still had his arm around the girl, who must be Gemma, but there was a gentle shift in the angle as he edged towards Lucy on his other side.

Gemma noticed it, pulling away from James and dragging his attention. He hadn't answered immediately. 'Are you seriously thinking about it?' she stormed.

James no longer had an arm around her and was apparently too tipsy to couch his thoughts. 'What do you want me to say?'

'I want you to say me,' Gemma replied. 'We are going out, aren't we?'

'Yeah.'

'So say me.'

'Fine.' He shrugged. 'You.'

Lucy was on James's other side and it felt as if she was carefully trying to keep a neutral expression. Sarah didn't blame her. From the context of the video, it seemed as if Gemma was James's girlfriend, and Lucy was his friend. Being asked to choose between them had no correct answers.

Well... there *was* a right answer – and James, being a teenager, had bodged it.

Gemma pushed herself away from him and stood as a couple of people off camera began laughing. The poor girl was humiliated and furious. 'You don't really mean me. You wanted to say Lucy.'

Sarah willed her husband's former self to redeem himself. It wasn't that hard. Say sorry, and tell the poor girl he definitely meant her.

Except James didn't do that. He shrugged again, swigged his beer and turned away from Gemma. 'Fine. I wanted to say Lucy.'

There was another laugh from off-camera, although even without seeing the person, Sarah could sense the unease.

Gemma stamped a foot, almost cartoon style. 'I don't get it. If you fancy her, why aren't you *with* her?'

'I told you, we're just friends.'

James glanced sideways to Lucy, who was squirming from the attention, though not moving.

'A friend you just said you love more than me?'

Sarah felt poor Gemma's frustration. The tone said so much more than the words. She was going out with a boy, and had known the entire time that he was more into his friend than her. Finally, surrounded by alcohol and her mates, it was coming out.

'It's complicated,' James said flatly. 'We're just friends. The day we're not friends will be because one of us is dead.'

He'd spoken so matter-of-factly, so without emotion, that the atmosphere was sucked from the room, from the video. Sarah felt the uncomfortable second of silence until a nervous laugh sounded off-screen. Someone said, 'It was only supposed to be a joke,' and then the video ended.

Sarah felt breathless after watching. She didn't think she was much of a rubbernecker. She tried not to get involved in the various dramas that went on in WhatsApp groups, Facebook groups, or the estate where she used to live. Life was too short and all that.

Except there was definitely a voyeuristic thrill to watching something that felt as if it should never have been taken. The video had been recorded when everyone was tipsy and inhibitions were loose. The question to James was clearly unfair, though his answer hadn't been great.

None of that stopped Sarah from rewinding and watching the end part again.

'... we're just friends. The day we're not friends will be because one of us is dead.'

It could have been spoken as some joyous expression of a person's love for another – but it felt so much colder than that. It was wildly over the top. Teenagers *could* struggle to explain their feelings and emotions, they *could* get caught up in the drama and importance of things. And yet... James spoke so clearly. So clinically.

Sarah watched a third time, trying to work out why it bothered her so much. And then she got it.

Because, not long after, one of them *was* dead.

THIRTY-FOUR

Sarah watched the other videos Dean had sent, though James was barely featured in either. One was a somewhat dreary shot of some vehicles racing around a car park, before it swung around to show a group of boys displaying varying degrees of interest in the race. James was smoking, looking thoroughly bored, offering no opinion.

In the next, a group of teenagers were on some grass, tossing a small beanbag around a circle, catching it one-handed, counting until someone dropped the bag at forty-three. There was a groan and then the footage ended.

The things people did to entertain themselves before phones was baffling.

Sarah started the slow walk back towards the village, somehow filled with more questions than before. James – her James – had said he and Lucy were friends and nothing more. The video seemed to back that up, especially as each of them appeared to have separate boyfriends and girlfriends – Lucy was with Eric from the garage, James with Gemma.

And yet… there was clearly a tight bond between them. Was it *really* likely for boys and girls to be such good friends at that age? It was obviously possible and yet Sarah hadn't known any relationships like that when she was a teenager in the 1990s. It felt like a time when boys were friends with boys, and girls were friends with girls. The only time everyone mixed was when people were coupling off.

But maybe that was her and her friend group?

Sarah was passing the school when the next thought struck her. Carnington was a place that so few people seemed to leave. There was Miss Callaghan, the teacher, following in her mum's footsteps. Then Eric at the garage and Dean at the butcher's shop. James's apparent girlfriend was Gemma. And the first shop Sarah passed on the high street was Gem's Gems.

It might have felt like a long shot in any other place, especially as Sarah was used to living in a city, but she knew the identity of the owner before heading into the shop. Sarah waited outside the door, wondering if she should do this. Wondering if Gemma wanted a weird conversation about some boyfriend who'd been a dick to her almost thirty years before.

There was only going to be one outcome, even if Sarah knew she was being selfish.

A bell jingled over the door as Sarah pushed her way inside. The gust set off a chain reaction as a series of dreamcatchers and charms, that were pinned to seemingly every surface, started to twist, flutter, and jangle.

There was incense in the air, something rich and spicy that tickled the back of Sarah's throat. It was quite the experience for the senses, almost overwhelming. Sarah was still getting her bearings as she noticed the woman behind the counter watching her.

'You're Sarah, aren't you?' the woman said.

It was a shock to be recognised by a stranger, though Sarah would know the other woman – even if her name wasn't on the sign outside. It hadn't been that long before that she had watched a video of a much younger Gemma stamp her foot in annoyance.

But Sarah didn't let on.

'That's me,' she said.

'I was wondering if you might come by,' Gemma replied. 'I heard from Dean that you'd been asking around. Then Eric. He said you found Martin.'

The only thing Sarah could manage was a somewhat perplexed: 'Oh...'

She'd been torn on whether to intrude on someone's day – but it turned out her visit was anticipated. It felt as if every interaction she'd had since arriving in Carnington had her underestimating quite how interconnected the locals were.

'I didn't find him,' Sarah added, talking about Martin. 'It was a woman who lives in the house. I called 999.'

It felt as if this particular piece of misinformation about her finding Martin had already done the rounds. Probably too late to cut it off now.

'What's he like now then?' Gemma asked.

'Martin? I don't know.'

'No! Abe. Well, they say he's James now. I always liked the name Abraham. I don't know why he'd change it.'

Sarah was stumbling, somewhat taken aback at quite how anticipated she seemingly was. Not only had Gemma suspected she'd drop in, she'd apparently already planned the conversation.

'He's, uh... good?' Sarah said, accidentally making it sound like he wasn't. 'He's a good dad. A good, um...'

She had lost the thread of whatever she was trying to say, ending up caught in a web of calling everything 'good' – not that Gemma was bothered.

'It was *ages* ago that we went out. Did Dean send you the video? I couldn't believe it when he sent it to me. We all look so young! That was Craig's front room. We used to go there on

Fridays 'cos his mum had a singing gig at the Conservative Club. She'd leave us a bottle of cider.'

It was a lot of information in one go, a testament to quite how much Gemma had been waiting for Sarah to come by. If she could get a word in, Sarah wasn't sure what she'd add – not that she could. Gemma was still going.

'Feels like yesterday sometimes – then, others, like it was a million years ago. I'm surprised Abe came back – what with Lucy and everything. All the things people used to say about him...'

She finally paused for breath – but not for long.

'Is that why you've been asking around?'

It felt much worse with the directness. Sarah *had* been asking around about her husband and his past but she hadn't realised the people involved had also been talking to one another.

With the spiel over, Gemma was waiting for a reply. Sarah was trying not to be distracted by the twirling, still jingling, collection of trinkets that were attached to what felt like every surface. She was having a fever dream.

'I was, um... dropping off my son at school on Tuesday,' Sarah managed. 'It was his first day and someone said she was surprised James was back after what he did. A few hours later, Martin knocked on my door, saying James had killed his daughter. It was all—'

'—A bit much. Yeah. I mean, Martin's always believed that. He never liked Abe and Lucy. After she disappeared, it only got worse. I thought that was probably why he left.'

Sarah was still a little taken aback at the other woman finishing her sentence – though Gemma wasn't wrong. It had all been a bit much. It was hard to know if she wanted real answers, or whether she was desperate for someone to tell her what she needed to hear. James was a good man, who'd never hurt anyone without reason.

She asked anyway. 'What do you believe happened with Lucy?'

Gemma had apparently anticipated the question, replying immediately, 'I dunno. I mean... you married him?'

It sounded harsh – and perhaps Gemma realised it, because she waited a beat, then added, 'You wouldn't have done that if you thought he was capable of killing someone.'

Sarah waited, nodding almost to herself. She *did* believe that. She'd had his child! He couldn't be a bad person.

'They loved each other,' Gemma added, a little more quietly. 'Not like you and him probably do. More like a... brother and sister, I guess.'

Sarah thought on that a moment. Both she and James were only children – and another of their vague plans involved giving Oliver a younger brother or sister to grow up with. It could have happened earlier, were it not for the idea of moving house. She sometimes wondered if they were going to end up with too big an age gap.

'I was so jealous,' Gemma said. 'I know you talked to Eric – and he was the same with Lucy. We'd talk about it all the time and joke *we* should be together because Abe and Lucy were devoted to one another, even though they always said they were just friends.' She held up a hand, showing a plain wedding band. 'I guess it worked out in the end. I've got two boys of my own. Everything happens for a reason and all that.'

The twirling, tinkling collection of tat had finally settled, allowing Sarah a moment to think almost clearly. It had been a very one-sided conversation.

'Did he ever talk to you about what happened with her?' Gemma asked, presumably talking about James and Lucy.

'Only recently,' Sarah replied, not wanting to say outright that James had never mentioned Lucy's name until he absolutely had to.

It got a gentle nod from Gemma. 'It's not like she disappeared, then he immediately left town. He was still here. There were people saying he killed her, sometimes to his face.'

She left it there a moment – but it was the first time Sarah had properly thought about things from her husband's point of view. She knew he didn't want to move back and had never given any real reasons until now. But it must have been awful to not only have a good friend disappear – but then be directly accused of having something to do with it. No wonder he left and didn't return.

'We'd been broken up for a few months by the time Lucy disappeared,' Gemma continued. 'I figured he'd leave in the end – but he stayed for a couple of years. We had a job in the same place for a while.'

'After you finished school?'

'Right. There was a candle-making factory on the edge of town. We were maybe seventeen, eighteen – so probably a year or so after Lucy went missing. We were on the same production line and I think it was only about three quid an hour back then. Really boring – but there weren't many part-time jobs in town.'

Sarah had known James worked in a candle factory – but hadn't realised it was in Carnington. She thought it had been while he was at uni. Sarah had temped in a lamp factory when she was sixteen or seventeen. It was her first job after school and she'd hated every moment of stacking boxes into other boxes for eight mind-numbing hours in a row.

Gemma was off again. 'There was this guy,' she said. 'Clive. One of those single old blokes who hate everything – but he *really* didn't like Abe. Made fun of him all the time. Called him a girlfriend killer.'

Sarah must have pulled a shocked face because Gemma nodded in agreement.

'I know. People kept saying he was out of order – but Clive was one of those blokes who'd worked there for years. Longer than any of the managers. Like a fly stuck in a house. He hated working there and everyone who worked there hated him.'

Sarah knew the sort. One of their old neighbours had worked at the local council for twenty-five years – and did nothing but complain. She hated the office but seemingly not enough to ever leave. A toxic relationship.

Gemma had said something about finding an article on her phone, though gave up almost as soon as she'd started.

'Clive left after a night shift and he was found in the canal the next day,' she said. 'He had head injuries but the police said he fell. He'd been sneaking whiskey on his breaks for years, so it wasn't *that* much of a surprise.' A pause. 'But people always talked.'

'Talked about what?'

'About Abe. Said he killed Lucy, then he killed Clive. Some were relieved when he said he was leaving town.'

Sarah couldn't get past the idea that every time she spoke to a new person, she found out something else about her husband she'd rather not know. It was obvious that whispers could go around a place of work – and a long-standing colleague drowning while drunk after a night shift was certainly gossip-worthy. And yet the fact he'd apparently bullied James was another dimension.

'I never thought Abe did anything,' Gemma said, a little more quietly now.

Sarah wasn't sure how to reply. How could she defend a person she didn't know? She had met James years after all this. They'd had late-night talks about their lives and hopes – but the topic of him potentially being a killer had never come up.

But he couldn't be. He just couldn't.

'I'm surprised he came back,' Gemma added. 'I guess all this was bound to happen. People have long memories around here.' She stopped a second, then added, 'Not that you aren't welcome. It's a great little town. You should see it in peak summer, when the tourists come. There's a proper buzz. We always—'

She cut herself off because the phone on the counter buzzed. Gemma picked it up and unlocked the screen. Within moments, her mouth dropped and she looked up to stare wide-eyed at Sarah.

'Martin Shearer's dead.'

THIRTY-FIVE

The sun was out as Sarah walked along the high street. The police car had gone from the house opposite the garage, but there was still a flicker of tape from the side.

Martin Shearer: Dead.

Lucy Shearer: Missing, presumed dead.

Christopher: Pamela's son, dead.

That Clive bloke: Dead.

That was four people from James's orbit who weren't around any longer. Two of them were men with whom Sarah's husband had definitely clashed. The third was a witness who saw blood on James after Lucy disappeared. With the fourth, Lucy, he'd said the day they were no longer friends would be the day one of them was dead. Was he saying it as a nod to being friends forever, or was there an undercurrent of threat? That if Lucy rejected him, he'd do something awful?

Sarah couldn't believe how quickly her life had shifted. They'd gone from a cosy family looking forward to a move to... this.

She had never seen violence in her husband but it was impossible not to see the trouble around him.

Sarah trailed down the slope out of town and let herself into the house. She headed upstairs and tapped on her husband's office door, then stepped inside. He'd been facing the monitor but turned to take her in with a thin smile that almost immediately turned to concern.

'What's happened?' he asked.

'Martin Shearer's dead.'

James stared at her for a few seconds and then nodded shortly. 'OK,' he said – as if they were having a conversation about what to eat that evening. He turned back to his computer but hadn't touched the keyboard when Sarah felt her anger spill.

'Is that it?' she said. It sounded harsh and she meant it to.

'Is *what* it?' he replied, not turning around.

'There's a video of you beating him up. Then, yesterday, someone smashed him over the head at the exact time you were out of the house. You lied about where you were – and that's all after he told me you killed his daughter.'

Sarah wanted a reaction. She'd have been happy for her husband to shout back, outraged that she'd dared to question him. At least that would be something. Instead, he didn't turn from the screen. 'I told you about Lucy,' he said quietly. Calmly.

'No you didn't – not properly – and what you did say was only this week. How has it never come up in all the years I've known you?'

'It just didn't.'

He leaned in a fraction and tapped something on the keyboard, before switching windows.

'We were always doing other things,' he added – which sounded like quite the cop-out. They had been together for more than twelve years and there was definitely time for him to have mentioned he was once good friends with a person who disappeared. Oh, and perhaps that some thought he might have been responsible.

Sarah was so angry that she couldn't get the words out. She started a couple of sentences that didn't quite come to anything before James spoke again.

'It wasn't *me* who wanted to move here,' he said. 'I didn't even want to visit that time. It was all you. We're here because you wouldn't let it go. Because you used our son to emotionally blackmail me.'

The prick.

Sarah took a breath, more annoyed that he was right than anything else. She had *definitely* used their son against him – but it felt far worse when it was pointed out. The fact James was doing it while not looking away from his computer was doubly annoying. It was hard to argue with a person when they were correct.

'How could I have known about any of this?' Sarah replied. 'You never told me. You weren't even here when we moved in: you flew to New York and let me arrive with my dad and our son. I had no idea any of this was hanging over you. If you'd told me, mentioned it at all, then I wouldn't have kept pushing to move here.'

Maybe they both had a point.

James's fingers were resting on the keyboard, not moving. 'I didn't know,' he said. 'It was so long ago. I thought people might have moved on.'

He sounded exhausted, not only because of jet lag or tiredness. As if he was sick of it all. Sarah probably didn't blame him. If he was *truly* innocent in everything, if he'd really lost one of his best friends and didn't know how, why, or where, it would weigh on someone.

The problem was, Sarah wasn't certain that he was *truly* innocent.

'Why did you beat up Martin Shearer in that video?' Sarah asked. The fourth time now.

'I told you last night – it's in the past.' He was clipped, annoyed.

'You're not answering properly. People aren't going to let it go. Someone put it on Facebook and half the village has seen it. He's dead now and there are going to be questions.'

James's fingers were still unmoving on the keyboard but Sarah felt as if she wasn't telling her husband anything he didn't already know. James mumbled something about 'supposed to be working', though neither of them moved.

Sarah needed an answer and couldn't walk away.

Wouldn't.

Eventually James slunk lower in the chair and sighed. He stared at the screen, because it was easier than looking at her.

'Lucy's dad hated us being friends,' he said. '*Really* hated it. He said I was leading her astray and that she was going to end up killing her mum if she didn't improve her attitude. He'd say she was a disappointment to them both. That he wished they'd had a boy. He'd be on at her every day – and the more he did it, the more she wanted to skip school and tell him to shove it.'

Sarah had wondered if she could tell whether her husband was lying. She still didn't know – but this felt like the truth. The mix of fury and sadness was too hard to fake.

'We weren't even together but he'd call her a slag,' James added. 'He never believed we weren't a couple. He'd say he was going to send her to boarding school, or even that they'd register her for home schooling, then lock her in the house.'

James spun slowly in his chair until he was facing Sarah. *Almost* facing her. He still couldn't look her in the face. 'That day of the video, we were walking along the tracks, probably going to The Den. I don't remember – but her dad was there and grabbed her wrist. Lucy screamed that he was hurting her – and I lost it. Completely lost it – probably for the only time ever. I don't remember it properly, only in flashes. I saw the video at the time and then yesterday. I thought Dean was going to delete it back then – but I guess not. It was like watching someone else.'

Sarah could still picture the seething fury on her younger husband's face as he was dragged away from Martin, kicking at thin air. She still wasn't sure she completely understood.

James was done explaining. He twisted back to the monitor and made a point of double-clicking an email that had just come in. When he next spoke, it was while he typed a reply. 'Martin's dead. So what? What do you want me to say? I'm not sorry. It's just a shame it took so long.'

That was final enough.

Sarah considered asking about the newest video Dean had sent, the one with James saying the day he and Lucy were no longer friends would be the day one of them was dead. Except, after his explanation, the fact she'd seen the video felt like more of an intrusion than before. No wonder he wanted to forget.

She hovered for a moment, wondering what to do next when there was the sound of gravel from outside. Sarah would have never noticed individual vehicles at their old place – and the quiet was going to take some getting used to. She crossed to the window, wondering if there was another delivery van – but gasped when she saw what was actually outside.

James twisted away from his monitor. 'What is it?' he asked.

Sarah watched as a car door opened and a man in uniform climbed out.

'It's the police,' she said.

THIRTY-SIX

James was gone.

The police officer had been nice enough. He'd shown his ID card and said James wasn't under arrest. He'd asked politely whether James would accompany him to the police station – and that was it.

It might not have been an arrest but James could hardly say no. He'd asked for a minute, changed from his jogging bottoms into a pair of jeans, set an out-of-office on his work computer, and then got into the police car.

As he was driven away, Sarah wondered whether Raina next door had been watching. If she was, she'd have tipped off Pamela, and then everyone would know.

The facts were clear enough. Martin Shearer had died and then, roughly an hour later, James had been arrested.

It wasn't good.

Sarah sat on the bottom step, wondering what to do. Should she take Oliver out of school? Should she try to get ahead of things and tell someone like Gemma that James was *voluntarily* assisting the police? She'd read a book about public relations a few years before but couldn't remember whether it was better to try to head off a story, or hope it didn't come out.

Is that what her life had come to? The police took away her husband, while she wondered what people would think?

Sarah headed upstairs, into her husband's office. She wasn't sure what she was looking for – but tried the drawers anyway. The top one was full of a kind of rubbish that littered every top drawer. There were paperclips and pens, rubber bands and Tipp-Ex – even though, as far as she knew, all James's work was online. The other drawers were full of envelopes, and various email printouts, all of which seemed unwaveringly dull.

As she was wading through that, Sarah's father called. It was a check-in, a *how-are-you-getting-on?*-type thing. Sarah was so desperate to tell him everything. She'd made an enormous mistake, she didn't know who her husband was.

But she couldn't. The admission of defeat so quickly after what felt like a victory would be too much. She enthusiastically told him things were brilliant, and that Oliver was loving it. James was busy, but that wasn't new. She had some leads on work. She'd had a fantastic lunch in a cute café. Gosh, wasn't life brilliant?

The truth would come out at some point, it had to. But not yet. For now, the balloon couldn't pop.

Her dad said he was delighted for her, then he said that he'd been playing golf but that his hip was acting up. 'That time of year', and so on.

Sarah listened, offering the expected 'That sounds good' when the times came. After the golf story, he said he'd leave her to it – and that was that. Back to the unpacking.

It was as she was putting everything away that Sarah realised James's mobile phone was sitting on the desk next to the mouse. James had definitely taken one with him – but Sarah assumed he must have picked up his work one by accident. Every iPhone from the past few years looked identical anyway.

The lock screen was a photo of James, Oliver and her, when they posed with the Westfield Centre Santa the year before. Oliver knew it wasn't the real Father Christmas, and might have twigged that the idea of the real Santa employing stand-ins was a load of old nonsense.

He didn't turn down the presents, though.

Sarah took a second to relive the photo and then remembered what she was doing. It was an unexpected invitation – and, though she knew her husband deserved privacy, Sarah wasn't going to miss her moment. She typed 0794 into the phone and waited for it to unlock.

It didn't.

Sarah tried the number again, taking more care this time, except it was still wrong.

0794 was their old address – flat seven, building ninety-four. She used it as her phone code, as well as the PIN for the joint account card. When they'd set things up, they had both gone with the same numbers. As a couple, they'd never been the sort to check each other's phone, and Sarah hadn't even known that was a thing until she'd read an article about it. There was a natural trust between them and Sarah had never felt the need to go snooping.

Except James had changed his phone PIN at some point.

Sarah re-locked the phone and returned it to the spot next to the mouse. She sat in her husband's chair and used her own phone to search for 'Clive canal Carnington'. All the Cs.

Google threw up very little of interest, certainly nothing about any drowning. Sometimes it really did feel as if a line had been drawn in the early 2000s, where everything before simply didn't happen.

Sarah tried a few more combinations, but didn't get any better results. It was close to noon and there were a few hours until Oliver needed picking up from school. She felt a desperate need to do... *something*.

This perfect home, this place she'd dreamed of, was becoming a nightmare. Before she knew it, Sarah was out of the house, along the drive and on the road. She turned in a circle, looking for twitching curtains that weren't there. She'd not long been home but bounded back the way she'd come, heading up the hill towards town. At first Sarah didn't know where she was going – but then she realised she needed a friendly face. Someone who'd make her a tea and share a biscuit.

Sarah passed the garage, refusing to glance sideways towards the house where Martin had died. Where he had been *murdered*. She continued along the high street, past the café until she reached Bonnie's bookshop. She headed inside, to where Bonnie was sitting behind the counter, paperback in hand, tea on the side, dog at her feet.

One of them had their life in order – and it wasn't Sarah.

Bonnie put down the book as Gary trotted across to sniff Sarah's ankles. 'It's good to see you,' Bonnie said.

Sarah's reply was somewhat shorter. 'Martin Shearer's dead.'

Bonnie's face slipped from happiness at seeing Sarah to confusion. 'Are you sure?' she asked.

A nod. 'Gemma from down the road told me.'

Bonnie looked towards the end of the street and then focused back on Sarah. Gary had decided Sarah wasn't carrying anything that could be construed as a treat, so headed back to the counter.

Bonnie had picked up her phone. She tapped the screen, sighed, then put it down. 'I'm always the last to find things out,' she said. 'When did it happen?'

'This morning, I guess. He was in a bad state yesterday.'

Bonnie was momentarily staring into nothingness and it felt as if she wanted to say something. As if she maybe already knew, though hadn't wanted to say.

Or perhaps it was just the dim light.

She almost immediately focused back on Sarah at the next news drop. 'James has gone with the police,' Sarah said.

'What?! He's been arrested?'

'They specifically said he *wasn't* under arrest,' Sarah replied. 'They asked if he would go to the station to answer some questions. He's there now.'

Bonnie's mouth was open. 'Wow. This is a *lot* of news for one lunchtime.' She put down her book properly and gulped a mouthful of tea.

'I can't believe he's dead,' she said. 'I mean... Martin *is* the town. He owns half of it. I wonder what's going to happen with his flats and the rest. I don't know if he has a next of kin.'

It felt as if they might spin off to a subject with which Sarah didn't want to bother. She didn't know the man and had little interest in the machinations of inheritances and the like.

'Can I ask you something else?' Sarah asked.

Bonnie had been staring into nothingness but blinked back until she was focused on Sarah. 'Of course.'

'Did you ever hear of someone named Clive, who used to work in the candle factory? He died in the late nineties after falling in the canal.'

Bonnie shook her head, as Sarah instantly realised her mistake. 'I didn't grow up here,' Bonnie replied. She'd said as much the other day. 'It does ring a bell, though. I think someone might have told me about a man who drowned in the canal. It might have even been one of the coven.'

She caught Sarah's eye and grinned. This moniker for the other mums was their little secret.

Bonnie didn't ask why Sarah wanted to know, which made Sarah like her a little more. Of everything that had happened since they had moved to Carnington, at least meeting Bonnie was a positive.

'Do you know anyone who might remember?' Sarah asked,

before adding a somewhat cheeky, 'Someone who isn't friends with everyone else...?'

She didn't spell out that she felt burnt by Eric, Dean and Gemma apparently sharing details of their chats. Talking to another of their potential group didn't feel like a good idea.

Bonnie got it anyway. 'I might be wrong on this,' she said, 'but I think the reason we were talking about the man who died in the canal was because his brother was the old head of the secondary school. I can't remember his name.'

Sarah did. Miss Callaghan had mentioned it a few days before. She'd even said where he lived.

'Sorry I can't be more help,' Bonnie added.

Sarah could have told her that she'd been more help than she thought – but it didn't feel quite right to say that she'd spoken to so many people in recent days that the fabric of the town itself had opened to her.

'Are you staying for a brew?' Bonnie asked, holding up her mug. 'I've still got most of those digestives – although Gary keeps eyeing them.'

She ruffled the dog's fur and a part of Sarah was desperate for a tea, a biscuit, and a chat about literally anything other than her life.

Except another part was so desperate for answers.

'I've got a bit of work at the house,' Sarah said. 'But we'll definitely do another time.'

She said goodbye and was at the door when Bonnie spoke Sarah's name. There was something serious in her voice now. 'Be careful,' she added.

Sarah paused. 'How do you mean?'

'It's just... the video. I watched it again after you left. All those punches and the kick. The way he hit Martin on the ground. It was so brutal. My dad used to beat up my mum and I've been thinking about it a lot since I watched it.'

Sarah gazed across the shelf of books towards her new

friend. Aside from her dad, her literal immediate family, Bonnie was the first person who seemed to be looking out for her since the move.

'James has never hit me,' Sarah said.

It got a small shrug. 'I don't know him. I'm not saying otherwise. But just... be careful.'

THIRTY-SEVEN

Sarah was back outside in the sun. The warmth stung her skin – or maybe it was her friend's warning.

Be careful.

Nobody had ever said such a thing to Sarah before and, perhaps for the first time, she wondered whether she did have to be cautious around the house. She had such trust in her husband, in the father of her son, that she'd had no hesitation in asking question after question. She'd trailed around the village, asking others their opinion, trying to figure out what had happened. At some point, with the way the locals talked and talked, that was going to get back to James.

Should she be worried?

Surely not – and yet Lucy Shearer, Martin Shearer, Pamela's son Christopher, this Clive Horlock guy... all dead. All connected to James.

Surely he wouldn't have agreed to move back unless he was certain he'd done nothing wrong? Sarah continued a little further along the high street, almost as far as Gem's Gems but stopped outside the old post office. It was the grandest building on the street, probably the village itself. The first time Sarah had visited the town, back on the day her life changed, when she'd fallen for the place, it was this building that had drawn her. There was a pretty steeple, a clock in the centre – then black-rimmed windows dotted around the sides, with a blue plaque above the door. As Sarah looked at it now, years later, she couldn't quite remember what had felt so charming. Like meeting an old boyfriend and wondering what had been attractive.

The building was no longer a post office. There was a note for tourists, saying it was private flats – presumably because too many people had knocked on the door, hoping to mail a letter. There was a second sign about no free newspaper or flyers, plus three doorbells.

One was labelled 'Horlock', so Sarah pressed that, then stepped away and waited. It wasn't long until the door opened to reveal a short man with not a lot of hair. He was probably in his seventies but trim, with pocked skin on his tanned arms. The sort of maniac still running marathons well into his nineties.

'I'm trying to work out what you're selling,' the man said. He didn't sound too harsh.

'I'm not selling anything,' Sarah replied.

'You're not one of my old students, so...?'

Miss Callaghan had said that he'd given her a reference and, with the way everybody knew everyone else, it felt as if he might be used to knocks on the door.

'I'm Sarah Parkinson,' she said. 'My husband is James Parkinson but I think you might know him as—'

'Abraham James Parkinson,' the man said. A person who never forgot a name or face. 'Why are you here?' he added.

Also a person never shy with a question.

'We moved here on Monday,' Sarah stammered. 'I took my son to school on the first day of term and a woman at the gates said James had done something bad. Then Martin Shearer came to the cottage, looking for James. He said James had killed his daughter. And now Martin's dead. This has all happened since Tuesday!'

Sarah was aware she sounded somewhat manic, though it reflected how she felt.

'Martin Shearer's dead?'

It was news to the man, who momentarily put both hands on his head, before removing them.

'He's really dead?'

'The police asked if James could answer some questions. He's at the station now and I suppose I have a few questions of my own.' She waited a second, then added, 'You *are* Mr Horlock, aren't you?'

The man seemed delighted to be known, puffing out his chest. 'As I live and breathe!' he declared, before apparently remembering someone was dead. 'I don't know what you think I can answer for you,' he said. 'It was a long time ago that I knew your husband.'

'Someone told me you had an amazing memory...'

Sarah had made it up on the spot, playing on the old man's pride – and he took the bait. 'I guess my reputation precedes me. Guilty as charged.' He held the door wider with a flourish. 'Did they tell you about my flapjacks?'

'Something like that,' Sarah replied, trying not to laugh because it sounded like a euphemism.

The inside of the post office was not what Sarah had expected. With its age, she'd thought it would be slightly run-down. Instead, there was a large open hall and indoor garden. Mr Horlock pointed out that the old counter had been turned into a fountain, even though the water was off. The high ceiling and bright skylight made the area seem as if it was almost outside.

There was a door on each of the three sides and the former head teacher walked towards the back of the fountain. He opened it with a key that was attached to a string worn around his neck. He led Sarah through to a study that was floor-to-ceiling books and wafted a hand towards them with an airy, 'If only I had time to read them all.'

An old computer sat in the corner, complete with a fat-back monitor and coating of dust. An upright vacuum stood next to it, almost like some sort of art installation.

'Do you want some tea?' he asked.

Sarah didn't, and almost said no, but she'd spotted a counter of photographs near the window – and fancied a minute or two to check them out. She said it would be great and then, as Mr Horlock disappeared into another part of the flat, Sarah started scanning his pictures.

Miss Callaghan had said he was the head for the bigger school – and he had a series of photographs that were a lot fuller than the ones in the primary school. It was still more of the same, with teachers along the sides and hundreds of students sitting and standing in the middle.

Some things felt the same wherever a person came from. There were the old-timer teachers with cord patches on tweed jackets, then the younger ones who looked barely older than the students. There was a PE teacher in a tracksuit, with a thick moustache – because there was seemingly a law that all PE teachers had 'taches.

Even the women.

Mr Horlock was there, dead centre, in a suit too big for him. He beamed brighter than anyone as his pride at the school and his position seeped from the photograph.

Sarah was looking for James, possibly even Lucy, but it was hard to tell in which year the photo had been taken. Miss Callaghan had said that Mr Horlock had been head for thirty years.

Sarah gave up when she heard footsteps – and then Mr Horlock was back with a tray. There were two mugs – plus a

Tupperware tub. After setting everything down, he unclicked the lid and offered it towards Sarah. 'My speciality,' he said.

There was a stack of crusty-looking flapjacks inside, and it felt impossible to refuse. Sarah took one and settled in one of the chairs. Mr Horlock was watching as she nibbled a bite of something that had clearly been overbaked. It was dry and crumbly but Sarah swallowed and smiled. 'It's so nice,' she lied.

The arse-licking was complete as Mr Horlock clapped his hands together. 'That's what everyone says,' he insisted – and, though it might be true, it only emphasised that there were a lot of liars in town. 'When I finished at the school, I had to find something to fill my time – so baking it was.' He resealed the tub and then took a chair. 'I suppose you want to hear about your husband,' he said, sounding a little too pleased about it all. People were dead, after all.

Sarah was resisting a second bite of the toasted wallpaper. 'It's been rare to hear people saying things about him,' Sarah replied – which was nearly true. Good things, at least. 'I gather he was best friends with Lucy...?'

'That takes me back.' Mr Horlock was in his element. He was rocking back and forth in his non-rocking chair. 'I did have some problems with Mr Parkinson and Ms Shearer but probably not as much as others might remember.'

'What do you mean by others?'

'Teachers, maybe students. Some always felt as if he was leading her astray.'

Sarah kept hearing the same thing, even from those who knew them well. 'You don't sound sure,' she replied.

Mr Horlock was watching expectantly, leaving Sarah no choice but to cough back another bite of the supposed treat. Even Gary would turn his snout up.

'I always tended to find that people were only led astray if they wanted to be,' Mr Horlock said. 'And who's to say it was him leading her? I found them both likeable. If I was to list the troublesome students from my career, I doubt Abraham would make the top fifty.' He let a little grin slip, which took twenty years from his age. There was a definite impish quality. 'But that's probably because we didn't always see a lot of him at school.'

People kept saying James was a school-skipper, so it had to be true, even though it felt so far from the man Sarah knew. If James said he was going somewhere, he not only went – but he was never late. People definitely changed but the descriptions felt *so* different to Sarah's James that she wasn't sure what to say.

She was so disorientated that she chose to nibble another corner of the flapjack – which was an immediate mistake. Like swallowing the contents of a vacuum cleaner. Sarah just about disguised the cough as a throat-clearing – and Mr Horlock didn't appear to notice.

'Mr Parkinson was certainly polite and courteous when he made it to school,' Mr Horlock added. 'If I remember correctly, his exams went well, considering.' For a second, Sarah thought he might reel off the precise results. She didn't doubt he knew. There was something of a raconteur to him.

'If it was only about the not-turning-up, nothing much would have happened,' Mr Horlock said. 'We'd notify the parents but there wasn't much we could do past that. Except, when he was off, Ms Shearer was often with him. Then her parents would be in to complain to me, even though we were the ones sending letters to tell them about the absences. When I said *I* couldn't do too much, they weren't happy. I'm sure they took it up the chain but don't know how far they got. The responsibility is on the parents to send their children to school, not the other way around. I tried to tell them that.'

It was more or less what James had said – except there was the added complication that his family was living in a flat owned by the Shearers at the time.

'The thing is,' Mr Horlock continued, 'school isn't for everyone. You might think it's strange for me to say – but there's no point in trying to pretend. Not everyone fits into a group environment. Some find it impossible to learn like that, with distractions of things on the classroom wall, or other children. Some don't like being talked at. It's nobody's fault – and everything's a lot better today – but some would, and will, always reject it.'

Sarah had found the former head teacher to be a bit quirky and eccentric until that moment. He spoke with such passion and understanding that she began to understand why he lasted so long in his role. She'd been at school not long after corporal punishment had been phased out. Even though teachers weren't allowed to hit children by that point, there were definitely a few who craved it. It sounded like Mr Horlock had never been one of those who missed the old days.

'Abraham was from a poorer family,' Mr Horlock said. He sounded softer now. 'I remember we helped his family with grants for school uniform and lunch money, that sort of thing.'

'I didn't know that...'

Sarah hadn't meant to speak. She'd known James didn't have a lot growing up but needing grants to pay for uniforms and food was a step further than she thought.

It got a small nod in reply. 'You hear things you can't necessarily act on, because you haven't seen it. But there is a stigma that comes with it. Children are so much more perceptive than people realise – and they notice these things.'

He wasn't wearing glasses, though he looked upwards at Sarah, as if he was. 'Do you understand what I mean?'

The word hadn't been spoken – but she got it. Things were the same at Sarah's school. The kids who got free school meals had to line up to collect their tokens. All that really did was single them out as kids to be bullied. It was like an adult had thought of a way to single out everyone poor, as if the vouchers couldn't have been handled in a better way.

'Some felt ashamed over something that was in no way their fault. I've wondered since if there was more I could do to prevent that – and the answer's obviously yes – but that's easy to say with hindsight.'

Sarah shivered, suddenly seeing her husband, seeing that teenager from the videos, in a new light.

Poor James.

Poor Abraham.

She could still picture those kids, standing in their line of shame, waiting for free meal vouchers, having to telegraph to the whole school that their parents had financial struggles. *Thank God, it's not me*, Sarah used to think when she saw them.

But it *had* been James all those years ago.

'Is that why he skipped school?' Sarah asked.

Something had changed in the room. The flapjack was abandoned on the arm of the chair and Mr Horlock no longer seemed bothered by whether she ate it.

'I suppose that's a question for him – but, seeing as you're asking me, I'd say there's a good chance.'

Sarah couldn't speak at first. This was the other side. When Dean had told Sarah her husband used to be one of the naughty kids, who skived off and got into trouble, she struggled to believe it. When it became clear it was true, Sarah hadn't known what to think. Except what one person thought was naughty could be another's shame. Easy to say he was skipping school, when the alternative was to get bullied for being poor.

No wonder James didn't want to talk about it.

Mr Horlock waited, perhaps to make sure Sarah knew what he was talking about.

'But then Lucy disappeared,' Sarah managed.

It got a nod. 'It was difficult for everyone. She was in year twelve or thirteen by then, so not necessarily supposed to be at school all day, every day. But we obviously felt a duty of care. Her parents were, understandably, furious. At us, at Abraham, at his parents, at the police. I'm not saying they weren't justified. Everything was so unbelievably sad.'

The oldest students at Sarah's school were sixteen. If they wanted to continue into further education, there were separate colleges. She knew that many schools in rural areas folded everything into the same building. That might explain why James had hung around for a while after Lucy disappeared. He had school to finish, as well as that part-time job in the candle factory.

It was that which reminded Sarah why she'd come knocking in the first place. She wasn't sure how to bring it up. 'Someone told me that James had a falling out with your brother...?'

The former teacher had been staring into nothing, lost in his thoughts and memories, though a cloud passed now. He blinked, rubbed his eyes, then peered towards Sarah.

'That's... um... I don't know why anyone would be speaking about that.'

'Some people like talking about my husband's past.'

Mr Horlock seemed to think on that a moment. He chewed his bottom lip, as Sarah wondered if she'd pushed too hard.

When he next spoke, he was careful with the words. 'Clive was... a bitter man. We never got on. I'd say it was because of him and the fact he didn't appear to like anything or anyone – but I accept everyone has their own story. He might have said something similar about me. We had incredibly different personalities. We lived in the same town but had no real contact.'

He stopped, thinking, then added, 'As for your husband, I was told a long time ago there were issues between them at the place where they worked. It sounded a lot like my brother's mean streak coming into play. I'm sure if you were told about that, you were told how my brother died. I think we're best leaving it there.'

Sarah wondered if he was about to usher her out, say they

were done. Mr Horlock definitely didn't want to talk about his brother and, from the things she'd been told, Sarah didn't blame him. Her impression of the man in front of her was the opposite to Gemma's description of Clive. Mr Horlock was kind and thoughtful; Clive sounded mean and vindictive.

She picked up the flapjack and nibbled the corner, wondering if it might buy her five more minutes. As it was, the former head teacher no longer seemed bothered by her opinion on his baking.

'Martin Shearer told me that James killed Lucy,' Sarah said.

Mr Horlock was nodding. 'He was saying the same back then – and I assume ever since. He was angry that Abraham was the last person to see her. That he left her at that place. I think everyone understood the anger but it was a big stretch to target all that on a young man. The only thing I can tell you is that Abraham was in school a lot following that. He concentrated on his studies and got the results he deserved.'

He waited a moment, until he'd caught Sarah's eye. 'I realise you're new to town but what you should understand is that there are people here who enjoy the drama. Every place is probably the same – but it is more concentrated here, because the village is small.'

Sarah thought that was probably true. There were people who craved gossip and histrionics everywhere. It was a lot easier to ignore in a city, where their noise was drowned out by normality.

There was quiet now and it was perhaps the end of the conversation. Sarah was seeing her husband in a slightly different way, perhaps understanding more why he'd not spoken about his youth. She doubted she'd have been keen on reliving some of what it sounded like he'd gone through.

'I suppose, after what's happened, Martin Shearer is even more of a tragic figure,' Mr Horlock said. 'First his daughter, then his wife to Covid, now this. I suppose they do say he did a lot for the community.'

It didn't sound as if he'd phrased it to specifically stir something up – but it was undoubtedly peculiar. Deliberate, too.

Sarah doubted the former head teacher said much without thinking it through.

'You don't sound sure,' she replied.

Mr Horlock was nodding again. 'It's not that he didn't do good,' he replied, carefully. 'But I suppose I often wondered how much good a person is doing if it's all about what they get in return. Whether it's planning permission for flats, council funding for a drama club, subsidies for a theatre when he's the director...'

The former teacher tailed off and the point had been made. Sarah might have worked it out herself – but it wasn't the sort of thing too many people around town would be saying.

'Martin gave a lot to Carnington,' the man concluded. 'But he also took a lot. I suppose it's up to individuals whether they see that as an acceptable compromise.'

THIRTY-EIGHT

Sarah was waiting a little away from the school gates, ignoring the non-subtle sideways glances from the coven. Bonnie would have already picked up Georgia after a half-day, leaving Sarah alone with her thoughts.

Perhaps she understood her husband a little better now – but there were still so many questions.

Oliver trotted out from school, happily saying that they'd spent the afternoon writing stories. His was about a woman who lived under his bed who told him facts about animals bigger than sharks. Sarah had shown him the bulb she found under his floor and, considering how it had affected him, he'd not been too bothered by it. He was happier with his imagination... but at least he was now sleeping through the night.

They walked through town and Sarah found it hard not to stare at the large poster, advertising the play in which Martin Shearer was supposed to be starring and directing. She found herself daydreaming about everyone else in town, how their lives seemed entwined with his. Everyone appeared to have a story about living in a flat he owned, or joining a society he ran.

She'd just moved to town and this would be her norm – but, for everyone else, life was going to change.

As they passed the garage, Sarah checked her phone, wondering if James had messaged from his work device. He hadn't, which meant he was likely still at the police station. Sarah had been wondering what to tell Oliver, because he'd be expecting his dad to be home. They continued down the slope, towards the cottage. When they reached the front door, Sarah took out her key, before realising the door was unlocked. There was a double-click mechanism that she'd not entirely figured out – though it was hard to remember if she'd failed to lock it properly, or if James was home.

Inside, and there was a clank from the kitchen. Sarah was fiddling to get her shoes off. She called a curious 'James?' through the house, wondering why he hadn't messaged to say he was home.

Except it wasn't James's voice that sounded from the kitchen. It wasn't a man's voice at all.

THIRTY-NINE

Sarah hurried along the corridor, getting in front of Oliver, wondering who'd walked into the house. She almost burst through the door, to where... a familiar face was sitting at the kitchen table.

In fact, there were *three* familiar faces.

Cara and Richard, their London friends, were giving it the full jazz hands. 'Ta-da!' Cara declared. 'Did we surprise you?'

That was an understatement to say the least.

Their son, Harry – who was Oliver's age – was tapping an iPad near the back door. Within a moment, the two boys were sharing the screen as Harry showed off some new game he was into. Oliver was utterly unfazed by the visitors.

Sarah wasn't quite sure what to say, or do. She'd been hoping James had returned from the police station – but now, there were *people* in the cottage.

'We messaged James at lunchtime,' Cara said excitedly. 'We thought he'd be working from home and could keep it a surprise for you. After everything you said, about how great the cottage was, we *needed* to see it for ourselves.'

Cara stood and leaned in for a hug, which Sarah felt obliged to go with. That was the problem with creating a web of lies – there was a point where a person ended up tangled in their own mess.

'We were surprised the door was unlocked,' Richard said. 'But I guess that's what it's like living out here. All a bit Enid Blyton, isn't it?'

Cara and Richard were one of those couple friendships in which gender lines were entrenched. Cara was Sarah's friend, Richard was James's. Sarah had never been able to work out whether she even liked Richard. He was the sort who could have a long conversation about interest rates.

Sarah said something about the door being old, and some sort of twisty double lock – but she was boring herself.

'Where is the old dog anyway?' Richard scoffed. 'We assumed he'd left the door open for us. We thought he'd be here.'

Sometimes Sarah forgot Richard was posh. She needed a moment to realise he was talking about her husband and not an actual dog. She could hardly say James was at the police station – especially not with Oliver in the room.

'James had to pop out,' she said. 'It's a bit of a trek to the supermarket from here.'

That got some nods of understanding. Sarah and Cara had talked more than once about the differences between city and village life over the past few months. Cara always liked to talk about the high walk score for where they lived, versus the much lower one of Carnington. Sarah almost laughed when she remembered that. It sounded so quaint, compared to everything else going on. Oh for the days when WhatsApped screengrabs of walk scores was her biggest worry.

'I'm sure he won't be long,' Richard replied, a statement based on nothing. He asked where the bathroom was, then disappeared upstairs.

With the boys occupying themselves in the corner, Sarah

sat across the table from her friend. It was hard not to sigh and let on quite how much of a nightmare the move had become.

Cara rolled her eyes anyway, nodding upstairs. 'I think men get to forty and their bladders go,' she said. 'Richard can't get through the night without needing to wee twice. Like a leaking bucket.'

The little laugh escaped Sarah before she knew it. A big part of her craved a nonsense conversation.

'James is the same,' she replied. 'If he's had a glass of wine, it's even worse.'

There were two bottles of wine on the table, one red, one white. Cara nodded to them. 'Richard picked these. House-warming – to go with the others.'

Sarah thanked her friend, then put the bottles in the fridge. She wondered if this meant they were planning on sharing the drink, then staying over. It wasn't what Sarah wanted – but she had been the one to invite them. That was the problem with open invitations that weren't really meant. Sometimes, the other party took things literally.

Cara made a point of looking around the kitchen. 'This is really great,' she said. 'We did have a bit of a poke around down-stairs when we were looking for James. We didn't realise the house was empty. We'd have waited outside otherwise. Harry loved the garden.'

They turned to watch the boys sharing the iPad. Sarah tried to be strict about screen limits and the like, but it had been a long week and she had bigger battles.

'We parked along the lane,' Cara said. 'Didn't want to spoil the surprise. I was telling Richard we should wait until one of you answered your phones – but he was insistent we try the bell, then the door. I'm sorry for not waiting.'

Sarah told her it was fine – and it probably was. Richard returned to the kitchen, still zipping his flies, before taking the boys into the garden. He didn't ask if it was OK and, even though it was, it would have been nice for him to check.

Another battle with which Sarah couldn't be bothered.

Oliver was still in his school uniform but it was Friday and it didn't matter too much if he got it dirty. Cara said Harry was on a half-day for teacher training, which is why they'd decided late on the surprise visit.

As Richard entertained the children outside, Cara told Sarah about the journey down and her surprise at how long it took to navigate the country lanes once they were off the motorway. She talked again about how much she liked the house – and Sarah gave her a quick tour. There were lots of oohs and aahs – and every room was met by an enthusiastic, 'Wow! There's so much space.'

They watched from the top window as Richard ran the boys around the garden. Sarah saw the weeds and the work; Cara saw the space and opportunity.

'I'd love to get out of the city,' she said wistfully. 'Richard's office wants him back in five days-a-week – so I think we'll have to wait a bit.'

Whenever they'd talked about the move in the past, Cara had sounded unsure if she wanted the same. Now she'd travelled and seen a small part of what was on offer, she sounded sold.

Sarah saw the similarity to herself. One visit and she was smitten. It was only now that reality was setting in for what moving to a remote village actually meant. Even if it wasn't for the chaos of the week, she thought she might have struggled.

They continued watching from the window, until Cara glanced to her phone. 'What time is James home?' she asked.

Sarah was wondering whether to tell her that she didn't know, that he was with the police and everything was a mystery. Depending on how long her friend was planning on staying, it was inevitable that Sarah would tell her at some point.

She was trying to think of how best to phrase things when the opening bars of Blur's 'Song 2' ripped through the upstairs floor. Both women turned, wondering what was going on, as Sarah realised it was James's ringtone. He'd gone overboard when the band had one of their various comebacks, re-buying all the old albums on vinyl, because that's what men in their forties did, apparently. The ringtone had come from that, even though his phone was usually on silent.

Sarah said she'd deal with it, then hurried along the landing, ducking into James's office and closing the door.

Sarah picked it up, expecting to see her husband's own name on the screen. She thought he might be ringing his personal phone from the work one, wondering where he'd left it.

It wasn't James's name on the screen.

Sarah was so shocked to see the four letters that she almost dropped the device.

LUCY.

FORTY

Time had frozen. Sarah stared, mouth suddenly dry until she remembered what to do. She pressed the green button and held the device to her ear.

'Hello...?'

It was a woman's voice with an American accent on the other end. 'Sorry,' she said. 'I thought I was calling James's phone.'

'You did,' Sarah said, with a stumble. 'This is his wife.'

She had spent the entire week hearing about the ghost of Lucy Shearer, how her husband had apparently killed her, and now a Lucy was calling.

There was a pause from the other end and Sarah heard a gentle inhale of breath. 'Is he there?'

'He's out at the moment. He left his phone at the house but I don't know when he'll be back.' Sarah waited a second. 'Can I help?'

An ice age came and went. There was hesitation from the other end of the call. 'Maybe,' Lucy said. 'We're pretty sure he left his laptop charger with us in the New York office, so I wanted to let him know. You can pass it on if you want.'

Sarah only realised she'd been holding her breath as she let out a long gasp. Lucy wasn't a particularly uncommon name – to the point that she had a client called that. She'd been so focused on Lucy Shearer all week that her head had gone.

'It was nice meeting you,' Lucy added. 'Well, not *meeting* you. You know. Bye.'

Sarah replied with a 'bye' of her own but the other woman had already gone. She took another breath, realising that the creak from outside the door likely meant that Cara was nearby. Sarah left the office, smiling at her friend and mumbling, 'James's phone,' as if that explained it all. They headed downstairs together, back to the kitchen, where they watched through the rear window as Richard continued to play with the boys. He'd found a tennis ball from somewhere and was trying to teach them French cricket with a rounders bat that also wasn't theirs. From what Sarah could see, it involved him thrashing the ball into the undergrowth, while both boys searched for it.

Not that either of them seemed to mind. Sarah wondered if they might be up for a bit of weeding while they were at it.

'A man in the village said James killed his daughter when he was young,' Sarah said.

There'd been no build-up and, until the words came out, she wasn't sure she'd actually say them. Cara coughed and patted her chest, spluttering with surprise.

'Sorry? What do you mean?'

'James says it was a girl he knew. They were friends when they were teenagers but then she disappeared. He was the last person to see her, so her dad blames him – even after all these years.'

Cara was silent for a moment, though Sarah felt the sideways stare. She was watching the boys as they dug out the ball and charged back to the bowling spot. Harry threw the ball and his dad smacked it to the far corner, when both boys set off after it, howling with glee.

'How long ago was this?' Cara asked.

'When he was sixteen or seventeen. Thirty years or so.'

'And her dad thinks James killed her, just because he saw her last?'

It was repeating what Sarah had said, though it sounded more incredulous in her friend's voice. 'It's not just only him,' Sarah said. 'Quite a lot of people in the village think the same. The police looked into everything at the time. James was never in trouble but I guess people have long memories.'

Cara ran a hand through her hair. The gloss of this perfect new life had well and truly been obliterated.

'When did you find out?' Cara asked.

'Tuesday – on the school run. Someone asked who my husband was and then it came out.'

'Didn't James say anything before you moved?'

Cara sounded as baffled as Sarah had been. 'I think he hoped it had all blown over,' Sarah said, which was being kind. She doubted her husband believed that, though didn't know what else to say. The talk with Mr Horlock, the idea of her husband being bullied for being poor, felt like something private. He'd never told Sarah and she didn't think she'd let on that she now knew.

Why had she forced him to come here?

The boys had found the ball again and, this time, instead of both of them standing at the bowling spot, Oliver headed towards the back fence, hoping for a catch. Harry lobbed the ball at his dad, who belted it towards an open patch of land. It was hard to see what any of the boys was getting from the experience – but, after the week she'd had, Sarah almost melted at the sound of her son laughing. He bounded around the edge of the garden, skipping with glee, before grabbing the ball and running back to the middle.

'There's something else,' Sarah said. 'The man who told me all that. The one with the missing daughter... he was attacked a day later. He died this morning. James isn't visiting the shops – the police are talking to him about it now. He's been with them all afternoon.'

Cara clutched her chest. 'This isn't funny.'

'It's not a joke.'

Despite the way their friendship was now split along gender lines, Cara and James had been friends before Sarah knew her. They'd been in a pub quiz team, a friend-of-a-friend thing from his work. When Sarah had first met her, there'd been a twinge of jealousy that, perhaps, he fancied her – or the other way around.

Sarah's old insecurities and worries felt so small now. It was hard to remember the little things she used to bother herself with.

'Did they arrest him?' Cara asked.

'No, they said it was for questioning. He went willingly.'

'I suppose that's one thing. Maybe it's all a misunderstanding...?'

Cara said it kindly, trying to make Sarah feel better – except when someone said it might be a misunderstanding, there never was.

'There's a video of James as a teenager beating up the same man,' Sarah said. 'I asked him about it and he said the man was being mean to his daughter. To James's friend. I don't know what to make of any of it.'

Cara didn't reply this time. They were past the point of meaningless platitudes, into the realm of complete mess.

Across the garden, it was Oliver's turn to bowl. He threw the ball towards Richard, who swung in a wild arc, missed, and was hit on the leg. For a moment, nobody knew what to do – then the boys charged the older man, running around him in a circle, as if he was a maypole. Richard was pretending not to be annoyed, saying it was someone else's turn anyway, but the grimace gave him away. He was perfectly happy belting the ball around the garden, not so much at being out.

'Sorry,' Sarah said. 'I know you wanted a quiet weekend in the country. It's been a strange few days.'

Cara stretched and touched Sarah's knee. 'Poor you. Gosh, this is a lot.'

Sarah snorted a little, and it was almost humourless. She liked Cara, she really did, but she was the only person Sarah had ever met who actually said 'Gosh'. If she and James were living in an Enid Blyton cottage, then they had an Enid Blyton friend.

'What does James make of it all?' Cara asked.

'It's hard to know. He was in New York, then he says he didn't do anything. It's all village gossip.'

'It probably is...?'

'I know – but in a town this small, everything sticks.'

Cara was quiet again, watching as Oliver bowled the ball to Harry. He swished the bat, missed, and was hit on the leg by the ball immediately. There was less celebrating this time as the boys swapped places. They were one leg strike away from Richard resuming competitive dad syndrome.

'The thing is,' Cara said quietly, reluctantly. 'James once told Richard that he'd killed someone.'

FORTY-ONE

Harry bowled and Oliver crouched, swinging from the hips, and leathering the ball past Richard towards the fence. Richard was so shocked that he almost spun himself off his feet in a reflex attempt to catch the ball. Oliver was so stunned he'd hit it that he froze, before throwing his arms up.

'Did you see?' he called across the garden.

Sarah was lost for words – but not because of the shot. She just about managed, 'I saw,' though it lacked the enthusiasm she wished she had.

'I thought Richard was joking,' Cara added a moment later. 'I didn't think he *actually* meant James killed someone.'

'What did he say?' Sarah asked.

'We were at some work thing. I think you must have been ill. James and Richard were talking about someone in Richard's office they didn't like. A dark joke. Why don't we throw him off the roof, that sort of thing.'

'That doesn't sound like a joke.'

'I know... but it was this stupid in the moment thing. Everyone had been drinking. Obviously it *sounds* bad – and I guess it was – but it was sort of funny at the time.'

In the garden, Richard had left the ball retrieval for his son. Harry had dug it out of an overgrown bush, then ran back to the middle. After watching Oliver smash the ball so far, Richard was now ready to take on bowling duties.

'What happened then?' Sarah asked.

'They were talking about Richard's colleague and the roof – then James said something like, "He wouldn't be the first person I've killed." Everyone took it as a joke and laughed along – but I suppose it always stuck with me.'

Sarah took a breath, tried not to sigh. She understood dark jokes among friends, especially if people had been drinking. Out-of-context, away from the moment, things sounded awful. She wouldn't have thought much of it, were it not for the fact her husband had been accused of killing someone.

Ahead, Richard bowled the ball at Oliver, who hunched once more, swung, and edged the ball in a direction he hadn't meant. Richard took a few steps and picked up the ball, then tried again – only to watch as Oliver smashed the ball through the older man's legs, off towards the house. Sarah's son had quickly reached the point of nonchalance, as if this was an untapped skill he always knew he had. He held the bat out horizontally and dropped it. She wondered where he'd learned to do a mic drop.

'I don't think James meant it,' Cara added, backtracking. 'I'm sure it's nothing. Why would you come back here if any of this was true?'

That was the point Sarah had been stuck on. If James *had* done something terrible, and got away with it, why risk everything to return? Her husband was many things – but not an idiot.

Did that mean he *was* innocent? Or was that old thing about people returning to the scene of a crime actually true?

There was a flutter of breeze from behind, a gentle *thunk*. Both women turned as footsteps clumped in the hall and then, a moment later, James appeared in the kitchen doorway. He stared at Cara momentarily, no doubt flustered by her presence. 'Oh,' he said.

Cara jazz-handed it once more, though with a good eighty per cent less enthusiasm compared to the first time. 'Surprise.'

'They did text,' Sarah said, somewhat pointedly. 'Your phone's upstairs.'

The boys were still playing in the back and hadn't noticed James's appearance. He glanced towards them, realising he'd not been seen, then stepped towards the hall. 'Can I have a word?' he asked.

Sarah followed him towards the stairs and the living room on the other side. With the warren of halls and corridors, it was unlikely Cara could hear – but they spoke in whispers anyway.

'What did the police want?' Sarah asked.

'They'd seen Dean's video on Facebook and I think someone had been onto them, saying I'd attacked him now. They were asking what happened then – and where I was yesterday morning.'

'What did you tell them?'

'The truth.'

He left it a moment, where Sarah wondered if *his* truth was *the* truth.

'I realised my watch tracked my run,' James added. 'I found the file. Everything's timed and mapped, so it wasn't just my word. There's proof of everything.'

Sarah looked to the chunky device on her husband's wrist. When he'd bought it for himself on a previous New York trip, he'd spent an evening boring on about its special features, none of which involved telling the time. Sarah had nodded along, giving it the whole *That's nice, dear.* She figured every woman had the same tone of voice for their husbands. I spent four-hundred quid on a giant *Star Wars* Lego set. *That's nice, dear.*

I'm going to spend thirty hours this weekend playing on the PlayStation. *That's nice, dear*.

And yet, Sarah was suddenly grateful James's customs fee-dodging had paid off.

'So… everything's fine?' Sarah asked. She'd spent an afternoon inwardly catastrophising that James was going to be arrested, tried, convicted – and that she'd end up raising Oliver alone, trying to pay this ridiculous mortgage, having to sell, living in a tiny flat somewhere.

But now…

'I think so,' James said. 'They asked about the Facebook video and I told them everything I told you. We went through where I live and work, then they drove me home.'

Sarah didn't know what to say. All that worry – for nothing. Maybe if she'd listened to her husband banging on about his watch in the first place, she'd have had the idea to check its history.

'Someone named Lucy rang,' Sarah said.

James was part-way through the start of a new sentence but stopped. 'What do you mean?'

'Your phone's upstairs. It was ringing, so I answered it. Someone from your work.'

It took him a blink, but then he said, 'Oh, right. Yes. Lucy from the New York office.' A pause. 'Why was she calling?'

'Something about a charging cable. I don't know why she didn't email.'

James didn't have an answer. He thought for a moment, then immediately moved on, nodding towards the kitchen. 'Did you tell Cara about where I was?'

Sarah felt almost embarrassed now. She'd had such visions of being a lone parent. 'I had to say something,' she replied.

James winced a fraction. 'I suppose. I didn't know they were coming.'

'I think I might have invited them. They're acting like I did.

I definitely said they should come for a weekend but maybe they took it *too* literally? Surely I didn't actually say *this* weekend?'

James seemed as blank as Sarah did – and, for a moment, everything was normal. They shared a thin smile that said everything. *How do we get rid of them?* It was nice to see friends – but it was nicer to see the back of them.

Before either could say something, there was a youthful yell from the back. Sarah and James locked eyes momentarily, each knowing it wasn't their son. They followed the passages back to the kitchen, where Richard and the boys were now inside. Cara was cooing at Harry, who was showing off a bleeding elbow. It was all fun and games until someone fell over.

Sarah couldn't remember where the unpacked first aid kit had gone, James thought it might be in the bathroom, Richard checked the kitchen cupboards, Sarah tried the living room, then Oliver said it was in his room – though nobody knew why.

For five glorious minutes, it was a normal life, filled with borderline comedic peril. Harry seemed unbothered by it all, in the way some kids became used to being gravity-challenged. Either way, by the time he was patched up, playtime was definitely over.

Sarah told Oliver to go upstairs and change out of his uniform, adding that he should leave it in the clothes hamper that she'd definitely unpacked into her bedroom.

The evening was a veneer of the life Sarah had envisioned when she'd pushed so hard to move. They ordered food from the only Chinese in town, then sat on the back porch, watching the boys play as they ate their food and drank their wine. They talked about old times, about the boys and school, about Richard and Cara leaving the city. James recounted his nightmare with the flight cancellations and they all agreed it sounded terrible.

Mediocre food, mediocre wine, nonsense chat. That was life.

At some point – probably when the wine was opened – it had been decided that Cara, Richard and Harry were staying over. They let the boys play an hour longer than usual, then put them both to bed in Oliver's room. It wasn't the first time they'd topped and tailed.

After that, Cara remembered they'd also brought cheese, that was at the back of the fridge. So they ate that, drank more wine, and even plonked on a bit of Ed Sheeran in the background. They were middle-class, dammit, and that's what middle-class people did.

Except... Sarah never quite switched off. She never quite stopped watching her husband, wondering whether those watch running files could be manipulated. Wondering if Pamela and the others might have a point. Wondering what actually *had* happened to Lucy so many years ago. Even by James's own admission, he was the last person to see her. She'd watched the video of him saying that thing about one of them being dead if they were no longer friends.

All this beautiful domestic bliss – and yet Sarah couldn't stop hearing the voice of a dead Martin Shearer, telling her that James killed his daughter.

They all went to bed a little after midnight. Cara took the bed in the spare room and Richard squeezed onto the camp bed in James's office. He was one of those 'I can sleep anywhere'-types: possibly the least-likeable trait for a human being. *Oh, you can snooze sitting up on a plane, while kids scream on all sides, can you? WELL GOOD FOR YOU. It was more acceptable to be a crack addict.*

'Good night,' she said, instead.

Sarah and James headed off to bed together but her doubts and insecurities were back. She'd drunk too much, probably had too much cheese as well. Her head swam as she struggled to get comfortable under the duvet. James was on his side, not quite snoring, but doing the heavy breathing thing that was almost as annoying.

Sarah stared through the gloom at the ceiling, fighting the draw of her phone on the nightstand, wanting to pick it up for a nice bit of doom-scrolling. That would definitely help her sleep.

She blinked, then opened her eyes – and James had disappeared. Sarah stretched an arm towards him, finding only a gaping space on the bed. The clock said a little over two hours had passed, so it must have been a long blink. Sarah pushed herself up onto her elbows, struggling with the disorientation from the time slip. She yawned, fanned it away, then yawned again, listening for the sound of footsteps from the bathroom. As she and Cara had said to one another: their respective husbands couldn't get through the night without a wee.

But there was no sound.

Sarah waited a few minutes, then pushed herself out of bed. She crept onto the landing, not wanting to wake anyone, then poked her head around the open door of the bathroom.

It was empty.

She thought for a moment, knowing there was a time barely days before that this wouldn't have bothered her. She'd have rolled over and gone back to sleep – except, now, she couldn't get past the idea that her marriage was riddled with secrets. What better time to deal with them than when everyone else was asleep?

Sarah trod carefully downstairs, passing into the empty kitchen, then retracing her steps to the also deserted living room. Nobody had closed the curtains at the front and she moved to the window, looking to where their car was still on the drive.

But if James wasn't in the house, and he hadn't driven anywhere... then where was he?

FORTY-TWO

SATURDAY

Sarah returned to the bottom of the stairs and listened to the drowning silence. She wasn't used to such quiet and was unsure if she liked it. That background city hum had been a part of her life for as long as she could remember. She'd thought she wanted rid – but now... there was nothing except the gentle *thump-thump* of Sarah's heart.

It was *so* quiet.

Sarah tiptoed along the hall, back to the empty kitchen. She opened the fridge, eyed the cheese, decided against it, and filled a glass from the water filter jug instead. Her phone was upstairs, though she hadn't noticed whether James's was still on the nightstand. If it was gone, she could probably call.

It was as she stood, shivering gently from the chill of the water, that Sarah noticed the shadow at the back of the garden. It was almost swallowed within the rest of the shade – but Sarah knew how her husband looked, even when it was only his outline.

Sarah opened the back door and crossed the lawn in her slippers. James was in the furthest corner, staring across the fence towards the quilted, moonlit fields beyond. He didn't turn as she reached him, instead, holding out a hand that she took. He was cold and she wondered how long he'd been outside.

'I shouldn't have come back,' he said quietly.

The wine had got to him, Sarah knew that, but perhaps this was the moment she wanted. Sarah released his hand and stood at his side, folding her arms, gazing across the vast expanse of gently swishing grass. This was the first time she realised there was such space past their land. It stretched almost to infinity, before dipping into a line of trees.

'Did you kill Martin Shearer?' Sarah asked.

She heard the hesitation in her voice, the worry that he might say yes.

'No,' James replied, solemnly.

'What about Lucy?'

'No.'

It was such a short word, yet riddled with sadness. Her husband let out a breath, and it spiralled ahead of them, kissed by the white of the cloudy moon.

'Are you angry I asked?'

'No.'

Sarah wondered if he meant it, tried to picture herself in the same situation, considering whether she'd be annoyed at the suspicion from the person she loved most.

She didn't know the answer. Maybe. Probably. Yes. No.

'I wonder if something's broken that can't be fixed,' Sarah said – and it was the wine talking for her as well. She wished it wasn't but perhaps they needed this. Husbands and wives couldn't be suspicious of one another and hope to be happy.

James didn't answer, instead stretching out his hand again. Sarah didn't take it, mumbling a 'Sorry' as he reluctantly withdrew it, tucking his hands under his armpits.

'Are you frightened of me?' he asked.

Sarah paused and the half-second of silence said so much more than the actual 'No'. She wished it didn't but it was too late. They stood together for a minute longer, not talking, knowing there wasn't much more to say. Their perfect home, perfect marriage, and here they were. Destroyed in less than a week.

'I'm going inside,' James said after a little while. 'Are you coming?'

'No,' Sarah replied. 'I think I need to be alone.'

She didn't turn as her husband twisted and headed back to the house. Sarah heard the gentle click of the door as she closed her eyes and listened to the whispering whistle of the grass. Maybe they shouldn't have had the wine – but maybe it was what they needed? Maybe this was always going to happen?

Sarah waited a few minutes, then returned to the house. She grabbed a hoody from the front door, put on her shoes, and let herself out. There was no particular plan for what was next – and she was in her pyjamas anyway – but she couldn't handle being in the cottage.

In their flat, in the city, she wouldn't have gone walking by herself so late at night. Here was different. Sarah rounded the car and started up the slope, into town. The air was crisp, the night unbearably empty. She passed Eric's garage, where the police tape was still fluttering on the house opposite.

There was nobody in sight, no traffic, no anything except uncomfortable, endless quiet. Sarah paused in front of the poster for Martin's play. It sat under a gloomy orange street light, advertising something that would never happen. The man was an enigma. Hero, villain, charming and menacing all in one – and that was only to describe her two short interactions with him.

On through the town and Sarah felt like shouting, making any sort of noise, just to interrupt the still. Life shouldn't be so silent. There was supposed to be a hum, there was supposed to be—

Something was glowing in Bonnie's bookshop. It was dim,

as if coming from the back room, rather than anywhere near the front. Sarah crossed the street, and approached the front door. There were no blinds or curtains, with space for displays along the shopfront.

Was the light on for security? Bonnie had said the police had been around with some sort of warning – but, aside from the street lamps, hers was the only light glimmering. It was almost three in the morning, so it felt unlikely anyone was inside. Certainly nobody with good intent. Sarah pressed her forehead to the glass, cupping her eyes to shield the glare. She couldn't see much of anything – and it was only as she stepped back that she realised the front door wasn't quite closed.

Sarah checked both ways along the road, hoping there was something obvious to explain what she was looking at – but the street was empty. She nudged the door, first with her knee, then her palm, edging onto the step where she paused and stared into the gloom.

'Hello...?'

There was no answer, so Sarah moved further into the shop, pushing the door shut behind her. She was used to the light now, scanning the shelves of books through the grey haze, looking for someone.

'Bonnie?'

Nobody replied, though a dim white still glimmered from the back room, where she'd first seen that video of a young James punching Martin Shearer on the ground. Sarah crept into the back space, sending the hanging threads of the cork and wood curtain *tick-tacking* into one another.

The light *wasn't* on in the back room – but there was a dim glow coming from a door in the corner, next to where the children had played with Lego. Bonnie had said something about a cellar – and Sarah could see the top step. The door was the same dark brown as the wall, though Sarah still wasn't sure how she'd missed it first time.

There was a creak as Sarah pulled the door open a fraction wider, standing on the stone, feeling the chill seeping up the stairs, and calling an echoing 'Hello...?' into the abyss below.

There was no reply.

Sarah had seen this horror movie. There was always a dark basement, always a woman who ignored the viewer screaming at them to turn around. She knew she *should* turn around – and yet... perhaps she understood why the people in those films did the wrong thing.

There was a mystery of her friend's open shop, with lights on at three in the morning.

'Hello...?'

No reply. Sarah moved down a step, as it switched from stone to wood. A long, low *creaaaaaaaak* rippled through the cellar. A light was on from somewhere below, though shadows stretched long and up the stairs. Sarah eased her way down, passing piles of books that lined each step, until she reached a wide, stone floor. There were boxes jutting out from the shadows, lining the walls and towering to the ceiling. Bonnie had said the basement was full of books – and she wasn't wrong.

There was a clothes rail off to one side and a thick dark-pink curtain folded underneath. The colour was so grim, it was no wonder it was on the floor, not the wall. The other corner had a desk, with a second computer that looked newer than the one upstairs, on which Sarah and Bonnie had watched James's video.

'Bonnie...?'

There was no reply and Sarah was beginning to wonder if her friend had forgotten to lock up. Nobody was inside the shop and, as far as she could tell, nothing had been stolen or disturbed. Sarah would leave, make sure the door was closed and then... she wasn't sure. It might be weirder to text her friend at three a.m. to say the shop was unlocked and she just happened to be in the area.

Perhaps it was better to leave things, and have Bonnie discover the unlocked shop in the morning?

Sarah was on the second step from bottom, about to head up, when there was a sharp *snap* from somewhere above. It sounded like a letterbox, or possibly something falling. Sarah called a soft, 'Hello...?' as she continued up, then out of the cellar, into the back room.

There was nobody there.

Except...

Sarah couldn't quite comprehend what was in front of her. She pushed the curtain to one side and stared towards the front of the shop, where – incredibly, unbelievably – a fire was burning on the welcome mat. If it wasn't for the warmth prickling her skin, Sarah might not have believed what she was looking at. She moved closer, rounding a shelf until she was in front of the door. Something purple – a flannel or a tea towel – was on the ground, flames dancing from the material and licking towards the door.

Had someone put it through the letterbox? Was that the snap she'd heard?

The flames were small, not far past Sarah's ankles, though dark smoke was already filtering towards the ceiling.

Sarah backed away, clipping her heel on a shelf and almost stumbling to the ground, before grabbing the counter to right herself.

Was there a back door? She hadn't seen one.

Sarah dashed into the back room, looking for a fire extinguisher. There must be one somewhere – except all she could see was the sink, with a row of drying mugs on the draining board. In the absence of a better idea, Sarah grabbed a cup, filled it with water from the tap, then rushed back into the main area.

It had been a few seconds – but the fire was already twice the size. Sarah launched the cupful of liquid towards the flames.

There was a soft sizzle, a blinking shade of orangey-black – but no impact of any real note on the fire. She could feel the smoke tickling the back of her throat, the heat nibbling her skin.

There was no chance she'd be able to douse the flames with mugs of water.

Sarah ducked around the counter, looking underneath for an extinguisher but finding only a pair of flip-flops and a dog bed.

Into the back room again. The door to the cellar was still open, though Sarah knew there was no exit that way. She'd not noticed that door – and wondered if she'd somehow missed another. Except... where? The sink was in one area, with the computer on a desk in another.

Surely there had to be a way out?

The heat from the fire was now so strong that Sarah could feel her skin itching, even from the other room. She couldn't see the smoke through the dark, but she could feel it scratching her throat. Sarah let out a little cough, unable to stop herself.

What could she do?

There was obviously 999 and the fire brigade – but there was no chance of them arriving before it was too late. If James was awake and answered, there was little hope of him getting to the shop and somehow stopping the fire in time.

Sarah stood in the doorway, watching the fire build in the main area of the shop. The flames had caught the lower part of a shelf – which meant it wouldn't be long before it touched the books and then exploded with the new source of fuel.

The next breath was a mistake as it caught in Sarah's airway, making her choke and wince. For a moment she couldn't breathe.

She was trapped – and there was no way out.

FORTY-THREE

Sarah crouched low to the ground, figuring that if smoke rose, then perhaps she'd be better off below it. The air tasted of sulphur and fury, her tongue tacky and numb.

She retreated as far as she could into the back room, towards the spot where the computer was on the desk. A ceiling-to-floor curtain hung across the wall behind – and Sarah heaved the desk away from the wall, pushing it towards the doorway to try to give her some sort of barrier.

Not that it would stop a fire.

She grabbed the large curtain, wondering if she could pull it down and douse it with water from the sink. If she threw that in the doorway, it could help stop the spread while she called 999.

The next cough burned Sarah's chest as she crumpled. Her eyes were stinging and watering at the same time. Rubbing only made it worse.

Think! Sarah whispered to herself. No, she hadn't whispered. It was a shout. Her throat burned, her eyes prickled, her skin was tingling.

Sarah grasped the curtain and pulled as hard as she could. It was heavy but something pinged at the top and then, before she knew it, the full weight of the drape had collapsed on her. Sarah was so disorientated from the smoke, the heat, the stress, that it took her a moment to realise she could throw off the material. It felt like trying to heave herself out from bed after a night of tossing and turning.

She blinked away more tears, though avoided rubbing her eyes this time. There was light coming from both sides, and—

There was light coming from *both sides*.

Sarah was feeling woozy and it took a few seconds to realise what was in front of her. The large curtain was blocking a window. She stretched, touched the frosted, dimpled, glass; felt the cool, soft chill, told herself it was real.

It was hard to see much of anything but Sarah ran a hand around the frame, looking for any sort of catch.

Nothing.

She pushed the glass with her hand, realised it was a bad idea, then tried her shoulder, wondering if that was worse.

Not that it had any give. It was the sort of pointless window that only existed in old buildings – glass as thick as her thumb, nothing to see on the other side, even if the glass wasn't frosted. No wonder Bonnie had covered it with the curtain.

Except Sarah was going to have to break the window somehow.

She turned back to the room, where smoke was trickling through the divide, swirling the ceiling. Wasn't there something about being killed by the smoke first, not the fire?

Sarah scanned for something she might be able to throw. The computer itself was far too heavy, but Sarah couldn't see much else, except the mugs on the draining board.

There was only one thing for it.

The Mr Tickle mug bounced off the glass, shattering with a splintering *thwack* on the ground. Mr Bump didn't fare much better, though he did at least live up to his name.

There were no other options. Sarah rushed to the cellar,

dipped her head through the door, took the largest gulp of clean air she could manage – and then sprinted back to the main part of the store.

The fire was everywhere now. It had caught one of the window displays – which Sarah realised – too late, she could have used to try to escape.

No time.

She darted around the counter and started hunting through Bonnie's things. There was a glasses case, lots of rubber bands, a box of tissues, a second glasses case, a phone cable, two more Mr Men mugs.

Sarah could feel her lungs scratching, craving oxygen, though there was no way she could risk a breath here.

She wrenched open a drawer, grabbed a handful of letters, then felt her chest tighten. The room was starting to spin.

Think, think, think!

There was some sort of box in the shape of a butterfly next to the till. The murk made it hard to work out quite what it was, though it was heavy in Sarah's hand. She could feel her body starting to strain, to give in, so it would have to do. Her eyes were closed as she danced around the counter and then ran for the back of the shop. She burst through the curtain, almost tripping over her feet, before finally, *finally*, letting out a gulp – and then breathing in gloriously fresh air.

Fresh-*ish*.

She was coughing, eyes streaming, sweat drenched her back.

Sarah moved around the computer desk towards the window. The butterfly thing was made of metal and she wondered if it might be a jewellery box. Sarah took a second, composed herself, breathed – and then hurled the box at the window.

It travelled in slow motion and she pictured it hitting the

glass, then bouncing off, no damage done, leaving her trapped and awaiting her fate.

And it did that... but not entirely. There was a splintering, rupturing crack as lines appeared in the window.

Sarah picked up the box once more, though it felt heavier second time around – or perhaps that was only her thoughts. Everything was sluggish, even her ideas.

The second time the box hit the glass in a spot slightly above the first impact. There was a quieter *tink*. It didn't sound like much, though more lines had appeared in the window.

Sarah took a moment, tried to remember where she was, what she was doing. She was seeing the world in slow motion, gently wheezing, chest heavy, eyes heavy, thoughts heavier.

The butterfly box was so clumsy in Sarah's hand that she could barely hold it. A part of her wanted to fold to the floor, to lie down and finally get the sleep she so craved. The other part of her forced her arm back and hurled the box a third time.

And then, there was a rush of air, a taste of the outside.

Jagged, deathly spikes of glass surrounded the frame but Sarah didn't have time to worry. She clutched the sleeve of her hoody around her hand and loosened some of the larger pieces, shunting them outside where they splintered on the ground.

But then, incredibly, Sarah was outside, not quite sure how she'd got there. She must have climbed out but time had jumped. There was blood on her wrist, more on the fingers of her other hand. Glass littered the floor and Sarah was in some sort of alley, next to a large bin.

Her head swam, her eyes felt so tired, but Sarah managed to find her phone – and this time she did call 999.

FORTY-FOUR

Sarah was sitting on the kerb at the front of Gem's Gems, her legs stretched in the road, eyes closed, listening to the chaos from a few doors down. She wasn't sure how long the fire brigade had taken to arrive – though it had been quicker than she thought. Or perhaps it wasn't. A fug was surrounding Sarah's thoughts, leaving her unsure exactly what had happened. It was late, but maybe it was early? She was home but this wasn't home.

A large hose stretched across the road, snaking through the door of the bookshop. Men and women were dotted around, wearing heavy coats and hard hats. Sarah should probably tell one of them what had happened but she was *so* tired.

She jumped as something tapped her shoulder. Sarah stood and twisted at the same time, only to see a woman in a police uniform. She was smiling gently, but maybe she wasn't. Sarah was starting to doubt everything. Her chest was heavy and the gentle cough was now a constant.

'Are you Sarah?' the woman asked.

'Yes.'

'I'm Constable Jackson. Was it you who dialled 999?'

'Yes.'

Sarah stood, but it felt like she had the flu. Something sat deep in her lungs and there was a soft, irritating scratch whenever she breathed.

'Why were you inside?' the officer asked.

Sarah momentarily wondered why the woman was so tall, before realising she was standing on the road, while the officer was on the kerb, a few centimetres higher.

'I saw a light inside,' Sarah said, although the memory was murky. 'My friend owns the shop.'

Constable Jackson produced a notepad and pencil from a pocket. 'Do you have their details?'

Sarah realised she was holding her phone, having somehow not noticed. It took a while for her fingers to work, though she found Bonnie's number and turned the screen for the officer to see. Constable Jackson wrote down the number and nodded to say she had it.

'How did you get inside?' she asked.

Sarah tried to remember. Her eyelids felt so heavy. 'The door was open,' she said, fairly sure that was true.

The officer scratched something on the pad. 'Do you mean unlocked, or actually open?'

'Open.'

'Do you have a key?'

'No, it was open.'

Sarah wasn't sure why she'd had to repeat herself, though everything seemed to be added to the pad.

'When did the fire start?'

'Um...' Sarah was trying to remember, Everything from the past hour or so was clouded in grey. 'I'd gone in to see why the light was on,' she managed. 'I was in the back and there was a clunk of what sounded like a letterbox. Then I noticed the fire.'

The pencil had been darting around the pad, though it stopped and the officer glanced up to take in Sarah.

'So you're saying you don't know how the fire started...?'

Sarah began to say something that was probably no, though stopped herself as a degree of clarity finally sunk in.

'Do you think I started it...?'

FORTY-FIVE

The sun was up and Sarah was back on the high street. It had been a manic few hours, in which she hadn't slept, though she had coughed up something black and slimy. Her lungs didn't feel as heavy as they had in the immediate aftermath of the fire, though there was still a niggling tickle each time she breathed.

After talking to the police, Sarah had been looked at by a paramedic. They'd taken her pulse, maybe her blood pressure, although she couldn't quite remember. There was probably an alcohol swab or two for her palm and wrist, some painkillers, general advice to visit a doctor if her breathing got worse. Sarah had forgotten that she didn't have a doctor. She'd been dropped home by the ambulance, even though the cottage was only at the bottom of the hill.

By the time she got in, reeking of smoke as if she'd been on a night out in the 1980s, James was awake again. They'd not had much time to talk, though she'd told him in broad terms what happened with the fire and the bookshop.

The police had let her go, of course, although it didn't feel as if that brief chat on the pavement would be the end of it. Constable Jackson hadn't answered the question of whether she thought Sarah started the fire, dancing around it by saying they were 'examining all possibilities'.

Yes, but one in particular, Sarah had thought but not said.

She and James hadn't talked about the things they'd said the night before in the garden, though he'd recognised well enough that she needed space. When Richard, Cara, Harry and Oliver were all up, he said they were going out for a special breakfast, and they all disappeared off to a diner somewhere in the cars.

That left Sarah to have a shower and get out of her reeking clothes.

It had been such a long night. Such a long week.

But Sarah couldn't stay at the house by herself, and knew she wouldn't sleep – which left her trundling back into town, this time in daylight. Her clothes were fresh, but her body wasn't. Three yawns in a row ripped through Sarah as she crested the hill and followed the high street towards where more police tape arced around the shop. That was two places the police had to section off on the same street, in less than a week. All since Sarah had moved to town.

A small crowd had gathered near the bookshop, and Sarah recognised some of the school gate coven. An officer was standing on the kerb, making unconvincing gestures that onlookers should move away, while not particularly bothering to move anyone along. Nothing to see here – except the burned building.

Sarah spotted Bonnie immediately. She was standing on the road, at the back of her car, talking into her phone while facing the opposite direction. As Sarah neared the shop, she realised there wasn't quite as much damage in daylight as she'd feared the night before. One of the windows had shattered, leaving crusty dark scorch marks around the frame. The other was intact, though a singed, blackened hardback was on the ground, where there should have been a door.

Bonnie lowered her phone and turned as Sarah reached the

shop. She sighed loudly, then looked up to spot Sarah. She reeled a moment, as if not quite believing what was in front of her.

'The police said you were here,' Bonnie said, no hint of a hello. 'You called 999...?'

As soon as she'd spoken, Bonnie's gaze slipped past Sarah towards the gathering beyond. She nodded in the opposite direction and Sarah followed her friend over the street, towards the post box, where a bench was next to a lamp post. They sat together, staring across towards the shop. It looked worse with the fuller picture: the black around the window frames, the shattered glass, the lack of a door.

'It was your dream,' Sarah said quietly, remembering what Bonnie had told her. She'd always wanted to own a bookshop, had pulled it off, and then this happened.

Bonnie had been about to say something else but stopped, acknowledging the point with a solemn, 'I know...'

Neither spoke for a moment but then Sarah knew it was her time to explain. 'I had an argument with James,' she said. 'We'd been up drinking wine and it was ridiculously late. I needed to be away from him and the house and found myself walking. There was a light on in the shop – and you'd said something about the police talking to you about security. I wondered if there was someone inside, or maybe it was you, then I noticed the door was open. I went in, looking for you – and then... the shop was on fire. I couldn't find an extinguisher. I didn't know there was a window at the back but found it by accident. I had to smash it to get out.'

She let out a little cough that sounded fake, even though it was real. The scratching at the back of her throat felt as if it might never go.

Bonnie sighed again, seemingly weighing it all up. 'There's a fire extinguisher under the sink,' she said sadly.

Sarah tried to remember whether she'd looked there, though presumably not.

'Did you see anyone?' Bonnie added.

'No, the light was on in the basement. I'd gone down, looking for you. I didn't realise how big the space was. I hope your computer made it.'

Bonnie didn't reply. She was holding her phone in one hand, staring across the street towards the loss of her life's dream. Sarah almost didn't want to ask the next thing. And perhaps it was none of her business anyway.

'Do you know how much survived the fire?' she asked.

There was a long wait for the reply. The devastation was unmistakable. 'I'm not sure. I've not been allowed in – and they said it might be a few hours. The marshal told me there's a lot of water at the front.'

For some reason, Sarah hadn't considered that putting out the fire was going to cause as much damage as the blaze itself. Fire and books didn't mix – but neither did water and books.

'They're checking some of the CCTV from the shops around,' Bonnie added. 'But I don't think anything overlooks mine.'

'You don't have a camera?'

'Never thought I needed it.'

Bonnie flipped over her phone, making the screen light up, though turned it back again almost instantly.

'The police think I was involved,' Sarah said. This is why she'd come to town in the hope of finding Bonnie. She wanted the other woman to know it wasn't her.

'It was wrong time, wrong place,' she added. 'If I'd not argued with James, or not walked through town...'

Sarah wasn't sure how to finish but she tugged up her sleeve a fraction and held out her hands, showing the grazes and thin scabs. The paramedic said she was lucky not to have any blisters from the heat, though she wondered if these wounds might scar.

In a way, it was right time, right place. If she hadn't been there, would other buildings have caught fire? Half the town could've gone up.

She waited, hoping Bonnie would say it was fine, that she believed her, though it never came. The other woman was staring towards her shop and, now Sarah had been told, she could see the puddles at the front. There was a chance everything inside was destroyed, even the parts not consumed by fire.

Sarah tried to think of something more to say, anything that might make her new friend believe her, except she had no idea. The simple facts were that she'd been in town less than a week. In that time, her husband had been accused of at least one historical murder, a current one – and now she was suspected of starting a fire.

It definitely wasn't the time for it, but what was that old saying about no smoke without fire?

No wonder it seemed as if everyone in town was looking at her and James with suspicion.

Bonnie hadn't spoken for a good minute or so. She flipped her phone around again, unlocking the screen, and tapping something, before turning it back.

'Can you do me a favour?' she asked. 'Georgia's at swim club until eleven. Could you pick her up and hang onto her for a few hours? The fire marshal's coming back and I'm going to have quite a bit to do here. I don't want her to see the shop like this...'

Sarah answered 'of course' with too much eagerness. She craved Bonnie telling her not to worry, that *she* didn't think Sarah was at fault, though it still didn't come. There was a different olive branch, though.

'I'm glad you got out,' Bonnie said. 'There's been enough death for one week.'

FORTY-SIX

By the time Sarah arrived at the cottage with Bonnie's daughter in tow, there was a full house. Cara, Richard and Harry were back from breakfast, along with James and Oliver. As well as Georgia and Sarah herself, that was seven of them.

The boys were full of sugar after being allowed a doughnut after breakfast, so they set off roaring around the garden – with Georgia apparently happy to join in, even though she was a little younger. They were at the age where gender didn't matter and everyone got on with it. A new playmate was a new playmate.

The adults gathered around the kitchen table, Cara told Sarah what they'd had and where they'd gone for breakfast. She talked about the boys and how excited they'd been to be somewhere new, and how much Harry was delighted to be playing in a garden. Chirped joy and laughter echoed through from the back, emphasising the point.

But things were different from last night. There had been cheese, wine, and chat then. Except Cara had since clearly had a word with Richard, telling him that James had been with the police. That he might be a killer.

Richard had barely spoken since they got back – and certainly not to James. They were sitting next to one another but angled in different directions, as if they'd never met.

Despite everything she'd said to him in the garden, it was impossible for Sarah not to feel bad for her husband. If he was innocent in everything, if he'd done nothing wrong, she had dragged him back to a place that was rejecting him. He could have told her the truth in the first place, but it was a bit late for all that. Then she'd told their mutual friends, who would likely never see him in the same way again. All that after one of his teenage best friends had disappeared.

Sarah hadn't told Cara about the overnight fire – and maybe she should have kept her mouth closed the night before, too. Cara didn't *need* to know what was happening in their lives, despite how badly Sarah felt about it all.

It didn't help that Sarah desperately needed to sleep. That was the excuse for her not going to breakfast that morning – that she needed a lie-in. In reality, she needed time alone, too, to try to process everything from the early hours. The fire felt like something of a dream.

Conversation had dwindled. It was probably time for Cara and Richard to head back to London. They all knew it but nobody wanted to say as much, especially as Harry was having so much fun playing with Oliver and Georgia in the back. Richard was on his phone, James on his, while Cara flicked through a cookbook that had been on the counter.

Sarah was the only one watching the garden, though it was through a miasmic haze. There were times at the playground when she'd send Oliver off to the equipment and then zoned out while watching him. It was the same again, until her thoughts began to clear and she realised that the children had stopped running. Instead, the three of them were near the back of the garden, acting in a way Sarah had never seen either Oliver or Harry behave.

She told the others she was going to check on the boys, then headed to where Georgia was posing as if holding a camera, while the boys faced the fence, then peered over their shoulders towards her. It took Sarah a while to realise they were role-playing photographer and subject. But the way the boys were posing was far too adult for a child. It felt strange. Definitely wrong. Harry was even sticking out his bum.

They stopped as Sarah approached. 'What are you playing?' she asked.

'It's a game,' Georgia replied. She spoke with such confidence that it was as if she was the eldest of the trio.

'What game?'

'Mum says I'm going to be a model when I grow up. I have to practice poses.'

'She was teaching us,' Oliver added, oblivious to the oddly grown-up nature of what they'd been doing.

'It's called statues,' Georgia said. 'You have to stay really still.'

Sarah thought for a moment, not sure what to say. She had an imprecise memory of something named statues they used to play at primary school. It involved standing still while someone faced the other way – but there was none of the posing part. But then, anything out-of-context could appear weird. There was every chance one of those *Next Top Model* shows was Bonnie's favourite programme. If not that, a similar Instagram thing. If this game was an offshoot of that, between Bonnie and her daughter, it wasn't *that* strange.

All three children were looking to Sarah expectantly – which was the thing with parenting. A child thought their mums and dads knew what they were doing, while the adult was making it up, hoping for the best. That was especially true when it was someone else's child.

'I'm not sure this is the best place to play it,' Sarah replied, with fake cheer. 'Maybe try a different game!'

Georgia's face fell a fraction – but Oliver suggested French cricket, saying Georgia could bat first, and that seemed to appease her. She'd never played before but it wasn't long until Oliver was showing her how to use the bat to defend her legs. Boysplaining was a thing, apparently.

Back in the kitchen, the silence continued to hang. Cara looked up from the book, asking if the children were all right, with Sarah saying they were. She wasn't sure anyone else had noticed the oddity of the game.

Sarah sat, continuing to watch the kids as they chased the tennis ball. Her throat still tickled from the smoke and Sarah let out a small cough, before trying to soothe it with a drink of water. Cara smiled a gentle, wordless, 'You OK?', which got a nod.

It was only as Sarah was turning the taps that she noticed the spot of blood on her sleeve. There was probably blood on her hoody as well, from when she'd clambered through the window. That reminded her she had to do a wash. It wasn't only her smoky clothes from the night before, Oliver would need his school uniform for Monday.

That was the truest fact of life. A person's existence could dissolve into a murky, secretive web of assaults, deaths and fires – but none of that stopped the need to put a wash on.

Sarah asked Cara to keep an eye on the children, then headed upstairs, into the main bedroom. James hadn't bothered to remake the bed after getting up, which was one of the long-held niggles they had as a couple. His point was that it was only going to get messed up again the next night, so why bother. Hers was that he was being a massive nob.

It would have been nice if this was the biggest problem in their marriage.

The clothes hamper was in the corner of the room, next to a stray box. Sarah had thought everything upstairs had been unpacked, except boxes were like rabbits in the cottage. Turn your back for a moment, and they'd multiplied. Sarah's hoody was at the top of the dirty clothes pile – and she picked it up. The sulphury, thick smoke was strong, and she found herself wondering if it would ever come out.

It was only as she was turning it inside-out that Sarah realised there were things in the pocket. She fumbled through the folds, almost tangling the hoody into a knot before retrieving what turned out to be a crumpled pile of letters. Sarah stared, wondering where they'd come from, before flashing back to the night before. There had been a moment when she'd been searching for a way to break the back window in Bonnie's shop. She'd dashed into the main part, by the counter, looking for something heavy – and there had definitely been letters then. Sarah thought she'd dropped them but, seemingly, they'd ended up in her pocket. She had been holding her breath, on the brink of a full-blown panic, so anything was possible.

Sarah figured she'd return the letters to her friend the next time she saw her. If it was something important, at least it had been saved from the fire and water. She uncrumpled the envelopes, palming them flat across the dresser, before noticing the details on the front.

The address was definitely the bookshop – but it wasn't Bonnie's name on the letter. It was someone far more surprising than that.

FORTY-SEVEN

Sarah knew she shouldn't – except it wasn't as if anyone would know. With the fire, plus the water used to put it out, Bonnie wasn't going to notice a fistful of missing mail. The letters were still sealed but Sarah fingered open the envelope and pulled out the furrowed pages inside.

It was an annual mortgage statement from the bank, the sort of thing that – if it was up to Sarah – went straight from letterbox to shredder. She scanned the top page, then flicked through the rest, before returning to the name at the very top.

Bonnie didn't own the bookshop.

Martin Shearer did.

Sarah re-read everything, just in case, but Bonnie wasn't even mentioned on the documents.

Had she lied about owning the store? Sarah tried to remember what she'd said when they'd been in the back room together. There was definitely something about having a dream to run a bookshop, about practically living in the library when she was young. She said the man who owned the Carnington Bookshop wanted to sell and retire... but what then?

Sarah was fairly sure she knew. She might not remember the exact phrasing but Bonnie had mentioned her ex-husband, their savings, and a loan. They had bought the shop as a couple – but it was always understood to be Bonnie's.

Except it *wasn't* hers.

It belonged to a dead man.

Sarah wished she could remember. Perhaps it wasn't an outright lie, because if Bonnie *had* said she'd taken a loan, she didn't necessarily say it was from a bank.

Perhaps she'd borrowed from Martin himself? More or less everyone had said that Martin owned, or had a stake, in places around town. There were the flats where his body was found, and Eric thought he owned the café, or bakery. Dean might have suggested a place as well, though Sarah knew nobody had mentioned the bookshop.

Sarah packed the letter back into its envelope. There was no way she could return it to Bonnie now, yet she couldn't bring herself to throw it away. Instead, she hid it at the bottom of her pyjama/lazy clothes drawer.

Another question, in a village that was full of them.

Except that wash still needed to be put on. Sarah sorted through the rest of the hamper, then carried it downstairs to the washer and put everything in. She returned to the kitchen but had barely sat down when her phone buzzed with a message from Bonnie. For a brief moment, Sarah thought the other woman somehow knew that she'd been snooping through her mail – but it wasn't that. Instead, Bonnie was saying she was finished at the shop. She'd had to pop home but could now collect Georgia.

The cottage already felt full and, with nobody talking to one another, but none of them admitting it might be time to call it a weekend, Sarah didn't want to add another person. She replied, saying she could drop Georgia home instead – and a response came not long after, with an address, and 'Sounds great!'

Sarah feared Bonnie thought she might have started the fire – but perhaps she'd misread things when they'd been on the bench. She was sleep-starved, still re-running the flames and the smoke. It was hard to know where her head was.

With that, Sarah said she was taking Georgia home, leaving her husband and friends to figure out whatever they had going on. She went into the garden, where the children were now hunched in a small circle, near the fence.

'We saw a frog,' Oliver said, when Sarah arrived.

'It wasn't a frog,' Georgia told him confidently. 'It was a newt.'

'What's a newt?'

'A skinny frog.'

Sarah considered pointing out that they were different creatures, but realised she had no idea herself. Perhaps newts *were* skinny frogs? She thought they could all be amphibians, but maybe they were reptiles? Either way, she told Georgia it was time to go home – and then the children said goodbye to one another. Sarah left the boys on the ground and took Georgia back through the house, where they got into her car.

Georgia was happily talking about Oliver and Harry, asking when they could all play again. Sarah offered the eternal 'sometime soon', not wanting to say that, with Harry living in a different city, and everyone's parents now acting awkwardly around one another, it likely wouldn't happen.

She also realised that Georgia had no idea what had happened to the bookshop. It was the place she went after school each day, to play in the back room as her mum worked in the front. Everything was going to come as quite the shock for such a young mind.

The drive across the village was a short one, avoiding the high street and following a narrow lane out towards a row of houses, almost hidden from the road by a line of high hedges. Sarah was so used to the pristine Britain in Bloom façade of the main village that it was a shock to see an area of town was so run-down. An abandoned car was on the verge, half in the ditch, along with a large pile of scrap metal at the end of someone's drive.

Bonnie's house was through a gap in the hedges that Sarah would've missed if not for Georgia saying 'It's here'. The patchy front garden had an upside-down trampoline in the middle, the strings broken, a puddle in the middle of the canvas. The house itself was like something from the opening scenes of a property programme. Now was the before part, where it looked like it might fall down – after was when some lunatic in a novelty beret had painted everything black.

Sarah parked and Georgia let herself out. Bonnie was waiting at the door with Gary the spaniel as Sarah climbed out of the car.

'Do you want to come in?' Bonnie called.

Sarah did, mainly because she was desperate to know that her friend wasn't blaming her for the fire. A part of her wondered if she'd ask about the letter, and Martin owning the shop, though knowledge of that felt like a betrayal.

Bonnie's house was a proper home. There were shoes cluttered by the door, coats on the hook, though two were on the floor, a random low beam in the cluttered hall which made everyone have to duck, doors everywhere, plus a stopped clock above the kitchen door. Sarah had always found something a little charming about a person who lived in a space, rather than managed it. In her cottage, the shoes would be in neat rows on the rack, coats would *all* be on hooks, the clock's battery would have been replaced.

Georgia was dispatched to her room to get changed, then Bonnie led Sarah through to a small alcove room that faced a bare backyard. There were two armchairs in a little nook and Bonnie flopped into one. Gary had followed Georgia upstairs.

'They let me into the shop,' Bonnie said, once Sarah had sat. 'There's not as much damage as there might have been – but the smoke and water wiped out much of the stock. They said it was lucky nothing spread to the other shops.'

'Does anyone know how it started?'

She'd forgotten in the moment but Sarah now remembered that purple rag on the doormat, when the small flames were starting to take hold. Had she told that to the police? She hoped so – but too much of the past day or so was a blur.

'They think arson,' Bonnie said.

'It was deliberate?'

'They've been checking cameras on the high street but said not to get my hopes up.'

'Why would someone want to burn down a bookshop?'

When Sarah had found out Martin was the true owner, she somehow hadn't connected it to arson. It felt important now, especially considering he was dead. Except Sarah couldn't let on that she knew his name was on the mortgage.

'I have no idea,' Bonnie replied. 'They asked me the same. They wanted to know if I'd made any enemies, that sort of thing, but what are you supposed to say?'

Sarah didn't know and didn't reply. She was still trying to remember whether she'd mentioned the purple rag to the police, or anyone from the fire brigade. She'd been so manic after escaping the shop that everything blurred into one.

'I'm going to have to go through the inventory,' Bonnie replied. 'There's probably a few things that survived but we'll definitely be closed a while.'

It was then that Sarah remembered something else she should probably say. 'I used this jewellery box thing to break the window,' she said. 'It was on the counter but I don't know what was inside. I threw it at the glass to make it break.'

Bonnie had been still for a moment but she angled forward

with a new interest. 'I was looking for that,' she said. 'It wasn't in the shop. Have you got it?'

'I don't know where it went.'

Sarah's thoughts were a foggy, smoke-drenched haze – but the alarm on Bonnie's face was apparent.

'Is it an heirloom?' Sarah asked.

'Uh... yes. It was my mum's.'

She sounded unsure and, from being settled on the chair, there was a fidgety unease about her.

'I think I'm going to go back to the shop,' Bonnie said abruptly, standing.

'Oh.'

Sarah stood too, not sure what she'd missed. 'The box might have gone through the glass,' she said. 'It shattered but I don't remember after that. It could have landed inside, or out.'

Bonnie was nodding along. 'I should have thought about it,' she said, though it sounded like she was talking to herself.

'I can help you look?'

The other woman looked towards Sarah, as if she'd momentarily forgotten she was there. 'It's OK.'

Bonnie moved through to the kitchen, Sarah a fraction behind. The other woman was muttering 'keys' to herself – and her house seemed like the sort of place in which something like keys could easily disappear. It was only as she opened and closed a drawer that Sarah noticed the tea towel hanging over the oven door handle. The kind you get in a set of three or four.

Not just any tea towel.

A *purple* tea towel.

She was staring, mouth open, when she realised Bonnie was looking between her and the oven.

'I, uh...' The words weren't coming for Sarah. She was back in the main part of the bookshop, watching the flames lick and leap from the purple towel blocking the door. She remembered the letterbox clanging – and she knew.

They *both* knew.

Bonnie was at the sink, her mouth open as well. Her eyes flicked upwards, towards where her daughter was walking around in the room above.

And then, very calmly, she picked up a kitchen knife from the draining board.

FORTY-EIGHT

Sarah was frozen, still trying to stumble over a sentence as Bonnie stepped across the kitchen and returned the knife to the block. She picked up the plates from the draining board, opened a cupboard and stacked them inside.

All the while, Sarah hadn't moved. Now she'd seen the purple towel, she couldn't stop picturing the blaze from the night before. The taste of the smoke was back, the way her thoughts had raced when she'd been holding her breath. That panic when she'd thrown a mug at the window and nothing happened.

'It's not what you think,' Bonnie said. She was trying to keep her voice level but the momentary quiver gave her away. Her back was turned, so she was gazing over the sink, through the window, towards the bare patch of dirt beyond. She wanted to speak, possibly to explain, but only if she didn't have to look Sarah in the face while she did it.

'What do I think?' Sarah asked.

Bonnie didn't answer, not really. 'I'd gone in to grab some things I didn't want to lose and taken them to the car. I suppose it's a good job I left that box, otherwise you'd have been stuck...'

She paused, waiting for a reply that Sarah didn't give.

'I got the tea towel from the car, plus the petrol. I'd been careful. I syphoned from my own tank because the police might've looked at footage from the petrol station and seen me filling a can. I parked in a dead spot, between the cameras. I had to walk the long way around but knew I wouldn't be seen. I'd thought about it.'

Sarah had no doubt the other woman had. If there was a time when she was thinking of setting a fire with petrol, it wouldn't have occurred to her that the police might check cameras for someone filling a can, instead of a vehicle. She had been unlucky enough to reach the bookstore in the window of time between Bonnie removing items important to her, then returning with the tea towel.

'I didn't realise I'd left on a light,' Bonnie said. 'I didn't know you were in there. It was so late and I hadn't seen *anyone*. I wouldn't have gone through with it if I had.' She waited, then added a solemn: 'Sorry...'

She sounded it, though she was still facing the window.

There were youthful footsteps from upstairs as Georgia left one room and moved into another. A quieter pitter-patter meant Gary had followed.

Sarah considered leaving. The village was cursed, but maybe it was her. Look at the destruction with which she'd been involved.

'Was it an insurance thing?' Sarah asked.

No answer came at first – but then it did.

'No.' Another pause. 'Well... sort of.' One more. 'No.'

Bonnie sank a little, cradling her head with both hands. 'The thing is, I don't own the shop. I know what I said but it's owned by Martin Shearer.' She stopped, then corrected herself. '*Was* owned by him.'

Sarah didn't think there was much point in letting on she already knew.

'I got into debt in my twenties,' Bonnie said. 'My flat was flooded and I wasn't completely insured, then my landlord sued. I put all my spending on credit cards but then the interest was high, so I got a loan...'

Something had shifted slightly for Sarah since she'd spoken to Mr Horlock and had been reminded of that lunch line of students outing themselves as poor. Sarah's family had never been rich, but they'd never been poor. She'd always had a roof, never had to concern herself about how to pay a bill, or whether she could afford food. She was struggling with how to cope with a husband she now didn't trust – but that hadn't stopped her seeing him in a slightly alternate way. They'd had very different experiences of early life – and perhaps it was unfair to judge him by her standards.

Maybe that was true of Bonnie.

Except Sarah had almost died the night before and it was the other woman's fault.

'Banks won't lend to me,' Bonnie added. 'I've got credit cards but the limits are low. I *really* wanted that shop. I wasn't lying when I told you it was my dream. I didn't know who to ask. But then Martin owns so many other things...'

Bonnie turned and her eyes were wet, cheeks red.

'Why burn it?' Sarah asked.

Bonnie was nodding, acknowledging the fairness of the question. 'We signed a contract and I read it all – even the small print. There's a clause that, in the event of serious damage, Martin had a choice. If he was unable to refurbish, or he didn't want to, then ownership falls to me.'

Sarah needed a moment to get her head around that – but then Bonnie explained anyway.

'He wasn't being nice. Martin took the profits and paid me a salary to run the shop. He set the amount and signed off on everything. But, if it went out of business, or got hit by lightning – something like that – the costs would fall to me. It meant he couldn't lose. I got my shop but he got everything else.'

'That was in the small print?'

A nod.

'But you signed anyway?'

Another. 'I wanted the shop.'

That was the thing with dreams: people chased them, even at the expense of everything else. Not that Sarah could blame anyone for such a thing. What else was the point of life, if not to chase those dreams?

She also got the rest. With Martin dead, the bank would get the shop... with the sole exception for if there was 'serious damage'.

Bonnie got the lot – and, if she could get insurance to pay for the refurbishment, the only thing she'd be on the hook for was the general mortgage payments. She'd be able to afford that, as Martin was no longer skimming the profits.

Sarah was impressed.

Bonnie must have seen something in Sarah's expression. 'I didn't want something bad to happen,' she said. 'Definitely not to you. I thought it would be a small fire, a bit of smoke. I read that contract so many times, making sure it said what I thought it did. There was nothing about deliberate fire, so as long as it wasn't traced to me, it was airtight.'

Sarah wasn't sure if 'airtight' was necessarily true, especially if there was a bank involved. In one way, it didn't matter – because that's what Bonnie believed. That's what had motivated her.

'I didn't mean for you to get trapped,' Bonnie added. 'I didn't mean for the police to suspect you. There's no way they can prove anything anyway.'

That was another thing that didn't sound entirely certain. It wasn't as if nobody had ever been accused of something they hadn't done.

'I don't know what to do,' Bonnie added. 'Please don't say anything.'

There were more footsteps from upstairs and Bonnie glanced up nervously, probably wondering how long until Georgia came down.

'What am I supposed to do if the police think it's me?' Sarah replied. 'What if they arrest me?'

'Just tell them what happened.' She picked up the tea towel. 'I'll get rid of this. It must've come as a pack of two and I didn't even think.'

'If there are cameras down the street, they'll have seen me.'

'Exactly – but you weren't carrying a petrol can, or a towel. You were just in the wrong place. If they ask, I'll tell them I trust you and you'd have never done anything like this.'

Sarah wasn't sure what to say. She didn't particularly want Bonnie to be in trouble – but there was no way she could take the fall if it came to that.

'*Please...*' Bonnie added.

Sarah was avoiding eye contact, knowing she'd agree if she looked at the other woman. 'I can't promise,' she said, staring at the crumbs around the toaster instead.

There was a hush between them as Bonnie realised it was probably as good as she was going to get. It was hard for Sarah not to feel sad. In a week that had lurched from one disaster to the next, making a new friend had been close to the only highlight. But, now, even if neither of them got in trouble over the fire, there was no going back. It was hard to be mates with someone who'd almost burned you to death, then asked you to keep quiet about it.

For now, at least Sarah had some idea of Martin's involvement with the bookshop. Mr Horlock's warning that he had given a lot to the town – but also taken a lot – suddenly seemed prophetic.

'Does Martin Shearer have this sort of loan arrangement with anyone else?' Sarah asked.

Bonnie had been looking elsewhere, lost in her own thoughts. She peered across to Sarah, as if she hadn't entirely heard.

'I don't know.'

'If he did, that might have been a reason to kill him...?'

For a moment, Bonnie's features froze, as if she thought she'd been accused of killing him herself. When it was clear Sarah didn't mean that, she started nodding, understanding why the question had been asked.

'He might. When he gave me the money, he said he'd only do it if I didn't tell anyone. At the time, he said he didn't want everyone coming to ask for money but maybe he had a lot more going on than I knew?'

That sounded possible.

Sarah was about to say she was leaving when Bonnie spoke unexpectedly. 'It's a good job he's gone. If it was James, he did everyone a favour.'

She spat the words and, though Sarah wanted to tell her it definitely *wasn't* James who killed Martin, it felt like a pointless conversation. She wasn't sure they'd be talking too much after this – and there definitely wouldn't be any more cosy tea and biscuits in the back room of the shop. For more reasons than one.

Sarah let out a small sigh and it was as if she'd lost something, even though she barely had it in the first place.

A timid-sounding 'Mum' echoed from the top of the stairs and both women looked up.

'I've got to go,' Sarah said, making up her mind about what she was going to do next. She'd been considering it the whole time Bonnie had been talking.

Bonnie started to reply, though stopped herself. 'I'm really sorry,' she said instead – and she certainly sounded it.

Sarah mumbled a 'bye' – and then she was gone. She waited until the front door was closed, and then *ran* to her car. If something was up with Georgia, she had maybe a five-minute head-start on Bonnie.

It was a good job Sarah knew where she was going, because she raced to the village centre, only slowing when she reached the THANK YOU FOR DRIVING CAREFULLY sign. It was the afternoon now, with a handful of tourists drifting around the high street as the sun shone. Sarah parked in the first space she could find and then hurried from the main road, into the side alley from which she'd emerged coughing and heaving barely twelve hours before.

The back lane was cobbled, shrouded in shadow. It was where the shopkeepers kept bins and loading pallets, the sort of place the Britain in Bloom committee definitely wouldn't be taken. Sarah followed the path ducking around various bins, boxes, barrels and containers. Memories flashed from hours before, when she was gasping for air, stunned to be outside – and it didn't feel much different in the daylight.

Teeny shards of glass signalled the back of the bookshop. Somebody had done a cursory cleaning-up job to get the larger parts, but minuscule splinters of glass still glittered through the gloom. The window Sarah had broken was boarded up, as she wondered whether there was still any of her blood on the frame.

No.

There wasn't time for that. She was here for a reason and almost certain Bonnie wouldn't be far behind. The other woman's reaction to the butterfly box had been curious. Sarah had asked if it was an heirloom and there'd been a hesitation before Bonnie said it was. If it wasn't for the other lies that had come out, Sarah wouldn't have thought much of it. Except it sounded as if Bonnie *really* wanted the box – and not because it was valuable.

With the glass still on the ground, Sarah was sure the box

would have gone through the window and landed outside. There was every chance someone had cleared it away – except, if they had, wouldn't it have been handed in? Bonnie had been allowed back in the shop, so had been around when the clean-up was happening.

Sarah turned in a circle, taking in the grubby space around her. There was moss between the grooves of the damp paving tiles and a general sense that it never dried out. The only thing in sight was a large metal wheelie bin. Sarah didn't particularly want to go hunting through it, especially as she didn't think she had a lot of time. She opened the flap anyway, peering inside and wincing at the acrid smell she should have expected. She turned, took a breath, and tried again – only to see a mound of black bags that she also should have expected.

She definitely wasn't going to hunt through the individual bags and if Bonnie wanted the box that badly, she could have it.

Sarah closed the lid and stepped away – which is when she spotted a large triangle of glass almost hidden behind one of the bin's wheels. It was much bigger than any of the other shards still littering the path, which meant it had likely been missed by whoever cleaned up. Sarah crouched, wincing as her knees creaked.

And then she saw it. A fraction out of sight, lost to the shadow, was the butterfly box that had saved her life. Sarah stretched and pulled it clear, again struck by how heavy it was. She gave it a shake and something shifted inside. Sarah tried pulling off the lid, though couldn't find the join. She twisted and turned it, prodding and poking, looking for a catch that apparently wasn't there.

Whatever was inside felt significant and so, rather than leaving it for Bonnie to find, Sarah gripped the box hard and ran for it.

FORTY-NINE

As Sarah arrived home, there was noise from the kitchen. She put the box on the windowsill nearest the door, and headed through to where Cara and Richard were saying an uncomfortable goodbye. When Cara realised Sarah was there, she stopped mid-sentence.

'Oh, I'm so glad you're back. We were just leaving. I was hoping to see you.'

They went through the motions – love the house – love the garden – thanks for hosting – have to do this again sometime – and so on. They both knew something was different, if not with them, then between Richard and James. It was a shame all round, but especially for the boys. Sarah had seen Oliver's *Do we really have to leave?* face enough to recognise Harry's. Apart from sleeping, he'd spent almost all his time in the garden. There were parks near to where they used to live but it wasn't the same as having an exclusive space to play.

James, Sarah and Oliver walked Richard, Cara and Harry to the door. There were more waves, goodbyes and promises to catch up soon – and then they were gone. Sarah doubted they'd be back anytime soon.

As Oliver took himself off to his room, likely tired after a day of running and chasing, James and Sarah stood in the hall. It was the first proper time they'd had to speak since the fire. Sarah had more or less told her husband what happened, though he didn't know how close she'd come to being trapped. Nor that the police were acting as if she might have started it.

It was also the first time they'd been properly alone since the wine-fuelled truth in the garden the night before. Alcohol might make people say things they didn't mean – but what Sarah really feared was that it had made her say what she *actually* thought. Perhaps the lack of trust she now felt towards her husband wasn't fixable?

'Are you OK?' James asked.

'Throat's a bit sore... but yes.'

He pulled Sarah to him and she let him. She wanted his hand on her back, to feel his fingers in her hair. They stood like that for a while, maybe a minute, maybe more, and Sarah could feel his heart beating.

'What's that?' James asked, releasing Sarah so abruptly that she almost fell forward. By the time she'd righted herself, she turned to see her husband holding the butterfly box.

'It was in Bonnie's shop,' Sarah said. 'I needed it to break the window.'

It didn't seem as if James was listening. He'd flipped it over, done something Sarah didn't quite see with his finger and thumb – and then there was a sold *click*.

He turned it back the right way, where a hidden drawer had popped out from the side.

'How did you know to do that?' Sarah asked.

James was preoccupied and answered without acknowledging her. 'It used to belong to a friend.'

'Who?' Sarah asked, though no reply came. James was fiddling with the box, shunting it from side to side until a pair of USB drives dropped onto the carpet. He stretched and picked up one – but Sarah snatched the other. He went to take it but she clamped her fist around it.

'Don't look at that,' he said. He spoke so firmly that Sarah took a half-step backwards, as if he'd pushed her. He didn't seem to notice as he shook the box, presumably to see if there was anything else inside.

'Why can't I look at it?' Sarah asked.

James put down the box and held out an expectant hand. Sarah had never seen him act in such a way, let alone towards her. 'Can I have it?' he said – although it was more of a demand. Sarah took another step away. Her laptop was in the living room and, if James didn't want her to look at the drive, she knew she absolutely had to.

'What's on it?' she asked.

'I don't know.'

'So why can't I look at it?'

There was no answer – but, as Sarah took another step towards the living room, James realised what she was doing. He darted around her, blocking the door, and making a snatch for the drive. Sarah pulled her arm away, just about avoiding his hand.

'Let me past,' she said – except her husband wasn't moving. He stared her dead in the eye, a different man to the person she'd married. She'd seen that stare – but only in a video. Only when he was punching Martin Shearer on the ground.

'Give it to me,' he said.

FIFTY

It was a stand-off. Sarah could feel herself shaking, amazed how quickly things had shifted. She and James had been hugging barely a minute before – and now he was blocking a door, demanding she hand over something he wouldn't explain.

And then, as if it hadn't happened, James stepped to the side. 'Go on then,' he said, defeat in his voice.

Sarah had no idea what was going on but she slowly passed, nervous over his intentions. She'd never been scared of him but... maybe she was.

'What's on it?' Sarah asked.

'I told you, I don't know.'

'So why don't you want me to look at it?'

'It's complicated.'

Sarah tried to read her husband's face. She had woken up next to him almost every morning for years. She knew the spot where the stubble grew a fraction thicker than anywhere else. She knew there was a singular long hair that only grew in one nostril, that he could only raise one of his eyebrows, that his ears twitched when he laughed.

She *knew* that face.

But not now. He was someone else as he watched her with clouded eyes.

Sarah shivered as a tingle of fear tickled her spine. She crossed the living room and grabbed her laptop from the coffee table, then sat in the chair facing the door. James had followed and was at the side, a fraction out of touching distance but not by much.

'What's on it?' she asked again, convinced he knew.

'I don't know.'

It had to be a lie, because she didn't understand his behaviour otherwise.

Sarah's laptop said it was low on power, so she stood again, hunting for the cable, finding it partially under the seat, then plugging it in and returning. James hadn't moved, hadn't spoken. Sarah's hand was shaking and it was a struggle to fit the drive into the USB slot. It scratched and scraped the laptop case before eventually clipping in.

Sarah didn't know what she was expecting. There was a gentle hum and then a green LED started to blink, before a pop-up appeared, listing a series of folders.

Oh no.

Sarah scrolled down, even though she'd seen immediately that every directory was tagged with a woman's name.

There were at least fifty, probably more – and the name of the top folder, the most recent one, made Sarah's heart jump.

Georgia

Sarah didn't want to look but she did. The contents should have been a surprise but they weren't. There was a host of new folders, each arranged by date, at least thirty in Georgia's.

Oh no.

Sarah double-clicked again, revealing a long list of thumbnail jpeg images, probably another sixty or seventy.

That was sixty or seventy images, multiplied by at least thirty different dates – and that was for Georgia alone. There were at least another fifty girls' names listed.

Sarah didn't want to load the image. She watched her finger shaking, felt her breathing slow, wanted it to stop.

'Did you know?' she asked, hearing the quiver to her voice – but James didn't answer. He'd not moved from her side, though she sensed him watching the screen.

Sarah held her breath and double-clicked the image. It was painfully slow to open, even though it happened immediately. Enough time for a million dark thoughts to sift through Sarah's thoughts. It had barely been an hour before that she dropped off the girl at home.

It suddenly became obvious why Georgia's game of statues in the garden had been so bizarrely grown up. The image was of her posing provocatively, wearing a short crimson dress. If it wasn't for the pose, it would have been *almost* normal. The outfit was short but Sarah had seen worse in those weird American child pageants.

Except there was the same pose Georgia had encouraged the boys to do in the garden: arse out, back arched, looking over the shoulder.

They take my picture.

Sarah remembered what Georgia had said in the garden now. She'd thought it was part of the game but now it felt worse. So much worse.

Who was 'they'?'

Sarah went to close the image – but then she spotted what was behind the girl. She'd seen the dark pink curtain before, folded on the floor of Bonnie's bookshop basement, next to an unused clothes rail.

Oh no.

Sarah closed the image, then clicked backwards out of the folder, before choosing another folder at random.

Georgia was in a swimming costume this time: similar pose, same place.

Sarah had seen enough. She clicked backwards until the screen was showing the base folder of the drive. There had been two computers in the bookstore: one in the basement, one upstairs. Sarah had never thought to question why, partly because she had been escaping the fire.

'Did you know these were here?' Sarah asked, fearing the answer. James *couldn't* have known – but then there was a time in which she couldn't have pictured him punching a helpless man on the ground.

'Of course not,' he replied quickly. 'How would I know?'

'Because you told me not to look.'

He let out a long, reluctant breath, though didn't elaborate. Not at first.

And then it came.

'It was Lucy's box,' he said after a long, long while.

That name again.

'She used to keep photos inside,' he added.

'Like these?'

'No! God, no. Nothing like that. Normal pictures of friends and herself. It was mainly Polaroids. We used to take her camera to The Den. She'd give away anything she didn't think was perfect – but she kept the ones she really liked.'

Sarah remembered the way the drawer had slid from the box. She could see how it was the perfect size for photos. James had known how to open it.

'I don't understand what's going on,' Sarah said.

She wanted her husband to spell it out but he was silent again. 'James!' she hissed and he jolted from the spot.

'What?'

'How did you know what was on the drive?'

'I didn't. It's just that box was hers. One of her prized possessions. The fact it's being used to store... *that*. It's a dig.'

'A dig at who? Lucy? Bonnie doesn't know her. She only moved here a few years back. She never grew up here. Lucy had disappeared long before that.'

James was nodding. 'I know.'

'So how is it a dig?'

'It's not Bonnie,' James said – and he was so firm that Sarah believed him.

'Who?' she asked – but a part of her knew. The same part that had known how badly things were wrong when she'd watched that video of a young James battering Martin Shearer on the floor. She'd seen the same look on his face a few minutes before – although it had been there and gone.

'Martin?' she asked.

There was no answer but maybe there was? James shifted a fraction.

'Is this why you beat him up all those years ago? It was something to do with this?'

Sarah still wasn't sure what 'this' entailed – and she didn't get an answer anyway.

'Give me the other drive,' she said. James was holding the butterfly box in one hand, the second USB drive in the other.

'No,' he replied, though the firm insistence of moments before was gone. He sounded deflated, defeated. Sarah stretched and snatched it from his palm and there was no resistance. She pushed it into the second USB port, angry now. Why could nobody ever give her the answers she craved?

A small circle turned on the screen, thinking about loading, but then a new window appeared, asking for a password.

'What is it?' Sarah demanded.

'How would I know?'

There was only one thing for it. There was probably a better way to describe things compared to what happened the night before – but if James was going to be like this, Sarah was going to burn the whole damned town to the ground.

'I'm taking these to the police,' she said.

FIFTY-ONE

Sarah didn't move. James had taken a few steps towards the door and, for a second, she thought it was to stop her leaving. Then he paced back and put the butterfly box on the arm of the chair.

'Maybe you should,' he said.

'Go to the police?'

'If that's what you think.'

From nowhere, it was Sarah who was unsure. 'What aren't you telling me?' she asked, though maybe it was more of a plea.

James sat in the armchair. Stood. Took a breath. Sat again. 'Do you tell me everything?' he asked. Sarah's husband was staring directly at her, though she still couldn't read him. She ejected both USB drives and snapped the laptop lid closed.

'Of course,' she replied.

'But do you really? You can't tell me about every thought in your head, or everything you ever did before you met me. You can't possibly share everything.'

Sarah started to reply, although it seemed like he was actually asking something else. 'I tell you the important things,' Sarah said.

'But who decides what's important?'

'I do.'

'Exactly.'

Sarah stared at James and her husband stared right back. She was looking directly into his soul, yet had no idea who he was. Maybe for the first time, she wasn't sure who *she* was, either.

'What did you do?' she asked, knowing it was something.

'I can't say.'

'Did you kill Martin Shearer?'

A shake of the head. 'No.'

'Did you kill Lucy?'

Another one. Déjà vu: they'd done this before.

'No.'

'But what can be so bad, you won't say?'

'If you're taking those to the police, you should go.'

James nodded to the drives in her hand and Sarah closed her palm around them. Was this some sort of double-bluff? Reverse psychology? He didn't want her to go and now he didn't mind?

Sarah stood but, immediately she did, she started to wonder whether there actually was a crime. The drive was full of photos, but, with the ones she'd checked, there'd been no nudity or obvious abuse. It was strange, probably inappropriate, but Georgia said her mum reckoned she should be a model. Perhaps this was part of whatever training Bonnie thought was necessary? Maybe that was true of whoever else was photographed? It felt weird, it gave her the ick, but Sarah doubted it was illegal. If anything, Sarah was the lawbreaker for stealing the drive – and the police were already suspicious of her for starting the fire.

She felt her knees tremble, though James didn't seem to notice. If he did, he didn't move.

'Do you know the password?' she asked, holding up the second drive.

'I told you I didn't.'

'Do you know what's on there?'

'Maybe. It's Lucy's box.'

'What is it?'

James bit his lip and they both felt the weight of his next words. 'Perhaps it's best not to know?' he said. 'Or maybe you should take it to the police? I don't know the answer.'

'What do you *think* is on it?'

They were stuck. He could either tell her or not. He trusted her, or he didn't. Maybe it was dramatic but it felt as if their marriage might rest on what he said. Sarah watched her husband's eye twitch, his lips press into one another. He was chewing the inside of his mouth.

'You should do with it whatever you think is best.'

He had chosen his words so carefully. In many ways, it was the ultimate offer. Sarah had complete choice over what came next – though that didn't mean she trusted her husband. It didn't mean things could ever go back to how they were.

If anything her own words from the night before felt even more meaningful now. Something between them was broken.

With James unwilling to say, Sarah had two options. Go to the police – which might get her in trouble; or ask Bonnie. She supposed there was a third – destroy the drives, maybe even the box. Pretend she'd never found them.

Except it was a bit late for that.

Bonnie was her only realistic choice.

Sarah put the drives in her bag, though left the box where it was. She'd not long arrived home from Bonnie's house, though was heading out again. She wondered if Bonnie would be at her house, or if she really had followed her to town to look for the box. Sarah told James she'd be back later, more from habit than courtesy. He nodded to acknowledge he'd heard, though didn't ask where she was going, nor try to change her mind.

Whatever he knew had to be bad if he was willing to put their marriage on the line.

Sarah left the cottage, knowing that if it wasn't for Oliver upstairs, she might not come back. Puddlebrick was a stupid name anyway.

It was bright and she fumbled for sunglasses, not wanting to squint into the sun while she drove, then she realised she hadn't unlocked the vehicle. By the time Sarah was ready to get in, a man was standing at the end of the drive. He stared at her, confused.

'I was about to knock on your door, see if you were in,' Dean said.

Sarah hadn't seen the butcher since the time he'd sent her the videos of James. It was the first time she'd seen him out of his uniform and he was wearing three-quarter shorts, showing off chubby, hairy ankles that were better behind trousers.

Instead of getting in the car, Sarah stepped around the vehicle, to the edge of the drive, where Dean was standing.

'Why are you looking for me?' she asked.

'It's kind of... um... delicate.' He shot a sideways glance towards Raina's house and Sarah wondered whether he knew her.

'What do you mean?'

'It's probably better if we're not *overheard*.' He leant in to whisper the final word, before shooting another look at Raina's house. Sarah had already discovered the old bat was a gossip, so she got the point.

'Where do you want to go?' she asked.

He nodded at her house. 'Is anyone home?'

'My husband and son.'

'Oh... um, I don't know. What do you reckon?'

Sarah hadn't expected the question to be turned around.

She half thought about telling him to get in the car, except she didn't know where to drive him. Then she thought that if Bonnie *had* followed her to town, she might be at the bookshop – which wasn't far from the butcher's. It wasn't a long walk either way.

'Is your shop open?' she asked.

Dean turned and looked up the slope, towards the centre. 'It's half day on Saturday but I've got a key. We can go there if you don't mind?'

Sarah told him it was fine and they set off together, striding towards the high street. They avoided everything important, talking about the sun and how good the summer had been. She wondered what he might have to say that could be delicate, though maybe fear was a better word. It was him who'd sent the videos of James, after all. He'd been the one with a camcorder at the time Lucy had gone missing. Perhaps he'd found a new video about James – and wanted to show her before deciding what to do with it?

As Dean unlocked the front of the butcher's, Sarah had given herself enough time to fear the worst. Dean had left his old camera filming at The Den and it had captured the moment her husband had done something awful to Lucy. Whatever happened then related to the USB drive with the password.

Not that Sarah had any idea what to expect.

Dean held the door open for Sarah to head inside, then clicked it closed behind. They were in the main part of the shop, where a chill hung in the air. There was no meat on any of the surfaces, though Sarah realised everything had likely been returned to fridges or freezers.

Dean was leaning on the side of the counter, Sarah by the door. She'd felt a twinge of worry when he'd locked it – but she could reach and unlock it if she chose. The past week had made her jumpy.

'I heard about the fire at the bookshop,' Dean said. He waited a moment, then added, 'You were there.'

It sounded as if he was going to accuse her of starting it but then said, 'I know you're friends with Bonnie, which is why I'm coming to you. I think she might have started it.'

Sarah tried not to flinch, or let her features shift. She didn't want to be in trouble for something she hadn't done – but she didn't wish any ill-will on Bonnie, even if the other woman had trapped her in a burning building. She didn't want to see Georgia left without a mum.

'Why would you say that?' she asked.

Part of her wondered why Dean would come to her at all. As far as Dean knew, she and Bonnie were friendly – but he had presumably known Bonnie for much longer.

'I checked the shop's CCTV. We've got two cameras. Dad handed the police the first lot but he forgot I'd put a second one in the window itself. It's hidden in the corner.'

He nodded – and Sarah followed his eyes to a white box in the window. It was the same colour as the paint and, if he'd not pointed it out, she'd have never noticed it.

The room felt colder.

'Bonnie was out late last night,' Dean added. 'She's on film carrying what looked like a petrol can. I don't know if I should tell anyone...'

Sarah doubted she was that good as an actor but she opened her mouth and stared at the man in what she hoped was shock.

The stammer was real. 'I, um... I suppose you have to be certain about something like this. She has a daughter.'

A good ol' bit of emotional blackmail. What could go wrong?

Dean was nodding. He knew that, of course, had probably run through the same. 'I thought about giving it to the police, letting them deal with it. Do you want to see what I've got?'

Sarah didn't really want to watch, though it wasn't as if she had much choice. Perhaps she could muddy things a little? Convince Dean the petrol can could be a bag, something like that.

She said, 'OK.' Then Dean held open the curtain behind the counter. He trailed her into the small back room where Sarah had heard the baby crying the first time she'd been inside.

There was a large metal table along the middle, an empty cot to the side, sitting *almost* underneath the rack of knives and cleavers, next to the back door. The rest of the space was surrounded by freezers, with a small gap for a desktop computer in the corner. It was cramped, no room for two people to get around each other, without sliding chest to chest.

Dean was standing at the computer, fiddling with something he seemed unable to work out. Sarah hovered a little behind until he moved away, pressing himself against a freezer and allowing her space by the machine.

'It's there,' he said.

The computer was definitely fifteen years old minimum. Sarah moved the mouse and the pointer darted sluggishly from one side to the other. There was a blank screen and she wasn't sure what she was supposed to be doing.

'Where do I click?' she asked.

Dean had slipped around her and was at the back door. She watched him check the door was locked and then casually reach to the rack of knives. He pulled a cleaver from the metallic rail and held it up to the light.

When he realised Sarah was watching, he stared dead-eyed at her.

'Where are the drives?'

FIFTY-TWO

Sarah should have listened to her instincts. She'd felt something off when she'd entered the shop at the front, and Dean locked the door. She'd been frazzled by the argument with James, figuring it was fine because this was *her* idea. She'd suggested the shop, even though she now realised Dean had subtly egged her into it.

He was so much cleverer than she'd given him credit for – and now he was a couple of paces away, holding a cleaver, expressionless, emotionless.

'What drives?' Sarah replied.

She hoped for something, anything. She'd have probably taken anger – except Dean's granite features didn't shift.

'I know you have them,' he said. 'You were there. I dunno why but you were there. You used that box to get out the back window. I told Martin the bookshop was a stupid place to leave stuff – but he wouldn't listen.'

A breath and then, 'Where are the drives?'

How could he know she had them? *How?* They were in her bag at that very moment and Sarah forced herself not to instinctively glance to them.

'I don't know what you're talking about.'

Sarah wished she was a better actor. She wouldn't have believed herself – and Dean definitely didn't. It was the first time he'd flinched, although not really. He sucked in his cheeks, weighing up what was next. The cleaver was gleaming from the white lights overhead, the blade razor-sharp.

And then, Sarah started to see the joins. Bonnie was essentially blackmailed by Martin Shearer. He skimmed profits in return for delivering her dream.

But the same had happened to Dean. He'd more or less told Sarah as much when they first met. There had been something about a massive order during Covid which kept the butcher shop afloat. As Sarah now knew, Martin didn't throw money around without caveats.

'Where are the drives?' Dean repeated.

'What drives? I don't know what you're talking about.'

He was annoyed now, that menacing calm replaced by the air of a man who didn't like being told what to do – which was ironic if he'd taken Martin's money.

'What's wrong with you?' Dean asked. 'I told you to go and you didn't. I put that message on your wall and you didn't flinch. Leaked that video of your husband but you kept asking questions, poking your nose in.'

He sounded equally confused as he was annoyed. It took Sarah a moment to work out that, if Dean had sprayed the graffiti, then he'd been responsible for many of the things that had gone wrong that week. Martin had lied about who'd sprayed it, manipulated her into not pushing things further by saying it was a child.

It was Dean all along. She even knew he'd leaked the videos and hadn't realised it was on purpose. All that stuff about his wife and a WhatsApp group was the same nonsense as Martin's lies about the graffiti.

'Where are the drives?' Dean repeated.

Sarah didn't answer: she had her own question. 'Did you kill Martin?'

It got a reaction, though not what she expected. Dean blew a raspberry of indignation. 'Are you joking? Why would I? He's saved this town over and over. Saved this shop, saved Bonnie's place – not that she appreciates it. So what? He likes pictures of kids. It's not *that* bad. Not like he's touching them. I don't know what her problem is.'

Sarah had anticipated none of what Dean said. He was so blasé. She was so shocked, she stumbled to the side, closer to the curtain that led into the main shop. Dean must have thought she was going to run for it because he lunged forward, blocking the way. The cleaver was at his side but he was close enough that Sarah could see the spots he'd missed shaving that morning. The drives were burning a hole in her bag, which was looped over her shoulder.

'Yer man killed him, didn't he? Everyone knows it. Payback for Lucy.'

Sarah backed away and Dean didn't follow. There was nowhere for her to go anyway. The computer was behind, a freezer was on one side, Dean the other. The large metal table blocked the rest of the space.

The thing was, Sarah still wondered whether James *had* killed Martin. He told her the running route from his watch exonerated him, and maybe it did, but he wasn't a stupid man. He could probably manipulate that sort of thing if he wanted. The fact she couldn't rule it out is why she'd told him it felt as if something was broken in their marriage.

'What about payback for Lucy?' Sarah replied. She was trying to buy time, wondering how to get out of this.

Dean snorted, bewildered she didn't know. 'Payback 'cos her dad had to start somewhere.'

Sarah had replied before thinking, 'What do you—?' But she

stopped herself because she knew. 'Lucy's dad was taking pictures of her...?'

Of course it was true. Lucy was Martin's first. When she disappeared, he moved on to taking pictures of other girls. The USB drives from the bookshop were his. He'd taken photos of Georgia, so many, many times. The poor girl called it statues.

Dean was frowning – and had clearly assumed Sarah knew everything. 'That's what Lucy told people at the time.'

'She told people her dad took photos of her? Why didn't anyone do something?'

Dean stared as if she'd asked what colour the sky was. Someone *had* done something. Sarah had watched the video. *Dean's* video. James had beaten the shit out of Lucy's father, punching Martin repeatedly on the ground, aiming wild kicks in the older man's direction.

'If Lucy told people what Martin was doing, I don't get why nobody stopped him.'

Sarah was stumbling. She'd grown up being told that violence was never the answer. It was why the video had so shocked her. Not only the ferocity but the fact it was from a person she loved and thought she knew. Wasn't there a better way than punching someone on the ground?

Dean was incredulous. 'You've spent all week sticking your nose in and you've not learned anything. Haven't you listened? Martin Shearer *owns* this town. He *owns* the people in it.' There was a pause, then a quieter, '*Owned.*'

Sarah *had* listened but it hadn't gone in, not properly. Mr Horlock told her that Martin gave a lot but took a lot. She was about to ask Dean why he wanted the drives, why he cared now that Martin was dead – but then she knew that as well.

Oh, no.

It was somehow worse.

She'd walked around the park, having a cosy chat with Dean while he wheeled baby Naomi in the pram.

Martin had *already* photographed her.

The photos would be on the drive. No wonder Dean wanted them.

'Where are the drives?' Dean asked.

'I don't know.'

She did. They were under her arm but Dean had apparently either not noticed the bag, or not considered the idea they'd be on her.

'I think you do.' Dean passed the cleaver from one hand to the other, bouncing it in his palm, acknowledging the weight. 'Are they at your house? Because I think I'm due a catch-up with your old man.'

It wasn't only James at the house, Oliver was there too.

'Where are the drives?' Dean added. 'Last chance.'

There was nothing else for it. Sarah would have to hand them over and Dean would get away with how he'd used his infant daughter to gain favour with the man that saved his business. Same for Bonnie.

Sarah plopped her bag on the metal table and reached inside, pulling out the two drives, pushing them across the hard metal.

Dean eyed them, though didn't pick them up. 'Are there more?'

Sarah assumed he knew exactly what he was after – but apparently not. He knew there were USB drives but not how many.

'There were only two in the box,' Sarah said.

'Did you make copies?'

'Of course not.'

'Who else has seen these?'

'Just James.'

There were a few seconds in which it seemed as if Dean was considering it all. Then he scooped up the pair of drives and shoved them into a pocket. He moved backwards, hovering in the main doorway momentarily and giving Sarah a small amount of room. Not that there was anywhere to go. She was still wedged in by the freezers and the large table, with Dean between her and either of the doors.

Dean was muttering to himself, the cleaver low by his hips, though still in hand. Sarah picked up her bag. Her phone was inside, though she doubted she could take it out and call or text before he noticed.

'Will you open the door?' she asked.

Dean peered up, as if he'd momentarily forgotten she was there. His gaze was dark as she realised he'd been talking to himself, psyching himself up like a boxer about to head to the ring.

'Of course not,' he said, too calmly. 'You could tell anyone. It's going to end here, then I'm going to find your husband and shut him up, too.'

Sarah gasped as Dean lifted the cleaver a fraction. In those moments he'd been talking to himself, the man's soul had departed. He was someone else now.

Sarah froze – but only for a second. It was all she could think of – and she reeled back, then hurled her bag towards him. There was such a short distance between them but, even with that, she somehow missed. Dean barely flinched as the bag sailed to the side of him, landing somewhere near the curtain. There was a solid *whump* and then a deathly, dangerous silence.

Sarah had nowhere to go.

FIFTY-THREE

Helllllooooooo...

The woman's voice creaked from the doorway. The bulb-like speaking module that had been under Oliver's floor had been in Sarah's bag ever since she had shown it to Bonnie. Landing on the ground had set it off.

Dean turned, wondering how a woman could have got behind him – but Sarah didn't hesitate. She ran at the man as he looked away, slipping to his side, darting around the table and lunging towards the instruments by the back door. Sarah grabbed the nearest thing, a serrated meat tenderiser. When she turned, Dean was upon her – but he was too slow and it was too late.

Sarah nearly took his head off.

She felt the squish of notched wood on flesh. She heard the crack, saw the blood spatter across the nearest freezer. Sarah reeled back to hit him again – but there was no need. Dean was already on the floor at her feet, neck bent at an absurd angle, blood pooling around his temples, cleaver halfway across the floor.

Sarah stood over him, panting, unsure what to do. Everything had happened in a flash. She almost materialised across the room and now...

Sarah crouched, reaching into Dean's pocket and removing what turned out to be a key. She delved deeper, finding the pair of USB drives as well. With that, she grabbed her bag, unlocked the door – and ran.

It had been a long, long time since Sarah had really run. She'd done a bit of hurrying in her time, the odd quickstep to get in front of an old person who looked a bit chatty when they were near a checkout. She'd dashed from one room to another when it sounded like Oliver had dropped something – which happened often – or grazed a body part – which also happened often. She could put on a bit of a trot if she was on the toilet when a delivery driver rang the buzzer.

But she hadn't *run*.

She did now, though. Sarah's lungs burned as she hurtled along the high street, flying past bemused tourists and locals, then jinking into the road to get around someone on a mobility scooter. She flew past the garage and, as she reached the downwards slope, it felt as if her legs were moving too quickly, as if she might overtake herself.

Her chest was tight, head spinning, bag heavy – but Sarah pressed on until she reached the end. The cottage was right there: Puddlebrick, with its stupid name in this stupid village.

But there was something else as well. A new car was on the drive, with a 'Budget' rental sticker on the back. Sarah didn't have time to take it all in, let alone try to guess whose car it was. She fumbled with her keys, almost dropped the bag, set off the *Hellllloooooo...* again – and then finally threw herself inside.

They needed to go: her, Oliver, James – right now.

Except, as Sarah burst into the living room, breathless, tiny green stars kissing the edges of her vision, there was someone sitting on the sofa, cup of tea in her hand.

They blinked at one another, one woman to another, before

James hurried in from behind. 'I didn't know when you'd be back,' he gasped, panicked breathless himself but for a different reason. 'This is—'

Sarah didn't let him finish. She already knew. 'Lucy,' she said. 'You're Lucy Shearer.'

FIFTY-FOUR

SUNDAY

There wasn't time for introductions or explanations. The rest of the Saturday was a panic attack-inducing rush of getting everyone in a car, driving to the police station, making sure everyone was safe – and then Sarah telling them everything she knew.

Almost everything.

It was nearly eleven on Sunday morning when they got back to the cottage, the three of them plus Oliver. He'd already been asleep at the station and in the car – and James had carried him to bed.

Sarah didn't think anyone had ever needed to sleep more than she did that night.

She didn't wake until it was gone ten the next morning, heading downstairs to where her husband and his oldest friend were sharing a coffee, while her son amused himself in the back garden.

But this wasn't the moment for what was next. Sarah needed to think – and, even more, she needed some toast.

A couple of hours later and Sarah, James and Lucy were sitting as a trio on a bench at the edge of a play park. It was a

Sunday afternoon and there were a good thirty kids charging around the roundabouts, swings, and climbing equipment. The screams of collective enjoyment filled the air as parents gathered in twos and threes, some watching, some staring at phones.

There had been a different park, not even a week before, where Sarah had gone for that stroll with the man who later wanted to murder her. So much had happened in such a short period that Sarah knew she hadn't yet processed it. At least, for now, she was safe – and so was Oliver. The police had found Dean where she left him on the floor of the butcher's shop. He wasn't dead – but wouldn't be going anywhere for quite some time. He was not only under arrest but would be in hospital for a while. One of the officers told Sarah that Dean would likely lose an eye. She couldn't work out whether she felt bad about it.

Maybe.

And now she was ready.

'I'd like to hear it now,' Sarah said. She needed to be on this spot to listen to what James and Lucy were going to say. She probably knew a lot of it anyway. 'If you don't mind.'

Sarah sensed a sideways glance between her husband and the person she now knew was his best friend.

'It was exciting at first,' Lucy said. She had a soft American accent that might have been New York, though Sarah didn't know the difference well enough. 'Dad would buy me clothes and shoes. He'd show me how he wanted me to pose, take a few photos – and that was it.'

They sat in a row, Sarah in the middle. She and Lucy were almost an identical height – and it was impossible not to notice they looked similar as well. Same colour hair, even though Sarah's was a little longer.

'When I got a bit older, maybe thirteen or fourteen, I started to think it was a bit odd. He told me not to tell anyone at school but I ended up asking a few girls and they didn't have to get their pictures taken. But Dad kept wanting to buy me new things, even give me pocket money, so I kept going with it. It was hard to say no. He was my dad.'

'What did your mum say?'

Lucy went quiet for a long time. They sat, watching a big brother push his younger one higher and higher on the swings.

'She never said anything,' Lucy replied eventually. It might be the accent, or maybe because they weren't looking at one another, but Sarah was struggling to read the other woman. She talked as if relaying something that had happened to another person. It had been so long, that perhaps it felt like that. Lucy Shearer was officially dead, after all. It was as Dean had said: Lucy had been Martin's first victim and it wasn't that much of a secret. She'd let slip to people at school and she had definitely told James.

'I know it's none of my business but did he ever...?'

There was another gap, more quiet watching of children being children. Childhoods being made in front of them – including Oliver's.

'Not like that,' Lucy said after a while. 'But he always wanted to see more. I'd tell him no but then he'd say he'd show the other photos to my friends. Put them in an envelope and post them to people at school. He had so many Polaroids back then. Everyone calls it revenge porn now but you don't expect it from your dad.' She took a breath and then angled to peer around Sarah. 'James saved me.'

Sarah had figured out that part. He could accept people thinking he'd killed the other woman, because if they thought she was dead, they didn't know she was still out there, hiding from her dad.

'How?' Sarah asked.

'At first, it was getting me out of town. We had dry runs, where we'd get the bus to the seaside and spend a day there. Nobody had cell phones back then, so no Find My Friends. Nobody could call or check. There wasn't CCTV.'

Sarah was amazed at how much she knew, even though she'd not slotted together the pieces. James had told her he and Lucy skipped school to visit the seaside. She'd pictured leisurely strolls along the front, vinegary chips in hand. The reality had been so much bleaker.

'On all those trips, we'd been looking through the local paper, checking noticeboards, that sort of thing, trying to find a rental. There was a card in a newsagent from this old woman, who had a room to rent. She was only after a tenner a week. I arranged to rent the place with her – and said I'd move in properly the next week. Then we went for it. We disguised ourselves on the bus – hats, coats, the lot. Then, at the flat, James cut my hair and dyed it black. I barely went out for three weeks. Only odd trips to get food from the corner shop, after dark. They said I was missing and it was in the papers – but nobody was looking for a goth girl with short black hair.'

James picked things up. 'I knew people would be watching me. That kid said he'd seen blood on my trousers – but it was hair dye on my legs. I *was* wearing shorts, which is why I convinced the police that Chris was wrong, or lying. They didn't realise we'd got on the bus and never gone near The Den that day. But, because I knew people would be watching, I couldn't visit Lucy for weeks. I went to school every day, got my head down, went home.'

Sarah knew that, too. Mr Horlock told her that James had concentrated on his studies after Lucy went missing.

'What about after that?' Sarah asked.

'I took that job in the candle factory, but I hardly spent anything. I started to take Lucy food and money. She didn't really leave the flat, not for months until things had died down.'

'Hardly anything happened for about a year,' Lucy said. 'I was bored out of my mind but it was still better than being at Dad's. My landlady didn't care as long as she got her money – and she preferred cash anyway. James and I would see each other maybe once every two or three weeks – but we were always careful, in case Dad was keeping an eye on him.'

'In the end, I went to uni,' James said. 'This was a bit over a year after Lucy disappeared. Nobody was paying me much attention by then, except Lucy's dad – but he wasn't going to follow me there. I picked a place hours away. I moved on my own, waited two weeks to make sure there was no sign of Martin – and then Lucy moved with me.'

For most of the week, Sarah had barely even considered the idea that her husband could be involved with Lucy disappearing. She'd put more weight in him killing the other woman, though it was hard for Sarah to know if that said more about her, or James.

The idea had felt so outlandish, and yet it sounded like they succeeded by keeping things as simple as possible. It would be harder now, with cameras everywhere and phones – but it felt entirely possible as something from the time.

'I ended up doing my own course up there,' Lucy said. 'By that point, we had our own friends and lives. We would see each other a lot but we weren't living together. I got a chance to move to New York, through an American who was doing a semester on my course. I never really came back after that.'

Sarah had known – and perhaps she had at the time – that the Lucy from New York who'd called James phone was *this* Lucy. *The* Lucy.

'Did you change your name?' Sarah asked. That was always the first thing people talked about. Some sort of fake identity document, new name, new start.

'Not really. I had my birth certificate and knew my national insurance number. I applied for a passport in my own name. You don't get declared dead until seven years but that's a big window. Plus there's no cross-referencing – or there wasn't. It's not like the police were monitoring every passport application, just in case.'

Sarah assumed that was true. If somebody had the correct documents and filed in the expected manner, why wouldn't they get a passport? Whoever made those decisions wouldn't be checking every local paper from the previous seven years to make sure the person wasn't missing. Either the applications weren't checked against a missing person database – or they weren't twenty-odd years ago.

'Weren't you worried your dad would find you?' Sarah asked. 'Maybe a private investigator? That sort of thing.'

Lucy was on firmer ground now, sounding much more confident about the story. 'Maybe. He kept accusing James of killing me but we were never sure if he actually believed it. James beat him up one time. It was—'

'She's seen the video.'

Lucy stopped at James's interruption. She didn't bother to question the existence of Dean's recording, adding a simple, 'Oh.' And then, 'He was protecting me.'

Sarah knew that now – but it was still hard to picture the younger version of her husband with such fury. But then she was a woman who'd smashed someone in the face with a meat hammer. Nobody knew better than her that people acted in extreme ways when they thought they had no other choice.

'After a few years, I suppose I thought it didn't matter whether he found me,' Lucy said. 'What was he going to do? I was in my twenties by then, an adult, doing my own thing. And, besides, if he tracked me down and made a fuss, I could tell everyone who he was and what he'd done.'

She stopped, coughed, then turned away. 'I didn't know there would be newer girls. I thought it was a me thing. A *daughter* thing. I wish I...'

The sentence was lost to the breeze – but maybe there was no way to end it fairly. Lucy had escaped an abusive father but was it her responsibility to make certain everybody else was safe? It wasn't *her* fault, even if she thought it might be.

'When you go to New York,' Sarah said, talking to her husband, 'is it to visit Lucy? Was this always the reason?'

James was watching Oliver, who was on the mini climbing wall. He scampered up one side like a little chimp, then reached down to help another boy to the top.

'Yes and no,' he said. 'It *was* always for work – but I'd deliberately volunteer for the New York trips. I'd see Lucy while I was out there. I didn't really lie...'

That might be the case, depending on whether a person thought omission counted. Sarah didn't know. Her husband had helped a vulnerable young woman escape an awful father. Could she really blame him for keeping it to himself?

James twisted on the bench, towards the reason they'd come to this park, above the others, or the garden.

The police station sat on the road behind. Sarah had already spent enough hours there, telling them more or less what she knew. This was the part she didn't.

'It's not my story to tell,' Sarah said – and it wasn't.

'Luce?' James had angled forward on the bench, to look at his old friend. Perhaps his oldest. 'You don't have to,' he added.

'It's why I came back,' she replied quietly. 'Now Dad's gone, I think it's time to bring Lucy Shearer back from the dead.' She said it with the gentlest hint of a laugh, although Sarah wasn't sure she meant it.

A storm was still coming once people found out Lucy was alive but, for now, the three of them shared their moment on the bench. Sarah had so many more questions but didn't know whether she truly wanted answers.

'Lucy's married,' James said – and Sarah knew why he was saying it. The two women could easily be mistaken for sisters. The implication of that was something she didn't want to think about too much. Sarah wondered if she'd seen herself in that thumbs-up picture of Lucy from all those years ago – or maybe both women had changed over time? She knew she didn't want to re-check the article to find out.

'He's still in New York,' Lucy added. 'He knows James is my friend from England but not the rest. When I'm done here, I'm going to have to tell him as well.'

What a mess.

'I wouldn't be here without James,' Lucy said quietly – but it was unsure for whose benefit she said it. Maybe her own, maybe James himself. Perhaps she simply wanted Sarah to know the man she knew?

Except Sarah had spent a week asking herself the same thing.

Who, exactly, was the man she'd married?

FIFTY-FIVE

FOUR DAYS LATER

It didn't take the police long to get access to the second USB drive. Nobody had told Sarah officially, but, according to the local newspaper, they had found pictures of children dating back to Lucy's own from the 1990s. Martin Shearer had scanned the old ones of his daughter and filed them away in folders, exactly like the more recent images.

There were videos from what appeared to be hidden cameras in some of his flats, going back years. The police had traced a few of the more recent victims – and their parents – but it was going to take a while to find everyone.

Sarah hadn't spoken to Bonnie since finding out she'd set the fire. The rumours were that Georgia had been taken away, though nobody seemed to know for certain. Neither Bonnie nor Georgia had been at the school gates – and the gutted bookstore was boarded up. Sarah had driven past her house a few times, not quite building up the courage to try the door. There was no car on the drive anyway. She wondered what had happened to Gary the spaniel.

Pamela and the others at those gates were suddenly very

keen to be friends. Sarah had the inside story on the hottest piece of gossip Carnington had ever seen. One day Sarah had been a pariah, and all it had taken to turn around her fortunes was nearly dying in a fire, then almost killing a guy with a mallet. Why hadn't she thought of that earlier?

Not that she went with any of the new attention. How did the inspirational quote go?

If you can't handle me when you think my husband's killed his friend, you don't deserve me when I've clubbed a guy in the face with a meat tenderiser.

Something like that.

Lucy had returned to New York. She'd told the police her story and explained who she was. Everyone now knew the missing woman was no longer missing – but Lucy had sensibly got out of town before the story got too far. She had her own life.

Her own husband.

Sarah was on the bench opposite the bookshop. She'd sat there with Bonnie the morning after the fire, when she didn't know what the other woman had done.

There was a lot Sarah regretted about her first week in Carnington – but, oddly, despite how she had nearly died at least twice, the thing she thought most about was losing the person she believed to be a genuine friend.

When everyone in the village could barely look at Sarah, Bonnie was the only person who wanted to know her. It hadn't benefitted her in any way and, in fact, with the way things had turned out, the opposite was true. But Bonnie had done it anyway – which left Sarah stuck between knowing the awful things the other woman had done, directly alongside the truth that Bonnie had gone out of her way to be kind to Sarah.

Sometimes, in the quieter moments – which were frequent when living in the middle of nowhere – Sarah could still hear Bonnie's: 'It was my dream to run a bookshop'.

That's what had done her, after all. She needed money to chase that dream and the only person who could help turned out to be a monster.

Martin's terms hadn't only been the formalities around the bookshop ownership. It had been Georgia. He promised Bonnie he'd never touch her daughter, that it wasn't his thing. That he *only* wanted pictures. She should have said no and gone to the police there and then.

But people made terrible decisions when they believed a life goal was sliding away for good. She'd already lost a husband.

There would have been a time when it was probably thrilling and enticing for Georgia, in the same way Lucy had said it was exciting to get new clothes and the attention. Especially as the poor girl's father had not long killed himself.

One thing Sarah had heard from the police was that the computer in the bookstore basement was 'air gapped'. There was no modem, no way of accessing the internet. Martin used it to edit and look at his photos. It's why he kept the USB drives in the same shop. The newest pictures were all of Georgia and everything was in Bonnie's store. Nothing could be traced to him, unless he was dead, and his daughter came back to life to tell her story.

Sarah sat on the bench, wondering if Bonnie would ever come by to look at her store. A part of her wanted it, if only to have another moment of connection. Another part of her couldn't stand the idea.

Other than that, Sarah's life looked as if it might settle – as much as it could when she'd destroyed the fabric of her adopted village almost single-handedly. She probably wasn't going to get a discount at the butcher's anytime soon.

Oliver seemed to be enjoying school, James was at work, and commuting on the days he needed to. Sarah had dropped off some cards to drum up business for her bookkeeping – and a few locals had been in touch. The cottage was unpacked and the perfect home wasn't quite a perfect home but it wasn't *that* far off.

But Sarah still sat on the bench every morning after dropping off Oliver at school. There was no Bonnie – and Sarah knew there likely never would be.

She stood and crossed the road, then started the walk towards home. It was as she was passing the garage that a man called her name. When Sarah turned, Eric was hurrying across the forecourt, trying to flag her down.

'I've been looking out for you,' he said.

Sarah hadn't spoken to him since the day she'd found Martin Shearer over the road, covered in his own blood.

'Have you heard anything about Martin?' Eric added.

'What do you mean?' Sarah replied.

'About who killed him.'

Police had released CCTV of Martin walking along the high street, on his way to his death. He'd disappeared out of sight not long before reaching the house. They were still asking for witnesses – though, with the knowledge of what he'd done, Sarah doubted too many were going to come forward. Most now seemed to think he could rot. The police apparently hadn't ruled out the idea that he'd slipped and hit his head – and, though Sarah doubted it, there was a general sense that it might be better for everyone if that's what happened.

'I don't know anything new,' Sarah said.

Eric glanced past her curiously, across to the spot where Martin had died outside the flats he owned. He beckoned Sarah onto the forecourt, then pointed up to a spotlight. 'There's a camera next to that light,' he said. 'The police asked if I had anything from the time Martin was killed. You're on there, ironically enough, because you came into the garage and we talked. I sent them all that – but Martin wasn't on there because he came from the other side and the camera doesn't cover that wide an angle.'

He was walking, expecting her to follow and, though Sarah was nervous after everything with Dean, she trailed Eric into the office, where a monitor was frozen on an image showing the street outside.

'This was about ten minutes before you came by,' he said. 'Maybe twenty, twenty-five before you found the body.'

He tapped a button and the video started to play. It was black and white, grainy, but clear enough. A jogger emerged from the hill and barely slowed before darting sideways, slipping through a gap in the hedge until he was on the other side of the hedge. The only thing beyond was the house and grounds where Martin had been discovered.

The clip was around ten seconds and Sarah knew what it showed – but she asked to see it again anyway.

Eric obliged, resetting the clip and pressing play. Sarah watched again but she already knew the identity of the jogger. Perhaps she always had.

She wasn't the only one. 'Maybe Martin Shearer deserved it,' Eric said quietly. Sarah didn't answer, although, yes, he probably did.

Without being asked, Eric reset the screen and played the footage a third time. It seemed so pre-meditated, so planned. As if the jogger knew Martin's routine of visiting the house at the same time, every week – just as the woman from the house had said. Martin went by every Thursday to clear the noticeboard and check the fire alarms. If someone had done their research, had paid enough attention, they would know.

'What shall I do with it?' Eric asked.

'Have you given it to the police?'

'No. They only asked for the stuff from when it happened. I think they were looking to see if the actual attack had been caught – which it wasn't. When they realised that, they lost interest. I reckon they probably think he deserved it as well. I didn't check this far back myself until yesterday, when it was time to wipe the drive. It's only me and you. I figured I'd ask what you wanted to do.'

Oh, that was a big question. Perhaps too big for one person?

'I can delete it if you want?' Eric added. He'd thought about this conversation. 'Delete and never speak about it. I don't mind.'

'Can I watch it again?'

That wasn't a problem – and Sarah watched the jogger duck through the gap in the hedge a fourth time.

Strategic.

Deliberate.

It wasn't that long before that Sarah had suggested to Dean they head to his shop, oblivious at what he had planned. He'd let her think it was her idea, which is why she'd felt so comfortable. Why her guard was down. Why he almost had her.

Sarah tried to remember whose idea it was to come to Carnington that first time, that single afternoon, six years before, when she'd fallen in love with the place. She thought it was hers, and maybe it was. It had been such a perfect moment at the perfect time of the season. Who *wouldn't* fall for the place?

In subsequent years, with the growing idea to *move* to the village, she thought that was her idea as well.

And maybe it was.

But that was how people played the long game, wasn't it? If somebody was certain the idea was theirs, they'd have no reason to suspect a bigger plan was in play. A plan that took many years, that relied on knowing where someone was at the same time every week. On knowing how to manipulate a GPS running route.

On needing to live in a specific village, possibly even a specific cottage, at a specific end of town.

Sarah knew who her husband was now.

He'd once saved a young woman, despite everything it

meant for himself. He'd given Sarah a beautiful, brilliant son, plus an incredible decade and counting.

But she knew who he was.

And, with that knowledge, Sarah told Eric what to do with the footage.

PUBLISHING TEAM

Turning a manuscript into a book requires the efforts of many people. The publishing team at Bookouture would like to acknowledge everyone who contributed to this publication.

Audio

Alba Proko

Sinead O'Connor

Melissa Tran

Commercial

Lauren Morrissette

Hannah Richmond

Imogen Allport

Cover Design

The Brewster Project

Data and analysis

Mark Alder

Mohamed Bussuri

Editorial

Ellen Gleeson

Nadia Michael

Copyeditor
Jane Eastgate

Proofreader
Tom Feltham

Marketing
Alex Crow
Melanie Price
Occy Carr
Cíara Rosney
Martyna Młynarska

Operations and distribution
Marina Valles
Stephanie Straub
Joe Morris

Production
Hannah Snetsinger
Mandy Kullar
Ria Clare

Publicity
Kim Nash
Noelle Holten
Jess Readett
Sarah Hardy

Rights and contracts
Peta Nightingale
Richard King
Saidah Graham

Made in the USA
Columbia, SC
12 July 2025